Mimi Lee

GETS A CLUE

Jennifer J. Chow

BERKLEY PRIME CRIME
NEW YORK

BERKLEY PRIME CRIME
Published by Berkley
An imprint of Penguin Random House LLC
penguinrandomhouse.com

Library of Congress Cataloging-in-Publication Data

Names: Chow, Jennifer J., author.
Title: Mimi Lee gets a clue / Jennifer J. Chow.
Description: First edition. | New York: Berkley Prime Crime, 2020. |
Series: A sassy cat mystery
Identifiers: LCCN 2019043264 (print) | LCCN 2019043265 (ebook) |
ISBN 9781984804990 (paperback) | ISBN 9781984805003 (ebook)
Subjects: GSAFD: Mystery fiction.
Classification: LCC PS3603.H696 M56 2020 (print) |
LCC PS3603.H696 (ebook) | DDC 813/.6—dc23
LC record available at https://lccn.loc.gov/2019043264
LC ebook record available at https://lccn.loc.gov/2019043265

First Edition: March 2020

Printed in the United States of America
1   3   5   7   9   10   8   6   4   2

Cover art by Carrie May
Cover design by Judith Lagerman
Book design by Alison Cnockaert

For my dad: You are always number satu *in my book!*

CHAPTER

one

STOOD IN THE warm L.A. sunshine, admiring the marquee sign above my store. "Hollywoof," it read. The tagline? "Where we treat your pets like stars."

A week ago, I'd celebrated my life's quarter-century mark. The best birthday present: this fulfillment of my lifelong dream. All those years of cat sitting, dog walking, and poop scooping had paid off. I was the new owner of a pet grooming salon.

When I entered *my* store, the golden bell above the door gave off a gentle chime. As the musical note faded, I found myself trapped in a deep silence. Not one bark or chitter.

Though I'd placed ads on social media, nobody had shown up. I'd even offered a special discount this week. Yesterday had been quiet, except for the arrival of Ma, Dad, and Alice. And family didn't count as real foot traffic.

Today seemed about the same. Half the day had flown by, and still no luck.

Finally, the phone rang, and I rushed to grab it. "Hollywoof. Can I help you?"

"It's Pixie," a smooth voice on the other end of the line said. "How's your business going?"

Thankfully, Pixie St. James hadn't called it "my" business, though she'd put up the capital for it. She even looked more of a business-woman than me, with her no-nonsense cropped brunette hair and polished pantsuits.

I sighed. "Things are slow. Not a customer in sight."

She clucked her tongue, and I could imagine a flurry of ideas rushing through her brain. "Tell you what, I'll text a few friends," she said. "Maybe someone can swing by."

I heard an excited bark over the phone. "Is that Gelato?" Pixie craved Italian desserts, and her sweet tooth had inspired the shih tzu's name. That cute puppy was the reason I had my grooming business.

"Yes, he's due for his walk . . . I swear he's trying to drag me out the door right this minute."

I could imagine that. Energy on four legs, Gelato had jumped into the choppy waves off Catalina Island this past summer. I had to dive in to save him. After the rescue, Pixie had promised to invest in the grooming business . . . as long as I offered Gelato free baths for life. Deal.

The barking increased. "You better go," I said. "Thanks for check-ing up on me. Have a great walk."

A few minutes later, I heard a familiar happy giggle as my sister entered the store. I bet Alice had shown up at noon to match Holly-woof's hour-long lunch closure. I greeted her with a warm hug.

I didn't need to reach up for the embrace, since we had the same five-foot frame. People often mistook us for twins despite our two-year age gap. We did have the same features: oval faces, elfin ears, and small button noses. We wore our hair differently, though—she in an Amy Tan bob, complete with bangs, and me with shoulder-length black hair.

Her light brown eyes glowed. "I brought you something to celebrate your grand opening week." She held up a cardboard box . . . that purred. "Take a look at the cutie I found at the shelter."

I backed away. "Please don't tell me that's a cat."

A furry white head popped up from the box and blinked at me with ocean-colored eyes.

"Mimi," my sister said, "how can you say no to these baby blues?" Alice was a sucker for waif faces. Maybe that's how she wrangled twenty-five kindergarteners Monday through Friday and still remained smiling by the afternoon.

I frowned at the Persian cat. "Alice, you know I prefer dogs."

She gave me her peppy teacher's smile. "Maybe you just need to have the right kitty."

I hesitated, imagining sharp claws and giant hairballs.

"Please." She placed the box in my hands. "For me."

How could I say no to my baby sis? "We'll see," I said.

"You'll love him, I bet." Alice squeezed my shoulder. "Time for me to get back to class. The new principal's a real stickler about time."

I waved to her as she left.

As soon as I took the cat out of the box, he sauntered over to the plateglass window and stretched out in a sunny spot to nap. This kitty put the "cat" in catatonic. While he slept, I made a quick trip to the pet store to pick up supplies, including a carrier for the car.

When I returned, business remained stalled. Over the next hours, though, a few people dropped in from the beach to check out the store. I hoped some of them owned pets, because their visits left me with a lot of mess. Surfboards knocked into displays, flip-flops left wet marks behind, and sand was wedged into every nook and cranny.

Near closing time, I finished the cleanup. Then I looked over at the white cat, who had finally opened his eyes, and mulled over possible names. His coat was so poofy, it made him shapeless, like a giant marshmallow. Hmm, that wasn't too bad of a name.

I cocked my head at Marshmallow, and he stared back at me with piercing sapphire eyes. We maintained eye contact for so long, it felt like a staring contest. I would show him who was boss.

Okay, I blinked first. But I had an excuse. The door swished open.

A petite blonde barreled in. She wore pink on pink on pink. The woman had layered a lacy camisole under a moto jacket and paired them with a leather skirt, all in the hue of Pepto-Bismol. I wanted to snatch the sunglasses off her head to shield my eyes, but their lenses were also bubblegum bright.

Thank goodness the dog she was holding wasn't dyed to match. Instead, it seemed to be a common tan Chihuahua, albeit with a pink rhinestone collar. The owner held the little dog tight to her bosom.

The blonde swiveled her head from left to right, surveying the shop's interior. I bit my lip. Had I done it up right?

Think: Oscars meets Fido. On the floor, I'd created a Hollywood Bark of Fame, complete with golden stars featuring Lassie and Toto. A large-screen television took up one entire wall and played classic doggie movies on an endless loop. Two cream pleather benches flanked a swirled marble table in the waiting area. And a searchlight shone down on the reception table. Maybe the decor was a bit over-the-top.

But I'd wanted to attract ritzy clients from the nearby beach cities. What did I know about the rich, though? I'd been raised a few miles out in Lawndale, close enough in distance but worlds apart from golden sands and beachfront mansions.

I must have passed some sort of litmus test, because the blonde nodded at me. "Just the place to drop off my handsome Sterling," she said.

4

She pinched his cheek, but the dog didn't appear fazed. In fact, he snuggled deeper into her arms.

"How did you find Hollywoof?" I asked, crossing my fingers. Had the online ads worked?

"Pixie told me."

"Oh." I relaxed my hand. Pixie had helped me with the funding, and now she'd given me my first customer.

The blonde perched her sunglasses on top of her head and extended shiny manicured tips toward me. "I'm Lauren Dalton. You've probably heard of my husband? He's a famous Hollywood producer."

Was I supposed to kiss her hand? I hesitated and settled for a more professional handshake.

Lauren continued, "Sorry about the getup." She gestured at her screaming pink clothes. "I came straight from the Help the Homeless fundraiser. I love all costumed charity galas—it was a movie theme this time, and I picked *Legally Blonde*."

"No problem." I cared about how the animals, not their owners, looked.

"Actually, I'm in a rush." She glanced at her diamond-encrusted watch, more jewelry than timepiece. "My baby has gym class in twenty minutes."

Oh, I knew how to ensure her ongoing patronage. In my experience, parents loved gushing about their kids. "Your child must be super flexible—a real Olympic contender."

She blinked at me. "Well, Sterling *is* my baby. My assistant Nicola got him just last month from a local breeder, Russ Nolan."

I tugged my ear. "Of course, that's what I meant . . . Dogs are like children, but better. All the love without any of the whininess."

"Sterling is a clingy puppy, but doggie gym should energize him. And a beauty treatment might lift his spirits." She smiled at me and

5

lowered Sterling to the ground. Bending over, she gave him a peck. "Be a good boy for Mommy."

As her short skirt rode up, I averted my eyes. "So, what would you like done for Sterling today? Something quick that would fit your schedule." A wash and dry would take longer than twenty minutes. Plus, who knew how much time it'd take to brave traffic to get to the class?

She examined me with her forest green eyes. "This is a trial run. I'd like you to get rid of all the dirt clinging to him. He needs to look his best for gym."

Sterling's coat seemed pretty clean to me. "Perhaps a quick brush?"

"Fine. I'll wait here." She strolled over to a wall rack and started fingering the glitzy collars and leashes there.

"Be back in a jiffy." I tried to coax Sterling over to the back area, but he crawled like molasses.

I turned to Lauren. "Are you sure he's okay? Maybe you should drop by the vet . . ."

"I can't fit that into his schedule as well, but he *can* get a brush right now."

"Fine," I said, scooping Sterling up to save time. He let out a sharp yip and wiggled in my arms. Huh. Pampered little Chihuahuas usually love being cuddled.

I entered the workstation at the rear of Hollywoof, which held two stark rooms with antiseptic white walls. They smelled of scrubbing and cleanser. I passed by the smaller room, a kennel area for holding animals. At least, I hoped I would get enough business to have pets needing to wait their turn to get shampooed.

The larger room was the grooming area. Huge industrial steel sinks took up half the space. A few drying tables covered the rest of the room. I moved toward one and placed Sterling on its textured nonslip surface.

"Okay, boy, we're going to do a simple groom." I reached for the leash hanging off an arcing metal arm and hooked his rhinestone collar to it.

"There you are. Clipped in nice and safe. Let me get my equipment." I chose a soft curry brush. When I had first heard the term, I had thought of a cooking utensil, something more fit to dole out Ma's spicy *rendang* than to tame fur.

I showed him the oval brush with its rubber bristles. "This soft comb won't hurt your delicate skin."

Sterling quivered.

Hmm, should I start with his tail? Maybe he'd be less nervous that way. But he soon stopped trembling, so I followed my usual routine.

First, I let him sniff the brush to get familiar with it. Then I worked on his head and moved on to the body. Near his right hind leg, I hit a snag. What was that? He yelped and backed away.

I apologized and patted him in a soothing manner. Maybe I'd brushed too hard. I used gentler strokes until he displayed gleaming fur, way smoother than my own frizz-prone hair.

Sterling now had a shiny coat, but I wanted to add a finishing touch. Scrounging through the accessory box, I found the perfect item to go with his rhinestone collar. I placed a bright pink headband on top of his sweet head.

When I returned Sterling to the front, Lauren smiled. "He looks like a champ. How much do I owe you?"

We walked over to the cash register, where Lauren got distracted by the jar of doggie treats on the counter.

"Homemade," I said. "Peanut butter and bacon flavor. Two dollars a biscuit." Would anyone pay that much? I'd wanted to charge a quarter at first, but I needed to cover the rent of this extravagant business space near the pier.

"A steal," Lauren said, adding a dozen treats to her grooming bill. When I rang her up, she pulled a crisp hundred from a sparkly pink clutch.

"Keep the change," she said. "The pink sweatband is perfect. Speaking of *purr*-fect . . ." Lauren sauntered over to the display window. "What's the name of your adorable cat?"

"Marshmallow," I said as I joined her at the sunbathing spot.

"Too cute," Lauren said and tapped the cat's nose.

Marshmallow hissed and raised his paw up, claws out.

I pulled Lauren away from danger. "He's not quite used to company yet."

"Well, besides the unfriendly kitty, I like your place. I'm going to tell my yoga sisters, and they'll bring their animal besties here, too."

"That would be lovely." Yes. My business was picking up.

After the bell jingled on Lauren's way out, I heard a baritone male voice pipe up. "Good riddance."

I turned in a slow circle, surveying the store. "Who's there?" Had someone waltzed in while I was beautifying Sterling?

I didn't see anyone. Only Marshmallow glared at me from his perch.

The voice continued. "You let her attack my face."

I looked at Marshmallow. No way the *cat* was talking to me. Plus, his mouth hadn't moved. Not one whisker twitched.

"What kind of name is Marshmallow anyway?" His fur bristled. "Are you fat-shaming me?"

I rubbed my ears. They felt normal. Maybe it wasn't a physical problem. Oh no. Was I experiencing a psychotic break? I should crack open the DSM from my psych major days to find a rational explanation.

"This isn't real," I said, closing my eyes.

"Hey, Sleeping Beauty. I'm not done talking to you."

Marshmallow growled at me, and I opened my eyes to find him staring me down. Then he uncurled from his spot and slinked my way.

"Are you *speaking*?" No, it couldn't be true. Maybe this was a hallucination. Ma had brought over herbal soup last night sprinkled with a weird Asian mushroom: cloud ear fungus. But I'd eaten that stuff before and suffered little besides a jaw ache from chewing the slippery but crunchy brown masses.

Marshmallow advanced on me, and I backed up until I got trapped at the counter.

"This isn't happening." I grabbed the treat container for defense. After all, it was made of heavy glass. Or maybe I could pelt him with dog biscuits.

He halted and sat on his haunches, seeming to consider me. The talking stopped.

Taking a deep breath to collect myself, I started closing up shop. I wiped down the counter with cleaner and turned off the lights. Then, massaging my temples, I headed toward the front door. When I reached it, I flipped the sign over to read "CLOSED." I grinned, glad that I made my own easy work schedule of ten a.m. to six p.m.

As I opened the door to leave for the day, Marshmallow budged in front of me with his nose in the air. He squeezed through the gap and out to the pedestrian-friendly paved plaza. Worried that he'd run away, I bent down to snatch him up, but the cat seemed content to sit there crowd-watching. People meandered around the stores, popping into the fresh juice bar around the corner and checking out the boards on display in the surf shop closer to the pier.

A gentle sea breeze blew, making the palm trees, planted in two parallel rows, wave their green fronds at me. I gulped in the salt-tinged air floating to me from the beach a few blocks away to center myself.

It had to be sleep deprivation. I'd gotten little rest while preparing for the big opening of Hollywoof. Or maybe it was the stress from this afternoon after seeing Sterling move like a glacier. His slowness struck me as very strange for the feisty Chihuahua breed, and I worried about the little guy as I headed home.

• • •

The drive on the 405 was as good (or bad) as usual. The major freeway ran north and south through Southern California, and people joked that it was well named because traffic moved at "four or five" miles per hour.

The pulsing sea of red brake lights before me and the rushing headlights speeding down the other side of the freeway put me in a sour mood. Though traffic wasn't bumper to bumper, I still appreciated the great gas mileage on my Prius. We finally reached home sweet home.

Seaview Apartments didn't live up to its name. No ocean view existed. In fact, it was miles away from any body of water. However, the nearby 405 offered ongoing traffic as a white noise substitute for ocean waves. The stucco walls of the modest complex had seen better days. I think the original color had been a cheerful peach, but now it looked more like a faded urine yellow.

Oh well, at least the rent was cheap. I could afford a one-bedroom in this area and not need to move back into my parents' ranch house.

"End of the line," I told Marshmallow as I unbuckled his carrier and lifted it out of the back seat.

At least I lived in one of the ground-level units. I'd hate to manhandle the cage up a flight of stairs.

In my apartment, I struggled to take Marshmallow out of his carrier. He didn't move and instead roared at me. I couldn't tell if he was carsick or hangry, but I was glad he was using a normal cat noise to express himself.

Pulling out a silver dish, I placed it on the linoleum floor of my cramped kitchenette. Marshmallow got a bowlful of kitty food while I slapped together an Elvis sandwich. Mm, peanut butter and banana.

Starving, I didn't even bother to sit down at my IKEA particleboard dining table. Instead, I chewed, leaning over the cracked porcelain kitchen sink. A glob of peanut butter slipped out of my sandwich and onto my top, a black T-shirt with a cartoon dog saying, "I PAWS for no one."

Time to do laundry. In fact, the wicker hamper in my bedroom was already overflowing. In the tiny space that held only a nightstand and a bed, the dirty clothes had taken over half of my full-size mattress.

I shucked off my T-shirt and put on a pair of faded plaid pajamas, the only clean outfit left in the apartment. After transferring the dirty laundry to a fabric bag, I grabbed a roll of quarters off my cluttered nightstand.

Dragging the stuffed sack out of the bedroom and past the kitchen, I noticed Marshmallow curled up in a ball.

"See ya later," I said.

He gave me a slow nod as I exited. I saw his empty dish and understood: Food coma. Good, because I needed a break.

When I emerged outside, I saw a brilliant orange and pink sunset, courtesy of L.A.'s air pollution. The vivid colors made even the inner courtyard of Seaview look pretty. The rectangular patch of artificial grass with its ferns in scattered pots seemed more inviting.

I whistled as I headed to the laundry room. Time for some quiet. The area held three sets of washers and dryers, but I had yet to run into anyone in my few months of living at the complex.

Maybe it was because the machines were crazy clunking old. Or how they took only quarters. Perhaps people hauled their laundry to proper Laundromats instead. Plus, the whole complex housed a mere fourteen units—

"Alamak!" my mother had exclaimed upon hearing the number. "Very unlucky."

"Fourteen?" I'd said, clutching the apartment key with sweaty fingers.

"Number like meaning for *sure die*."

Remembering, I shook my head. Ma with her superstitions and old beliefs. You would've thought marrying outside her race meant a more modern mind. Guess she'd taken emotional baggage along with her physical luggage when she emigrated from Malaysia.

I stared at the laundry room. An unusual sight—the door had been propped open with a rock. Someone was inside sitting on a plastic chair and reading a huge book. A cute someone.

Even from the threshold, I could tell. His dark brown hair flopped down, hiding his face as he read, but I still saw his lean body.

He wore a white tank top with cargo shorts, and I could see his biceps move as he flipped the page. I felt my cheeks ignite. If only I wasn't wearing these frumpy pj's.

I backed up, but my heavy laundry sack hit the side of the door. The loud thwack made the stranger look up. Ack. He was even cuter when I saw his face uncovered: intelligent, dark brown eyes, kissable lips, and a small dimple as he grinned up at me.

He beckoned me forward. "Come on in." He gestured to the row of unused washers. "I'm up for grabs. I mean, *they're* up for grabs. My stuff is in the dryer."

"Uh, okay." I marched in with a straight back, trying to appear taller and also less ridiculous in my plaidwear.

I stuffed my delicates into the machine first, hoping the handsome stranger would remain engrossed in his book. After I'd finished, I turned around to find him staring at me with those dreamy eyes.

He waved. "Hi, I'm Josh Akana. Moved in about two weeks ago."

My mouth felt dry, and I swallowed. "Mimi Lee," I said. "Not related to Bruce."

His thick eyebrows rose up. The unasked question lingered in the air.

I rubbed the back of my neck. "People think I know kung fu when they hear my last name. The thing is my dad's white. Joke's on them." I babbled when I got nervous. This was why I worked with animals. Zero social skills.

"*I* wouldn't have assumed that." He closed his thick book and motioned for me to sit next to him.

Oh my gosh (or *Josh*). Did he want to keep talking to me? I sat down and peeked at his book. "So, what are you reading?" That was my opener?

He swept his bangs out of his eyes. "A casebook. Boring law stuff."

"Are you a lawyer?" He looked around my age. "Or maybe a law student?"

Josh coughed. "I was a 3L last year."

"Meaning . . ." I tucked my frizzy hair behind my ears.

He reached into his wallet. Pulling out a business card, he waved it in the air before placing it on top of his book. "I'm an attorney now. Last year I finished law school at USC."

Don't say it, I told myself, but it was like a Pavlovian response. "USC. University of Spoiled Children."

He chuckled, a fun laugh I wanted to continue hearing.

I kept dishing it out. "Or University of Second Choice." I clapped my hand over my mouth.

He stared at me with widened brown eyes.

Ugh. I'd insulted his alma mater twice. The Bruin had come out in me. Rivalry between UCLA and USC ran deep. Then again, my alma mater had its own nickname: University of Caucasians Lost among Asians. Ma had loved the moniker, thinking I might graduate with an MRS degree instead of a bachelor's.

Before I could fix the situation, my phone piped out "Chapel of Love," as though thinking of her had summoned Ma like a genie. I'd chosen the tune tongue in cheek to symbolize Ma's ultimate goal for me.

I held up one finger to Josh. Ma would go paranoid if I didn't pick up. She worried about me working by myself in the shop at nights all alone.

I hit the speakerphone button, letting Josh know it was a harmless conversation. Me? No boyfriend. Single and free. I held the phone up with my left hand, facing it toward Josh, so he could see my empty ring finger.

"Hi, Ma," I said, chirping out her name.

"Mimi. Where you are, eh?" Ma's voice came out bold, like a lioness.

"I'm home, safe."

Ma kept yell-talking. "I at store. Need anything?"

Boy, was she loud. Should I take her off speakerphone? But then maybe Josh would think I had something to hide. I edged closer to the running washer to muffle her volume.

"No. Actually, I'm busy." I glanced over at Josh, who'd opened his book again, at least pretending to give me some semblance of privacy.

"I need tell you: Date at *kopi tiam* in two days. Starbucks."

I hazarded a glance at Josh. He hadn't flipped the page, and his body was angled toward me.

"Ma, now is not the time."

Nearby, the dryer dinged. Josh got up to put his clean laundry away.

Ma's voice rose an octave in excitement. "Ah, guess what I find on sale? Perfect for you. Rubbers."

I slapped my forehead. The tips of Josh's ears turned red, and he shoveled his clothes into the basket.

Covering the phone, I said, "That's not what it sounds like."

"No need to explain." He scurried away with his full basket, grabbing his book on the way out.

While Ma gabbed about prices, I shouted at Josh's back, "I'm not that kind of girl."

He must have heard I had a date. Then Ma talked about rubbers. He put one plus one together.

"Ma, how many times do I have to tell you? They're called *erasers* in America."

"Sorry lah. I forget."

No matter how long she lived here, Ma still held on to some funny English. I blamed it on Malaysia's roots as a British colony.

"You need or not?" Ma continued. "Good for bookkeeping. If you need erase number . . . Or maybe Daddy come help you."

I blew out a long breath. "No, I can do it myself. Let Dad enjoy retirement."

She gave me a kiss over the phone. "Don't forget. *Kopi* date."

"I don't even drink coffee, Ma."

"Have fun," she said and hung up.

A few seconds later, my phone pinged with a text giving me the Starbucks details.

Ma had too much free time on her hands. Dad golfed as a hobby after retiring. Ma match-made. And she told me she'd up her efforts now that I had turned twenty-five, claiming that after rounding up, I was practically thirty.

Well, I could find guys on my own. Or not.

I looked at the empty chair Josh had vacated. Something small and rectangular lay on the ground beneath it. His business card. He'd probably dropped it while running away from me.

Aiyaa, my love life sucked. At least four-legged mammals adored me (with the possible exception of Marshmallow). Animals gave me sanctuary, and I looked forward to a peaceful day at Hollywoof tomorrow. What could possibly go wrong in that safe haven?

CHAPTER

two

I WOKE UP GRUMPY. Maybe last night at the laundry room had been a bad dream. But I saw Josh's business card peeking at me from the nightstand.

To top it off, Marshmallow had crept under my covers. And as his blue eyes peered into mine, I heard: "Where's my breakfast, Owner?" I had thought the delusion would stop after a good night's rest.

I groaned and covered my ears. Somehow I managed to feed us and get out the door.

We arrived at the store at ten on the dot. A few minutes later, a woman looking like a Bollywood star waltzed in. Except she wasn't wearing a single piece of jewelry, not even a wedding band, and wore workout gear.

She had on black spandex pants with a leather fanny pack and a sweat-wicking top. The exercise clothes didn't diminish her star quality, though. Long, flowing raven locks framed a slim face of high cheek-bones, luscious lips, and doe eyes. A fashion designer's model face.

"Can I help you?" I asked. Had she come in by mistake?

"Lauren recommended your place because you did such a great job with Sterling."

Then I noticed the leash trailing from her hand. At her feet sat a very quiet and well-behaved Chihuahua. I smiled at the dog and said, "I see you've brought in—"

"Ash. And my name is Indira."

"Nice to meet you both." I peered at the brown Chihuahua. "Wow, Ash could be Sterling's double."

One of Indira's groomed eyebrows curved up. "Except she's a girl."

"Fraternal twins, then." I held out my hand for the leash.

"Ash needs a bath." Her full lips pressed into a thin line. "No need for frivolous accessories like a headband or bow."

I nodded several times. "Got it."

Indira peeked at her Apple Watch. "Can't stay. I have an errand to run."

"Sure, no problem," I said as she finally relinquished the lead to me.

I brought Ash to the back. She was a quiet thing with an odd limp that troubled me.

I made sure to plug her ears with cotton to protect the ear canals. Then I placed her on the mat in the sink and turned the water to luke-warm. Shampooing Ash, I reveled in the foamy suds as I massaged her body. When I rinsed her off, she stayed stoic. She didn't even look tempted to try and shake off her fur.

Even when I moved her to the finishing area and turned on the high-velocity dryer, she didn't balk. A lot of dogs would've been startled by the sound.

As I returned to the front with a groomed Ash, the bell above the door jingled. Indira showed up, reaching for Ash's leash. She inspected her dog from head to toe, even sniffing at Ash's body. Thank goodness I'd used a "classic fresh" scent.

Indira gave me a brief nod before heading over to the cash register.

"Biscuit?" I said, pushing the half-full glass jar on the counter forward. I remembered Lauren's buying spree.

Indira looked at the price tag. "Not for two dollars a pop."

"They're homemade."

She shook her head. Before she opened her bag, she paused. "And don't forget to give me the grand opening discount."

All right, lady. Like you can't afford it. I gestured to her bag. "Love your fanny pack."

She unzipped it with a hard tug. "It's a fitness fashion pack."

"Oh, I see. Hands-free. Quite useful for athletes." I rang her up and gave her the total.

She checked the prices against the ones listed on the nearby board and seemed to calculate the sum in her head. Then she forked over her gold credit card.

"Indira Patel," it read. Underneath her name: *Indira's Designs.*

"What kind of company do you own?" I asked.

She tapped her leather fanny pack. "Luxury bags for the woman on the go."

"Very fashion forward." I stuck the card into the machine.

As we waited for the chip to process, she said, "I can expense all sorts of things, even this grooming, because Ash is the company mascot."

"She's a lovely dog." I gave her the receipt. "Where'd you get her?"

"From a breeder I found in the classifieds."

"What city?" Imagine if I could make a networking connection. I might expand my customer base.

Indira waved her slender hand around. "Somewhere in the Valley. Funny thing is the breeder had two first names."

"Could it be Russ Nolan?" I asked. The same breeder Lauren had used?

She shrugged. "I can't recall."

Sterling had been lethargic, and now Ash was limping. It didn't seem like it could be a coincidence. I frowned and said, "I wanted to tell you before, Indira—Ash has an odd limp. I think you should go to the vet pronto."

"She'll be fine. The breeder said that's normal. Besides, vet bills add up." Indira looked at her Apple Watch. "I have to go. My meter's almost out of time."

Though parking did cost an arm and a leg in this area, her comment sounded more like an excuse. I needed to say something to save the conversation and keep her as a customer. "Glad you came by. And say hi to Lauren for me." I put my palms together. "Namaste."

Her lip curled like she'd tasted durian, the rotten-smelling spiked fruit.

"Er, aren't you yoga sisters?" I fiddled with the buttons on the cash register. "I thought Lauren mentioned something."

"We're yoga parent-mates. Our dogs are in the same Mommy-and-me class."

She tossed her lustrous hair and exited the store, pulling Ash along.

Watching the Chihuahua leave, I shook my head. Something was wrong with the dogs I'd groomed over the past two days, and I intended to find out what.

I googled Russ Nolan and found an address in the San Fernando Valley. The Valley was close to the mountain ranges of Southern California, north of the urban skyscrapers that made up the downtown

L.A. skyline. People lived in the Valley because it offered affordable housing and greater acreage—at the unfortunate expense of hotter weather.

If I left now, I could avoid the dreaded five o'clock rush hour. Because another play on the name for the 405 was "four or five" hours to get anywhere using it.

As I drove, Marshmallow batted at the bars on his crate. "Where are we going?" he kept asking.

I hummed something to tune out the voice. My mind needed to remain clear for the task at hand.

Although I'd imagined a rural plot of land fit for a farm, complete with open spaces for puppies to run wild, I instead found Russ Nolan's neighborhood near the freeway exit. The residential street held a number of old-style bungalow houses clustered together. All the homes looked worn-out, with their cobwebbed porches and weed-filled lawns. One towered above the rest due to an additional but lopsided second floor.

Russ Nolan's dilapidated house sat in the tall home's shadow. His residence looked worse than the rest of them combined. It had cracked siding and peeling paint, and the front yard seemed more dustbin than grass.

I couldn't imagine Lauren setting foot in the house. Then again, her assistant had done the deed. Indira, though, might have gone in . . . if it meant a bargain to be had.

"Okay," I told Marshmallow. "I can't leave you in the car, so I'm taking you along. But you better behave." No more speaking, I hoped. I crossed my fingers.

He peered up at me with wide baby blue eyes.

I carried Marshmallow over to the front porch and placed him down on the splintering wooden boards. The bell didn't work, so I had to bang hard against the door.

A few pieces of brown paint flaked off after I knocked.

From inside, a deep voice boomed, "Hold on."

A few seconds later, and I heard the dead bolt slide. The door opened partway, and a man with shoulder-length red locks and a stubble beard looked out at me. His hair appeared purposefully messy, and his biker jacket and ripped jeans screamed grunge.

I cleared my throat. "Mr. Nolan, I presume?"

He nodded but didn't open the door any wider.

"I have a few questions about your dogs."

He squinted his hazel eyes at me. At least, I thought that was their color. Under the shadow of his bushy eyebrows, I couldn't quite tell. "You here about the ad? For a teacup Chi? Less than three pounds, even as an adult."

I stammered. "Healthy Chihuahuas grow up to be four to six pounds."

Russ closed the door an inch. "Who are you? Why are you here?"

That's when Marshmallow streaked into the house. Startled, Russ lost hold of the front door, and it flew wide open.

Worried about the damage Marshmallow might do, I scooted inside. Marshmallow kept on going, so I chased him. While running, I noticed the house smelled horrible. It needed a good airing and a vat of vinegar, if not kerosene and flames.

The front door closed behind me, and I heard Russ say, "I ain't prepared for company."

Marshmallow dashed to the end of a shabby living room and scratched against an opaque sliding door that divided a hidden back area. His imaginary voice piped up. "There are dogs trapped inside."

I managed to grab him and started to leave, but he slipped out of my arms. He pawed at the door again.

"Wait a minute," Russ said as his lumbering steps caught up.

My curiosity won out, and I slid open the door. Both Marshmallow and I froze at the scene before us.

Thick blankets covered the entirety of the walls, making a soundproof space. A foul stench arose from the cramped area. The enclosed back room was filled with Chihuahuas. I lost count after twenty.

The little dogs started yipping like crazy, and Marshmallow responded by yowling at them. Bowls of food had been knocked over. Half-empty water dishes spilled murky trails. A few tennis balls lay scattered around, drool-soaked and defuzzed.

However, most of the stink came from dog waste piled all around the vinyl floor.

I turned to face Russ. "What kind of hellhole is this?"

He scratched at his stubble. "You caught me at a bad time."

"I don't believe you. This looks like it's been going on for a while."

"You're trespassing," Russ said, flexing his muscles. "Take your cat and go. Or I'll make you leave."

I held my hands up. "Fine, we're going. I've seen enough."

I took Marshmallow, and we retreated to the front porch. At the door, I told Russ, "You can bet I'm reporting this to animal control and the police."

He curled his meaty hand into a fist. "You wouldn't dare."

I stared him in the eye. "I'd consider it my duty. You're harming those puppies."

He shook his fist at me.

I yelled in a voice as loud as Ma-speak. "Don't you dare threaten me, you monster. You hurt those dogs, and I'll hurt you!"

Russ slammed the door in my face.

A voice floated down to me from above my head and over to my left. "Cut the racket," it said. I looked next door and saw the upstairs window slam shut from the two-story behemoth of a house.

After I got into the car, I placed the calls right away. I got the answering machine at animal control and left a message. But at the local police station, an efficient-sounding woman picked up.

"I'm concerned about the care of some dogs," I told her.

"Yes, miss. Is this a neighborhood disturbance?"

"Litters of puppies are being mistreated. Here's my cell in case you need it." I gave her my number. Then I added my work line. "You can also reach me at my pet grooming business, Hollywoof."

"Did you say *litters* of puppies?" She paused. "Is this regarding a pet store?"

"A breeder." I provided Russ Nolan's name and address.

"Okay, I have the info, but you'll have to file an official complaint with the USDA."

"You're kidding, right?" I'd never reported animal abuse before. I didn't even know the Department of Agriculture had to get involved.

"No, I'm afraid not." She gave me the website.

I ended the call and pulled up the USDA site on my phone. Grumbling about red tape, I clicked on the section to file an animal welfare complaint. While I filled out the form, Marshmallow plopped himself on the dashboard.

After I finished typing, he meowed at me and said, "See, wasn't my talking helpful?"

Not now. Why did I continue to dream up his voice? I took deep breaths. "This isn't happening."

He hissed at me and moved in close. "Face it. This is real, sister." His nose came within inches of my own. "I just gave you proof back there, when I told you about those puppies."

That fact hit me hard. He'd told me about the trapped dogs *before* I'd seen them with my own eyes. How could my mind make up something without first seeing it?

Maybe the talking was real. "But how?" I asked.

"I have a special talent," Marshmallow said.

Wait a minute. His mouth hadn't moved, but I'd heard his voice. If this was truly happening, did that mean . . . "Do you have cat ESP? Telepathy? Or maybe, tele-*pet*hy?"

His whiskers twitched. "Thank heavens, no. Imagine suffering through human thoughts all day long."

"But you can talk to me. Er, think to me."

"Yes, the communication is one-way." Marshmallow blinked at me. "All pets try to speak to their owners, but you don't understand us."

I snapped my fingers. "Right, like those cat translators . . ."

"Useless." He purred. "You humans can't figure it out, so I decided to take matters into my own paws."

My fingers drummed the steering wheel. "You learned English?"

"Watched TV and picked up the language. So much simpler than cat talk. But I can't use my mouth to make the right noises."

"Thus the mind thing." I licked my lips. "So, you can speak to humans?"

"Weren't you listening? Only owners. A shame, because I wanted to thank Alice for rescuing me." Marshmallow's ears flattened. For a brief moment, I wondered about his personal history.

Then the sound of prolonged yipping interrupted my thoughts. I turned my attention back to Russ Nolan. I hoped it wouldn't take too long for the authorities to rescue the dogs.

I looked at his house. In the strange haze of dusk, it seemed to change color. If Ma were here, she'd call it a bad omen. The house glowed white . . . according to Chinese superstition, the color of death.

CHAPTER

three

SLEPT LIKE THE dead. Maybe the mental trauma from visiting Russ Nolan had overwhelmed my brain. In the morning, I only woke up at half past nine because a series of pings came from my phone:

> You wake yet? XOXO Ma

> Kopi date in ten minutes.

> P.S. His name Deeter. Such nice profile on Excite.

I groaned, threw on the first clothes I saw, and shoved a comatose Marshmallow into his carrier.

"Five minutes," I guaranteed Marshmallow when I left him in the Prius and entered the coffee shop.

Needing a caffeine boost but hating the jitters of coffee, I ordered a tea. Before doing so, I had a brief look around but didn't see anyone holding up a rose or using any kind of romantic signal. Then again, Ma had registered me on a dating site called Excite.

Well, I'd at least have some tea if the guy didn't show up.

Just then I heard the barista call out, "Detour."

"It's Deeter," a scratchy voice said.

Like the barista had said, I wanted to take an alternate route when I saw who had spoken up. A guy with orangey sunless tanner skin and a creepy smile. He wore a sweater tied around his shoulders and penny loafers with actual coins in the slots. Definitely not Josh drool-worthy.

First impressions aren't everything, I reasoned, and I had promised Ma to give it a try. I went over and tapped him on the arm. "I'm Mimi."

"Enchanted," he said. He made to swoop in and kiss my cheek, but I backed away.

The barista called my name, and I grabbed my drink. When I turned around, Deeter had already secured a cozy table in a dim corner.

I joined him but moved my seat a safe distance away. Figuring one cup of tea would take five minutes of conversation, I asked him an easy question. "What do you do?"

"Manage people's assets." He patted his shellacked hair. "Oh, I'm sorry. I hadn't meant to use words that went over your pretty little head."

Two more minutes with him, max. "I understand numbers. My dad's in finance, and I have my own business."

"That wasn't in your profile." He checked his phone. "Mimi *Lee*? Haiyaa!"

He made a chopping motion, and I managed to keep the scream inside my head. "Please, no kung fu references."

"Kidding." He held up his hands. "Can't you take a joke?"

"You sure you're ready to date?"

He waggled his eyebrows. "Who said anything about dating?" Looking at his phone, he quoted, "'You want kopi or not?' Sounds like a code word to me."

I almost spit out my drink at him. "Kopi means coffee in Manglish. Malaysian English."

Draining the rest of my tea, I fiddled with my phone under the table.

"Exotic." Deeter leaned forward. "You know, I don't live too far from here."

The alarm rang on my phone, and I picked it up. Pretending to take a call, I held a conversation with myself: "An emergency? I'll be right over."

I ran out the door, not bothering to look back. Once outside, I texted Ma to delete my Excite profile forever. What kind of site had she signed me up for anyway? I'd rather spend the rest of my life with Marshmallow than with that Deet-bag.

In the Prius, I saw the car clock. Ten o'clock already. Crap. I was late to open the store. As we peeled away from the coffee shop, Marshmallow asked, "What? Did you rob the Starbucks?"

Hollywoof didn't have its own parking lot but shared the metered spaces behind the shops, which made me even tardier. As I bustled across the palm tree–lined plaza, I passed by stores already in full swing. The taco shop had its doors open, and fried fish flavored the air. A table displayed sarongs in front of the swim store. Only the late-night sports bar hadn't opened up yet.

I sprinted over to Hollywoof, where I saw a suited man with his back to me. He stood peering through my shop window.

The stranger didn't seem to have a pet with him. And not one strand of fur decorated his dark gray jacket and slacks.

I jingled my keys to get his attention. "Excuse me, can I help you?"

When he turned around, I saw a man about six feet tall with sandy buzz-cut hair. He had hard features with a sharp nose and a square jaw. His light blue eyes reminded me of ice cubes.

"Mimi Lee?" he said. He brushed his sport coat with a subtle move of his hand, and I spied a badge at his waist.

"That's me." I scrunched my nose. "Is this about the dog breeder?"

"You could say that." His voice had an edge to it.

Marshmallow sat at my feet and bristled. "Don't trust guys who don't own pets," he said, as I opened the door to the shop.

I flipped on the lights and welcomed the officer in.

We sat in the waiting area on the pleather benches. I thought Marshmallow might stay near me to provide emotional support, but he strode over to his roost near the plateglass window. Figured.

I frowned at the cat, and the officer caught my look.

"Something wrong?" he asked.

"Nothing," I said.

He perched at the edge of his seat. "Here's my card," he said, handing his info over.

"'Detective Brown,'" I read and started trembling. "Homicide division?"

He tapped the shiny badge at his waist. "Yes, and I'm investigating the death of Russ Nolan."

"What?" I gasped. Out of the corner of my eye, I saw Marshmallow's ears prick up.

Detective Brown's cold eyes gazed into mine. "You were at his house yesterday. A neighbor heard your argument."

I nodded. I remembered the window slamming shut. "Russ Nolan was mistreating those poor Chihuahuas."

The detective made a noise in his throat, neither affirming nor denying my claim.

I wiped my suddenly sweaty hands against the pleather. They left a slight streak.

"The neighbor quoted you as saying, 'You hurt those dogs, and I'll hurt you.'"

My jaw dropped. "But I didn't kill him. I meant I'd report his activities to the right agencies."

Detective Brown straightened up and nodded. "Yes, that's how we found you so quickly. You filed a complaint with the local police. Intake said you seemed miffed the department couldn't help you more."

Shifting in my seat, I said, "I felt annoyed about the paperwork. It could take a long time to go through the red tape."

He quirked an eyebrow at me. "So you took justice into your own hands."

I shook my head. "No, Detective, I didn't."

"Do you have an alibi for last night?"

I glanced at Marshmallow. "My cat was with me . . ." If only he could talk to the detective as well. Use his mind powers.

"I see." Detective Brown gave me a knowing look. "I'm still gathering evidence, but I'm sure I'll be back soon."

I swallowed hard. "Yes, Detective. Er, have a good day."

He got up and dusted off his sport coat. With one hard push, he swung the shop door open and left.

I began pacing the floor. Was I a murder suspect? How had this happened?

"Calm down," Marshmallow said, his eyes following my movements. "You're making me dizzy."

I halted and threw my hands up in the air. "You're the reason I got into this mess. I traipsed through his house because I was running after you."

I needed to call somebody. Who? Not my parents. They would worry too much. Alice?

She'd be teaching class about now, but I hoped she'd pick up. Her cell went straight to voice mail, so I dialed her classroom number.

After several rings, I got through. I didn't let her speak as I said, "Alice, I need—"

A shrill voice came down the line. "This is Principal Hallis. You are disrupting this class. To whom am I speaking?"

My mouth opened and closed.

In a fainter voice, I heard the principal say, "Miss Lee, no personal calls during classtime. I thought you'd be more professional." The line disconnected.

I slumped my shoulders, while Marshmallow licked at his coat without a care in the world.

I pointed at him. "I'm taking you back to the shelter as soon as I can."

"You've got bigger fish to fry. Looks like you're murder suspect number one."

He was right. I plunked down on the bench and put my head in my hands.

"Perk up," Marshmallow continued. "You know a lawyer, right? I saw his card on your nightstand."

I spluttered. "You can read, too?" And who was he talking about?

"Learned it from closed-captioning. The card said '*Josh*.'"

My cheeks flamed. How could I face him again? But Marshmallow had a point. Josh was a lawyer. Actually, the only attorney I knew.

I looked at Marshmallow. "Okay, I'm keeping you, but only until I clear my name."

CHAPTER

four

JOSH WORKED IN downtown Los Angeles, which featured an eclectic mix of modern metallic buildings and certified historical gems with detailed artwork sculpted by hand. I navigated across a dizzying array of one-way streets until I located the right address. Giving up on any vacant metered street parking, I opted for one of the lots scattered throughout the urban area.

Josh himself worked in a conservative sandstone building that looked frumpy compared to its gleaming skyscraper neighbors. It was made of dull gray brick, and I was surprised ivy didn't creep up the edifice's stodgy walls.

Thank goodness I'd found a spare blouse at Hollywoof and changed out of my usual T-shirt. At least they wouldn't kick me out of the building on sight. I'd switched outfits, convincing myself I'd changed to better support my plea for Josh's help.

Here goes my second chance at a first impression, I told myself. What could I use for my new line? *Hey, Josh. I'm actually a great catch—*

just ask the cops. Shaking my head, I pushed through the skyscraper's glistening glass doors into the enormous lobby.

A rush of frigid air hit me in the face as I entered. Shivering, I jostled the oversized Hello Kitty tote bag on my shoulder.

A soft growl came from inside the giant purse. "Watch it," Marshmallow said. "And where am I anyway? Feels like a meat locker in here."

I shushed him. "The building's got heavy-duty air-conditioning, I guess." Checking the business card, I saw that Josh's office was located on the fifth floor. I headed toward the brass elevators and called for one.

When it arrived, I breathed out a sigh of relief. "All clear," I said, stepping inside the empty elevator car.

Marshmallow popped up his fuzzy head for a breather once the doors had slid shut. "Do you know how cramped it is in there?"

"Well, I can't waltz into a fancy law firm with a cat in my arms."

Using the reflective interior walls of the elevator, he proceeded to preen himself. "I still can't believe you stuffed me into a Hello Kitty bag."

"It's the biggest purse I own," I said.

He twitched his whiskers. "Did you know that Hello Kitty isn't even a real cat? No mouth. I mean, how is she supposed to eat? Or talk?"

"Doesn't stop some cats I know," I mumbled as the elevator dinged. When we arrived at our destination, the doors started sliding open, and Marshmallow crouched back down into the tote with a grumble.

I walked down a long hallway with plush carpeting until I found the unit number. Heavy wooden doors barred entry into the illustrious law office. To the right of them, I saw an impressive-looking bronze plaque tacked onto the wall. "Ooh, it's the firm of Murphy, Sullivan, and Goodwin," I said. "*Good win*—that's a positive sign, right?"

"Too bad that's not Josh's last name."

I brushed Marshmallow's comment aside and entered the auspicious law office. Right away, I felt overwhelmed. People wearing sleek dark suits scurried left and right. They seemed to weave around one another in a purposeful and coordinated dance.

I took a deep breath and made my way to the walnut reception desk, where a middle-aged blonde reigned. She sat there with erect posture, her hair tucked into a prim bun, and spoke into a headset.

When she saw me hovering, she held up her hand. She continued listening to the person on the other end and said, "I see. I'm transferring you over now. One moment, please."

Then she completed a complicated maneuver with her fingers, pressing various buttons on the phone with a flourish.

Finished, she turned to me. She scrutinized my appearance before asking, "Do you have an appointment?"

I rubbed my sweaty palms together. "I'm here to see Josh Akana."

She blinked at me with her ice blue eyes. "Who? I don't recognize that name."

I bit my lip. Pulling out his business card, I showed it to her.

She examined it and flicked her polished nails at me. "Must be an associate. Fresh blood. You won't find him in one of the actual offices. He'll be sitting at one of the tables in the open area." She gestured behind her at the straight rows of desks.

"Associate?" Marshmallow said. "He's not even a proper lawyer yet?"

"Associates *are* real lawyers," I said.

The receptionist raised her overplucked eyebrows at me. "Of course, dear. I'm sure your boyfriend is quite the catch." Then the phone rang. She squeezed the bridge of her nose and waved me away.

I'd been mistaken for his girlfriend. Josh and me together? The thought made my heart flutter as I walked past the receptionist's large desk.

The main room held row after row of solid oak tables, though I spotted a side hallway that must have led to more private senior offices. Placed back-to-back, the desks didn't offer much privacy, though tall hutches did block each lawyer's view of their opposite neighbors.

The tables took up so much space, only a narrow corridor of a few feet separated them from the walls on the side. Instead of artwork, framed mirrors were spaced along the wall, perhaps to give the entire area a more spacious feel. I moved down the tight aisle, looking for a familiar flop of dark brown hair at one of the tables.

I found Josh five rows down, his back toward me. I could recognize those muscular shoulders anywhere. But he sat slouched with his head in his hands. Nearby lay a crinkled fortune cookie wrapper. Its accompanying slip of paper read, "A smile uses less muscles than a frown."

I stepped closer to him. "Josh? I'm sorry to bother you, but . . ."

He lifted his head and registered me. Even under the fluorescent lighting, his eyes appeared a heady shade of brown.

His nose wrinkled. "Mimi? Did you tell me you were coming? I haven't had a chance to check my voice messages yet."

Oops. Guess I should have called first. Being accused of murder had made any sense of etiquette disappear.

The tips of his ears started turning pink. I wondered if he was reliving the last time we met, the awkward scene in the laundry room. "Er, sorry about the other day," I said. "My mom was really talking about *erasers*. She uses British terms sometimes as a force of habit. I don't really need rubbers for, um, other uses." Nervous babbling had overtaken me. I chewed the inside of my cheek to stop talking.

He held up his hands. "Hey, I don't need to know the intimate details of your private life."

I took a deep breath. "Actually, I'm here for legal advice. A cop showed up at my work and started questioning me about a murder. I panicked and rushed right over."

"Uh-oh. You're involved in a homicide investigation?" He drummed his fingers against the table. Hmm, he had the nice long fingers of a pianist. I bet he had a gentle touch.

Marshmallow whispered to me. "Psst, say something. Otherwise, he might think you're guilty."

"Um." I stopped watching Josh play his fingers against the burnished wood. "I didn't do it, of course."

That's probably what every guilty person says. I tried batting my eyes at Josh, and he stopped moving his fingers.

Instead, he stood up and brought his face close to mine. Was he about to kiss me? "Mimi," he said, "are your eyes okay?"

"What? Um . . ." The batting must have confused him. I rubbed my eyes. "A loose contact. It's back in place now."

"Look, even if I wanted to"—Josh gestured at a teetering stack of file folders—"I'm really busy right now." The whole pile seemed ready to crash into a nearby glass jar filled with wrapped fortune cookies. Did he collect those?

I wrung my hands. "I've never been in trouble with the police before. Not even a speeding ticket. Please help me out. Maybe I could give you something in return for your legal help?"

He seemed to choke at my words.

"Gosh, you're direct," Marshmallow said.

I felt my face burn up. "I mean, I groom animals for a job. Perhaps you have a pet?"

He shook his head. "No way. I used to kill *schools* of carnival goldfish. And that's only a slight exaggeration."

"Or . . . I could do your laundry sometime?"

"No thanks. Plus, maybe you wouldn't want me to represent you anyway . . ." His shoulders slumped. He picked up his fortune and reread it but, despite the advice, continued frowning. "In fact, you actually caught me at a horrible time. Just came back from court, where I lost my first case in ten minutes flat."

Marshmallow piped up. "You sure know how to pick 'em, Mimi."

I swung my bag toward the desk, stopping just shy of hitting the wooden surface.

A hiss erupted from the tote.

Josh's eyes widened, and he lowered his voice. "Do you have a . . . cat . . . in there?"

I hid the bag behind my feet so he couldn't look inside.

"No pets allowed in the office," Josh said. "Only service animals."

"Sorry. It's because I came straight from my shop."

Marshmallow huffed. "What a load of kitty litter. It's clear you can't focus around lover boy and need me here. Now, go get his legal advice."

Right. I clasped my hands together. "Can you help me out, Josh?"

He pointed an elegant pianist finger at the Hello Kitty tote. "I think you'd better leave now. The partners will have a fit if they find an animal, and then we'll both be in deep trouble."

Josh hadn't answered my question. He wouldn't help me, then. I'd messed up. I had driven away not only a talented lawyer, but someone I really liked, all through one conversation. "Um, I'll see you around the apartments," I said.

Josh didn't respond and focused on organizing his teetering files. I slunk away from the open area—and not a moment too soon.

Because near the front desk, my phone started blaring out "Chapel of Love." The receptionist placed a finger against her lips, and I silenced the ringing.

After I went down to the lobby, I called my mother back. "You called, Ma?"

"Finally use hand phone," she yelled. "Fast come home. Help me make dim sum."

I spluttered. "You're calling me about your food cravings?"

Sometimes Ma's spontaneous calls involved satisfying her taste buds. She often got a hankering for crisp roast duck or a sugar-crusted pineapple bun. Then she phoned me, because she hated eating by herself. If she ate with a partner, she could call it "bonding time," not "gorging."

"I'm really busy, Ma. You can't even begin to imagine." I paced back and forth by the brass elevators.

"Aiyaa! You not understand. Food not mine, for your *meimei*."

My little sister. "Alice wants dim sum?" I said as I stepped out of the law building and braced myself to walk the several blocks over to the exorbitantly priced parking lot. "I don't follow, Ma."

"She call me. Sound so sad."

I stubbed my right toe against an uneven ridge in the concrete sidewalk and flinched.

Ma continued, the pitch of her voice swooping high in victory. "I know how make better. *Dan tat* her back to happy."

Egg tarts would cure my sister's sorrow? Though, truth be told, they were her Achilles' heel. She never passed up a dim sum cart laden with the sweet pastries.

Those fresh homemade egg tarts took time to craft, too. Ma's recipe required a precise method of making the dough to create the exquisite crust.

"Why is Alice sad?" I asked.

"No say much. School trouble," Ma said. "So, help me can?"

I froze at the edge of the parking lot. Something had happened at Alice's workplace. Did it have anything to do with my emergency call to her classroom? Was she in trouble because of me?

A hot flush of shame bloomed in my body. "I'll be right over," I said as I sprinted toward my parked car.

CHAPTER

five

M A PUT ME to work in the kitchen making the egg tarts. The filling required whisking together sugar, eggs, vanilla, salt, and milk. However, the crust took more fine-tuning. Creating the extra flakiness required two dough mixtures: the first used all-purpose flour combined with oil, salt, and water; the second mixed together low-protein flour and oil. Then the two versions were flattened and rolled together and folded multiple times before being shaped into circles and fitted into cuplike molds.

After putting the tarts into the oven, Ma made sure to also brew a pot of strong tea. She placed the full red ceramic teapot embellished with a serpentine dragon on the lazy Susan. She'd made sure to add the portable spinner to the Formica dining table, the better to serve family meals. A spiral of steam came out of the teapot's spout, bringing with it the fragrant floral scent of chrysanthemum tea.

The timer dinged. Ma and I moved to the oven door. As she pulled out the baking sheet of egg tarts, I said, "Those turned out well." Each tart, about the size of my palm, featured a crimped buttery crust and a smooth golden center of egg custard. After they had cooled, I organized them onto a platter with double happiness symbols and added it to the lazy Susan.

Footsteps sounded near the front door. We heard a key turn in the lock.

I recognized those heavy, sturdy steps. Not my sister's, but those of—

"Dad," I said, flinging open the door.

He dropped his black bag filled with golf clubs on the threshold. "Princess Number One," he said, enveloping me in a big bear hug. His familiar scent of cedar and spice washed over me. Even though I was full-grown, he towered over me by about a foot, and I still felt as secure in his arms as I had as a child.

After he let go, he strode across to Ma and pecked her cheek. "Hello, love." He spotted the full plate of egg tarts on the table and said, "I see Alice hasn't shown up yet. Guess I made it back in the nick of time."

When he made to pilfer a dan tat, Ma swatted his hands away. "Alice get first pick." She eyed his clothes. "Anyway, you need change, Greg. Quick lah."

"Winnie, what I'm wearing is fine."

Dad wore his usual golfing outfit: belted shorts and a striped polo—generic, of course. From far away, the symbol on his shirt looked like a player on a horse wielding a stick. On closer inspection, though, the horse turned out to be a unicorn. "Same material, half the price," he often boasted, highlighting his figures-oriented accounting mind.

"No, you wear wrong. Like dis, do more style." Ma smoothed down her own batik dress. The special customized fabric from Malaysia featured hand-painted butterflies flitting around in a garden.

The physical contrast between my parents seemed striking at

first glance, but like their love, the fusion worked. Their unique combined style even invaded our home through the decor. Lucky goldfish sketches hung on our Benjamin Moore muted-color walls. Fancy brocaded silk throws decorated our long leather sofas.

The doorbell rang, one sharp chime.

"Too late now," my dad said as he stuffed his golf bag into the hall closet.

Ma wagged her finger at him even while she shuffled over to the door and opened it. "Alice," she said. "Why you ring bell? I always say no need guest air."

My sister walked in with plodding, weary steps. "It's only polite. I don't live here anymore." She rolled her neck to get a kink out. "I've had such a horrid day. Thanks for letting me come by, Ma."

She slipped her shoes off in the foyer and froze as she spotted Dad and me standing across the way near the dining table. "What are you guys doing here?"

"Ma wanted to surprise you," I said. "We showed up to provide moral support."

Dad gave Alice a big wink. "Actually, I'm here for the dan tats."

"Ooh." Alice made her way over and grinned at the display on the table. "For me?"

I dusted my hands against my slacks, leaving a streak of white flour behind. "Ma and I baked them fresh."

"And I stopped in the middle of a great golf game," Dad added. "We love you, Princess Two." He engulfed Alice in his arms.

Then, once we were all seated at the table, I poured out the tea for everyone in the matching red dragon cups. Although it was tradition to have the youngest serve the elders, I figured Alice needed a break.

For a few minutes, we munched on delicious egg tarts and didn't say a word. Enjoying the creamy sweetness of the custard, I reveled in the bites. Joy also spread wide across Alice's face as she licked crust crumbs off her fingers.

I saw Ma nudge Dad with her elbow, probably hoping he'd broach the topic of Alice's sadness. He, in turn, stared at me. *"Psych major,"* he mouthed.

Clearing my throat, I spoke up. "So, Alice, is there anything you'd like to talk about?"

She took another dan tat and placed it on her plate.

"Sometimes it helps to *process* your feelings," I continued. Ack, the words seemed ripped right from one of my old college textbooks.

She split her egg tart in half with a strong twist of her hands. An earthquake-like fissure severed its golden center. "Work is stressful right now, but I'm sure I'll manage."

"Um . . ." I poured her more tea. Wasn't the chrysanthemum flower known for its calming properties? "Does the stress have anything to do with a phone call?"

"How did you—" She stopped and took a sip of tea. Then she touched the tip of her pinky to her chin, our sister promise to keep things mum from our parents. "Never mind. It wasn't because of any *phone call.* I got in trouble when a new kid with an IEP acted up in class."

Ma gasped. The teacup shook in her hands, and she spilled a few drops. "Kid make classroom explode?"

Dad placed an arm around Ma's shoulder. "No, love. That's an IED, improvised explosive device. An IEP is . . ." He faltered and raised his thick eyebrows at Alice.

"An individualized education program. Some kids need certain adjustments to learn better. They usually have an aide, but the assistant called in sick at the last minute."

"The principal got mad at you about a *child* acting up? Come on, it's school," I said. "What does she expect to happen?"

"Principal Hallis was in my classroom observing my teaching today. The kid started screaming and throwing a tantrum. Afterward, the principal said I couldn't control my classroom and that 'any teacher worth her salt' would be able to maintain an 'optimal learning environment.'"

Alice started biting the fingernail on her thumb, a nervous habit she'd never outgrown. "The principal said the school might have some budget cuts soon."

I sat upright in my chair. "She doesn't mean . . ." Could the principal be threatening Alice's job?

"I don't know." Alice picked at the crust of her dan tat, scattering flaky bits across the table.

"Oh, princess," Dad said, placing his hand on top of hers. He beckoned to the rest of us. "Time for a group hug."

Scraping our chairs back, we bustled over to Alice's side. After the family hug, the crease on her forehead lessened, and Alice could nibble at an egg tart again. "Thanks, I feel better."

We settled back in our seats, and Alice turned to me. "What about you, Mimi? How's the new shop going?"

I looked at each loving person around the table: Alice, her eyes sparkling with kindness; Dad, a wide grin splitting his face; and Ma, her head tilted toward me with interest. How could I tell them the truth? That no customers came by? Even worse, that I could be on the verge of getting arrested?

I snatched a dan tat and stuffed it in my mouth. "Everything's fine," I said with my mouth full.

They exchanged puzzled looks with one another. Just then, I saw some white fur waltzing by. Ah, the distraction I needed.

I swallowed. "Marshmallow," I said, picking him up. He'd finally woken up from his power nap on my childhood canopied bed. "Thanks for giving him to me, Alice."

Marshmallow swished his tail at me. "And thank you for lifting me up closer to the treats," he said. "I'm famished."

"What a cute name," Alice said. Her light brown eyes seemed to glow. "May I hold him for a minute?"

"Be my guest." I placed Marshmallow on my sister's lap, where she fussed over him. She petted him until he sounded like a running motor with his continuous purring.

"Maybe the food can wait," he said, stretching across Alice's legs.

Seeing the fragile peace that existed while Alice stroked Marshmallow's head, Ma and Dad gave each other thin smiles. Their heads swiveled her way, watching my baby sis with anxious eyes.

With Alice's problem revealed, I couldn't add to the stress and dump my troubles onto my family, too. I'd have to get out of the mess on my own. And after Alice had finished pampering Marshmallow, I knew one place where I might go to gather clues.

• • •

Marshmallow and I stood on the sidewalk near the dried-up lawn of Russ Nolan's house. It looked shut up tight. In fact, a coroner's notice sealed the front door. Could I sneak in without getting caught? After all, the fading sunlight might mask my movements.

Even if I did, though, would I leave behind more incriminating evidence to get me locked behind bars? I shuddered at the thought of seeing Detective Brown again, this time with handcuffs held out to me.

If only I had some sort of camera. Or a drone. Something to be my eyes and ears without stepping foot into the actual crime scene. But wait a minute—I did.

I turned to Marshmallow. "Want to have an adventure? Bet you could wander inside and nobody would know the difference."

He trained his blue eyes on me. "Are you kidding? I don't need a record."

"You watch too much *CSI*. Cats don't get arrested." I pointed to myself. "People do."

He licked his paw with long, even strokes. "What's in it for me?"

"Justice and doing the right thing?" I said.

Marshmallow continued grooming.

I tried something more persuasive. "Catnip?"

"No drugs for me, sister."

"How about you get to keep me as an owner?"

He gave me a slow blink.

"If that happens," I said, "you'll get to see Alice a lot more. You two seem to have a great bond."

His ears perked up at that. Could he be convinced to do the deed? Before he even made a move, a loud screech sounded from behind us.

A sleek Mercedes SUV bumped up to the curb, and a woman in her midthirties got out. She was dressed much younger than her age, having adopted an artificial teenager look by wearing a teal cropped tank with sequined letters that read "Armstrong Academy." However, everyone in La La Land seemed to look for youth, whether by procedures, cosmetics, or attitude.

Her auburn hair was pulled into a high ponytail, and she sported oversize tortoiseshell sunglasses. The woman clomped her way toward us in rhinestone-encrusted sandals.

"Oh no. Russ Nolan must've gotten on someone else's bad side, too." The woman plucked her sunglasses off and stuffed them inside her leather crossbody bag with metal rivets on the sides. Her face appeared caked with bright makeup, just shy of obvious clown material.

"I don't know anything," I said, shaking my head multiple times, as though that could sever invisible connections to the murder. I'd been seen arguing with the man before he'd died. I wondered if I seemed guilty, not only to Detective Brown but to strangers like this lady. "Actually, I only met Russ Nolan yesterday."

Maybe I'd said his name with distaste, because the woman said, "Did he do you wrong in a day? That's a record. Welcome to the sisterhood, then. I'm Tammy." She offered her hand to me. When I went to shake it, she started making a complicated hand jive motion.

"Um." I stepped a bit back from her.

"You're not in the know? Guess not everyone's in tune with the latest and greatest." Was she trying to sound retro hip?

I wonder how well she knew the breeder and if she could provide me with any useful info. "Tammy, how did *you* meet Russ Nolan?"

"Bought a teacup Chi from him recently." Tammy's fire-iron red lips curved down in displeasure.

I thought back to my interactions with Indira and Lauren, who'd both bought tiny yippy dogs from him. "Did your dog happen to get sick?"

"How did you know? Do you own one of his dogs, too?" Her chestnut eyes locked on to Marshmallow, sitting beside me. "Guess not. I see you're more of a cat lover."

It would take too long to set the record straight for her, how this gift of a cat was not exactly so desirable, so I decided to nod instead.

"Well," she continued, "imagine my surprise when Kale's kneecap slipped. She started dragging her lame leg."

All the little Chihuahuas from the breeder seemed to have similar problems. Why was that? "How's Kale now?" I asked.

"Not good. And I wanted to give that breeder a piece of my mind." Tammy strode toward the sealed door and started shifting the tape. "I wonder what happened to him. Was it an accident? Revenge of the Dogs?"

"Don't touch that sticker. That's a real crime scene."

She turned to me with her hands on her hips. "Do you know something I don't?"

"No, not much," I stammered. "I heard, uh, a rumor that it was a homicide."

She narrowed her eyes at me. "How come you know about the sick dogs? Are you in cahoots with Russ, too? Buddies with that breeder Magnus down the street? He was supposed to be a top-notch guy, according to my mommy gal pals, but now I'm not so sure."

"I have no idea what you're talking about. I'm just a pet groomer and stumbled upon a few odd-acting puppies recently."

"Mm-hmm." She sized me up. "I'm a great judge of character. As acting president of the PTA, I keep kids safe from predators."

"Honest to goodness, I'm a groomer. Let me get you my business card." I scrounged through my tote. How could I find anything in this humongous and unfamiliar Hello Kitty bag? "Or perhaps I can give you some references? I've worked with Lauren Dalton—"

"Oh, Lauren." Tammy gave a gasp of delight. "She's generously donated to the school. If you know her, you should be in the clear. Plus, she's my pet yoga buddy."

Yoga again. "Do you know Indira as well?" I asked.

"I've probably seen her around." Tammy dug into her small purse, pulling out her sunglasses and slipping them on. "Did you say you're a groomer?"

She could be another viable customer. "One minute," I said as my hand finally closed around a familiar rectangular shape. I handed my card to Tammy.

"'Hollywoof,'" she read, giving me her fiery red smile. "I like it. Sounds happening. Catch you on the flip side."

"Sure. Goodbye." I waved to Tammy as she opened her car door and slid into the driver's seat.

As she screeched off in the SUV, the neighboring house's upstairs window popped open. "This is a residential street, not a racetrack," a familiar-sounding voice said.

A woman with a haggard face and frizzy hair trapped under a sweatband peeked over the windowsill. "You again," she said, her face puckering like those shriveled red dates Ma put in her herbal soups. "Don't move a muscle. I'm coming down right now to have a word with you."

CHAPTER

= six =

THE NEIGHBOR MARCHED over to the sidewalk to confront me. However, she wore lounge pants and a sweatshirt that read "I'd rather be watching YouTube," and she didn't look ready for company. In one hand, she held a rolled-up newspaper, which she brandished at me. I felt like a pesky fly she couldn't wait to swat.

"What do you think you're doing traipsing around this lovely neighborhood?" She shook her head and muttered, "We all used to keep our doors unlocked on this block. Except for Russ Nolan. At least I convinced him not to chain up his side gate. But ever since Russ moved in, things have gone downhill."

So the breeder had been a new arrival. Could he have brought unsavory characters with him to the area? "When did Russ Nolan buy here?" I asked.

She stopped waving her newspaper and snorted at me. "Please. Russ Nolan couldn't ever own a house in this neighborhood. That wretched Kevin Walker, my old neighbor's son, started renting out the place last year after his mother kicked the bucket. Not that she was a great neighbor, either, always taking the borrowing-sugar rule to the extreme."

She stood there, tapping her foot against the concrete, and waited for a response from me. I couldn't shed any light on her neighbors, but I did apologize for my presence. "Sorry to disturb you, ma'am. I had to come back today because my cat, uh, lost his collar." I pointed at Marshmallow.

His blue eyes narrowed at me. "How dare you pin the blame on me."

The neighbor did a double take. "I didn't notice him. Smart choice on your part. Cats make great pets, so quiet and clean." She aimed the newspaper tube at Russ Nolan's front door. "Not like those pesky dogs Russ kept, with their constant barking. Worse than those puppies the dog collector Magnus Cooper has on Oak Lane. Lives two streets away, but still walks his dogs around here."

One of her comments caught my attention. "Did you actually hear those puppies?" Hadn't Russ soundproofed the dog room with thick blankets?

She puffed out her chest. "I've got quite the hearing, even though I'm pushing seventy. I told Russ plenty of times to knock it off. Their constant noise caused me migraines." Massaging her brow, she continued, "Called the police station once, but they said it was my neighbor's right to own a few dogs."

So she didn't know how many dogs Russ actually owned, or that he'd bred them for profit.

She squinted at me. "You don't look like his usual type."

"Excuse me?"

"Russ. Not a single male buddy, but always parading his girlfriends around the neighborhood. Men nowadays, dating multiple women at the same time. Whatever happened to old-fashioned courtship?" She smacked the newspaper against the palm of her hand. "Loose morals."

I choked. "I wasn't dating Russ."

She harrumphed at me, clearly not believing a word I said.

My mind flashed to a comparison of Josh against Russ. I couldn't help but cringe and said, "For crying out loud, didn't you hear me argue with Russ? We're not a couple. I don't like him one tiny bit."

"The lady doth protest too much. You two had a lover's spat," she said, nodding her head. "And it caused a major neighborhood disturbance."

Those words echoed what Detective Brown had told me. "Aha, so you were the one who reported me to the police." My hands started clenching and unclenching.

Marshmallow nudged my leg. "Cool it," he said, but I shook my head. This lady had practically handed me over to the police as a murder suspect.

I shook my fist at the neighbor. "I'm in deep trouble now because of your big mou—"

Meow.

The neighbor and I both looked at Marshmallow, who'd let out the huge cry and had now shrunk himself into a fluffball. He peeked up at us with wide baby blue eyes.

An involuntary *aww* came out of the neighbor's mouth. "You definitely have much better taste in animals than in men."

I took a deep breath and relaxed my hands. "Thanks." I said it in response to Marshmallow saving my hide, but she didn't have to know that. My anger would only give this nosy neighbor more ammunition for the police to use.

Marshmallow twitched his whiskers at me and said, "Watch this." He held up a paw to the woman.

She unfurled her newspaper and fanned Marshmallow. "Do you think your cat's okay? He's acting weird. Is it heatstroke?"

"Tell her to shake my paw," Marshmallow said.

"What?"

The neighbor stopped fanning and peered at me. "It's those rock concerts, right? Makes young people lose their hearing. I said, *Do you think your cat's okay?*"

I gestured to Marshmallow's paw. "He's fine. Just waiting for you to shake his paw."

"Huh?" She stretched her left hand out to Marshmallow—and he tapped it.

After shaking hands with him, the neighbor smiled at Marshmallow. "What manners. How do you do? My name is Shirl, and you are . . ."

"His name's Marshmallow," I said.

She clucked her tongue. "He needs a more suitable name. How about Emperor?"

"Shirl's got great taste," Marshmallow said. "Emperor *would* be a more fitting name."

Shirl tapped her chin. "Have you taught him to do any other tricks? I saw a cat flushing the toilet the other day on YouTube."

"Oh, he has plenty of skills." I patted Marshmallow on the head. "But I can't show you them right now." I didn't know if he had any more tricks up his sleeve.

"Maybe when you practice and perfect them?"

"Yeah, sure. I take it we're okay. You won't call the police on me?"

She nodded, but her eyes were fixed on Marshmallow. "Not today, anyway."

"Thank you again," I whispered to Marshmallow as we headed back to the car. Near the door of my Prius, I paused and tried to give him a high five. He left me hanging.

Licking his fur, Marshmallow said, "Tricks are my secret weapons, Mimi. I can't give them out to people like party favors."

"Fine." I settled us into the car. Right after I buckled in, my phone rang. It played "We Are Family" by Sister Sledge.

I picked up. "Alice, is everything all right?"

Her voice sounded muffled. "I locked myself in the bathroom so I could talk to you. Ma and Dad are still trying to cheer me up. She started making another batch of egg tarts, and he almost suffocated me with his last bear hug. They even asked me to sleep over here, like a little girl."

A text pinged in the middle of our conversation. I ignored it.

"Sorry I left you with them, but I had to go and take care of something," I said.

"Does this have anything to do with your phone call to my classroom? I swear I won't tell Ma and Dad."

I didn't need Alice to worry about me. She already seemed plenty stressed by her work. "Oh, that? An accidental butt dial."

I heard the water faucet turn on from her end. "Almost done," Alice shouted. Then, in a lower voice, she said, "You called my cell, too, Mimi. That means you wanted to talk to me."

"Um, double butt dial?"

"I don't believe you." She shut off the water. "But I need to go before Ma breaks down the door. Please let me know if you need anything at all."

After she'd hung up, I remembered the ignored beep and checked my messages. Who had texted during the call? Ma. Of course.

Your sister lock herself inside washroom. Crying. You jiejie, big sister, can go fix. I call already school office and make you appointment. Tomorrow morning, eight.

CHAPTER

seven

LOCATED IN THE San Fernando Valley, Roosevelt Elementary was a prim schoolhouse made with storybook red brick construction. A giant American flag, alongside a bear-emblazoned state banner, flew high above a shiny metal pole. Every morning, Alice told me, the students recited the Pledge of Allegiance with their hands over their hearts.

Climbing the stone stairs, I crept past the stately columns guarding the front. I moved at a snail's pace through the hallway, dreading the upcoming confrontation.

After Ma had scheduled the appointment, I couldn't cancel it at the last minute and unleash even more ill will against my sister. Since I knew I needed to be the protective older sister, the burden rested heavily on my shoulders. I would have to help Alice and save the Lee family name from dishonor.

I paused before the school office and took a deep breath to steady myself. Marching inside, I noticed a long counter in the front, lined with bright neon flyers advertising various activities, all emphasized with exclamation points: "Sculpt with Clay!" "Engineer Through Legos!" "Cheerlead by Waving Fuzzy Pom-Poms!" The harried-looking receptionist, glued to a phone, peeked at a sturdy clock on the wall and mouthed, "Mimi Lee?"

I nodded, so she pointed behind her to a closed door with a frosted glass window. Walking over to it, I saw the word "PRINCIPAL" etched in faded gold on the opaque surface. I tried to peer through the murky glass but couldn't see a thing. I wondered what horrors might meet me inside.

My hand deposited sweat marks on the knob as I turned it. I entered to find Principal Hallis sitting in a high-backed chair behind a metal table that looked more like a butcher's block than a desk. Its uncluttered space held a desktop computer and a picture frame with its back to me.

The principal narrowed her eyes at me. Not only did her gaze cut me, but everything about her appeared sharp and dangerous. She had severe, gaunt features that made her chin, cheekbones, and nose look like jagged knifepoints. Even her cropped dark brown hair with stylized bangs seemed razor-edged.

She frowned at me and pointed toward the door. "Do it again. And this time, knock before you enter."

I hung my head, walked back out, and knocked.

"Come in," her stern voice said.

I entered with mincing steps. I'd never been reprimanded by a principal or a teacher ever in my life.

"Close the door," she said.

I complied and sat down in the armchair facing her. Made of steel, it seemed to suit the principal's personality.

She looked at the circular black clock on a side wall. She let it tick for a few seconds before turning to me. "What did you need to discuss?"

I tucked my hair behind my ears. "It's about my sister, Alice Lee."

Her nostrils flared, but she nodded for me to continue.

If I owned some of the blame for yesterday, maybe the principal's frustration would transfer from Alice to me. I looked Principal Hallis in the face and launched into my prepared apology. "The phone call was entirely my fault, Principal Hallis. Please don't blame Alice for that."

Her eyes narrowed at me again. "Fine, I blame you." She jutted out her sharp chin. "And why did you feel the need to call Miss Lee and disrupt her classroom?"

Oh, I hadn't prepared myself for actual questioning. Better to be vague. No doubt being related to someone in trouble with the law, possibly for murder, wouldn't improve my sister's standing. "It was an emergency situation," I said.

"Not a school issue." Her lips pinched together. "Your personal emergency, I gather. One that should have been redirected to a cell phone and left as a message."

I cast my eyes down and bowed my head to emphasize my contrition. "Yes, Principal Hallis. I've learned my lesson."

She glanced at the wall clock. Uh-oh. I was running out of time, and I still needed her to clear Alice's name. I jiggled my foot under the desk. "My sister really enjoys teaching here. She's a hard worker, and the kids love her."

The principal cocked one thin eyebrow at me. "I'll be the judge of that," she said. "One of your sister's pupils acted out of control during class. You know, I'm currently evaluating staff to see if they're even qualified to teach at an establishment like Roosevelt Elementary. And typically, when budget cuts occur, the newest members are let go first."

I swallowed down my panic. Alice had only recently finished her student teaching position and obtained her credentials. Would she stand any chance against the more tenured teachers here?

"Glad I made myself clear. This discussion is done." The principal turned to her computer and peered at the screen.

However, to end things on a more positive note, I stood up to shake her hand. She didn't seem to notice my gesture, so I walked over to her side of the steel desk. The sole framed picture on her desk showed the principal handling a hedgehog. It figured that she'd enjoy the company of prickly animals.

"Thank you for your time," I said, offering my hand.

She didn't shake it, instead waving me away. "Your appointment's done, and I have a school to run. Don't forget to close the door behind you."

I did as she asked. Outside her door, I stared at the wooden barrier. "Principal Hallis?" I mumbled under my breath. "More like Principal *Hellish*."

I passed by the receptionist, who seemed busy fielding questions from a long line of parents snaking out the front door. Checking the clock, I realized that although the meeting had felt drawn-out, the principal had booted me out of her office in little time. I wondered if I'd helped or hurt Alice with my rehearsed apology.

As I drove back to the 405 on-ramp, I saw a line of traffic blocking the major road, so I decided to go around through some residential streets near Russ Nolan's neighborhood. A sign for Oak Lane caught my eye.

My mind must have recognized the name somehow, because my hands moved the steering wheel and I made a sharp turn down the street. What a change from the worn-out look Russ Nolan's neighborhood sported, even though the two neighborhoods were within walking distance.

This street looked elegant, filled with European flavor. In fact, many of the houses had overdosed on Spanish flair. They featured crisp white stucco exteriors that contrasted with the brilliant red of their stylized tiled roofs. I bet mosaic-lined pools could be found in a number of their backyards. And instead of Spain's popular olive trees, regal palm trees sprouted in trimmed front yards up and down the block.

I remembered that Shirl, Russ Nolan's neighbor, had griped about another multi-dog owner named Magnus who lived on Oak. Also, PTA President Tammy had mentioned the same name as someone "in cahoots" with Russ Nolan. As his breeder buddy, wouldn't Magnus know about Russ Nolan's possible enemies? People with more motive than me to get rid of Russ? Maybe I could even compile a list of real suspects to present to Detective Brown.

How could I find Magnus? Cruising down the street, I didn't have to wait long before I spotted a dog walker. The young woman held five puppies on leashes. Who else would own so many dogs?

The cute Chihuahuas who trotted next to her wagged their tails. I parked at the curb a few paces behind her. Then I followed the happy pack of dogs on foot.

The group entered an enormous two-story house at the corner, its width extended the size of two houses. A homey anomaly on Oak Lane with its clapboard siding and buttercup paint, the house exuded a rustic charm. Above the doorway of the double front doors, a wooden sign in the shape of a poodle swung in the breeze. I'd found Magnus Cooper's place.

When I knocked on the door, the young woman, a couple of years past her teens, said, "We're open." Distracted with the puppies who'd managed to tangle their leashes, she waved me into the house.

While she tried to separate the dogs, I moved past a steep stair-

MIMI LEE GETS A CLUE

case in the center of the foyer. Past the entryway, I noticed a large muscular man sitting behind an office desk in the space where a dining table could have been.

"Do you have an appointment?" he asked, looking at me. "I wasn't expecting anyone." His broad shoulders and football player frame almost dwarfed the impressive oak desk in front of him.

"I don't. Sorry." I moved closer to him. "Would you happen to be Magnus Cooper?"

The man stood up. At his full height, he towered over me by more than a foot. I had no doubt his trunk-like arms could squash me like an ant if he wanted to.

"Yes, that's me," he said, crossing his arms and making his muscles bulge. "And you would be?"

Was he possibly shady like Tammy had implied? My voice squeaked when I replied. "Mimi Lee. I'm here about your dogs." I bit my lip. What would be the best way to guarantee my safety? Flattery often yielded great results. "I'm a pet groomer at Hollywoof. A friend told me about your doggie business. She said you're one of the best breeders around."

He uncrossed his arms, and his gaze softened. "Oh, you want to see my babies? Let me warn you, though—I have a year-long wait list, and it's only getting longer. But I do have time to give you a quick tour."

"That would be fantastic."

He addressed the young woman settling down the puppies. "Zel, please stay near the front while I'm gone."

Then Magnus led me past the dining area into what would have been a living room in a traditional floor plan. In this home, though, there wasn't any furniture. Instead, I saw a large pen with what appeared to be props. I noticed comfy cushions, plastic flowers, and silk ribbons inside the gated area. Seeing me stare at the space, Magnus said, "That's for staging our photo shoots. I also sell puppy cards and calendars."

We wove our way across an open kitchen with sleek marble counters and chrome appliances.

"Nice place," I said.

"Gone to the dogs, though," he said, slapping his thigh with a chuckle. "At least on the ground floor. The upstairs is still mine. Anyway, this way to the puppies . . ."

He led me through the kitchen door and out back. I marveled at the immense backyard, complete with a fenced-in dog run and toys scattered across the ground. At the rear of the yard stood a warehouse-looking structure, which backed up to an industrial road. Beyond the concrete wall, I could see businesses and hear zooming cars. I wondered again about the vast amount of space Magnus owned. "Gee, this is enough yard for two houses," I said.

He grunted. "It *is* two houses' worth. I bought lots next to each other. Well, I inherited one and made a deal for the other that the previous owner couldn't refuse."

What kind of an offer? He didn't seem to scream money with his twill shirt and Levi's, but he owned two properties and had upgraded his kitchen to include modern amenities. And the warehouse we were strolling toward looked like it had cost a fortune to build.

Without using a key or an entry pad, he slid open the door. "It's not secured?" I asked.

"I keep it unlocked on purpose," he said. "In case of a fire. That way we can get the dogs out quickly."

When we went inside the warehouse, an immediate cool breeze hit my face. "Is that air-conditioning?" I asked.

Magnus pointed to a thermostat near the entrance. "Climate control makes sure that my dogs are healthy and happy."

From the cacophony of happy yipping at our arrival, I estimated a fair amount of dogs in the warehouse. We walked past rows of cages, and most of the dogs seemed curious about us. A few, though, remained occupied with some elaborate play items. Each puppy space seemed well-furnished with chew toys and soft bedding. No unwanted odors permeated the building. In fact, it smelled a bit herbal.

I sniffed the air. "What's that fragrance?"

"Lavender," Magnus said. "The scent calms the dogs' nerves."

"You seem to really care about your animals," I said. He didn't seem very shady. How could Magnus stand being associated with Russ Nolan?

"Let me show you my prize stud," Magnus said, grinning.

He took me inside a pen where a tan Chihuahua strutted his stuff. The dog's eyes seemed lively, and he tried to jump and lick-attack me upon my entry.

"What a charmer," I said, stroking him under the chin.

"Bogart. He's a real ladies' man." Magnus winked at me. "Sired a number of award-winning pups, in fact. Of course, his latest offspring are in the nursery—"

"You have a nursery?" I glanced around the warehouse.

Magnus jerked his thumb to the hidden recesses at the back of the building. "Sure do. Those little guys are too young to be out here alone. They need to be with their mamas."

"Wow, you really run a top-notch operation." I hesitated. "I'm not sure why you'd partner with Russ Nol—"

"Russ Nolan?" Magnus ground out the name through clenched teeth. "You think I've worked with him? No way. I can't stand the guy."

"But I thought he was your fellow breeder."

"I don't call what he does breeding. Breeders take care of their babies." Magnus patted the silky coat of Bogart. Not a hair was out of place, and his toenails also seemed to have been trimmed.

Remembering the extreme disarray at Russ Nolan's house, I said, "That's what I don't get. You two seem polar opposites. But I heard your names mentioned together."

Magnus frowned and led me away from Bogart's space. I followed the breeder as he stomped his way back to the main house. "Russ isn't in the same league as me. For one, I'm accredited by AKC, the American Kennel Club. I think he got approval from some sketchy organization known as American Dog Makers."

When we entered the house, I saw Zel kneeling in the photo shoot pen, arranging the five puppies she'd just finished walking. She wanted to place them inside a white wicker basket, but they kept scrambling out.

Magnus climbed over the gate to organize the dogs, and I couldn't help noticing how he picked up the puppies with such ease. He seemed more like he was plucking blueberries from a bush than hauling wiggling animals.

He lined the pups in a row, his large hands stroking their backs to calm them down.

Curious about how Magnus would react to the news, I said, "By the way, did you hear that Russ Nolan died the other day?"

His hands continued their smooth motion. He swiveled his head toward me. "I didn't know that. Well, I hope you enjoyed the tour, Mimi." Then he turned his back on me, the bulk of his body shifting like a powerful ocean liner.

I walked out of his home, confused. I couldn't quite figure Magnus out. He seemed so gentle with his dogs. Yet he hadn't masked his extreme dislike of Russ Nolan. He also hadn't seemed surprised about the other man's death. In fact, his hands hadn't skipped a beat as he'd stroked his dogs. Perhaps he'd already known about the grim news. Could he, in fact, have killed Russ Nolan?

CHAPTER

eight

STILL THINKING ABOUT my uneasy visit with Magnus, I picked up Marshmallow from home and drove to Hollywoof. On autopilot, I opened up shop. Had I been speaking to a dangerous murderer? It was hard to say without any more details about Russ Nolan's demise to shed light on the actual killer.

I kept my hands busy tidying up the store, but my mind remained spinning in circles. After an hour of dazed cleaning, I heard the bell jingle.

A familiar female figure entered. She swung her handbag with metallic hardware as she strode in. Behind her, I spied a poor pooch trapped in a metal contraption. The dog was strapped into the open front space of the doggie wheelchair, while two wheels took up the rear of the device.

"Tammy?" I said, putting the cleaning supplies away. "What a nice surprise."

"I'm pretty much at Armstrong Academy every day, but I had a free spot between manning the school library, coordinating the bake sale, and preparing for my class—I'm also a docent in the volunteer parent-led program. Poor Kale has been stuck in the house, and she really needed to get out. It's too bad they don't allow dogs on campus."

From his prime window seat, Marshmallow's ears pricked up. "Kale? I still can't believe she named her puppy that. And I thought *Marshmallow* was bad."

I coughed to hide my laugh. "Let's see about the poor dear," I said to Tammy.

Kale's coat looked shiny and well-maintained. She seemed less than peppy, but given the wheelchair situation, I could understand her sore attitude. "What can I do for Kale? She looks great already, and I don't want to put any undue stress on her limbs."

"It's a simple task, and I've got exactly what you'll need in my purse." Tammy pulled out a Ziploc with a tiny bottle in it. "Can't have any paint spilling and ruining my precious bag."

"What exactly is that?"

"Puppy polish."

How would I prep for that? I didn't have to push back cuticles. Did I need to buff the nails first?

She mistook my bewilderment. "Sorry, I brought my own organic version instead of having you use whatever you've got in stock."

I hadn't even known they sold beauty products like this for dogs. I'd have to increase my awareness of special grooming techniques, and I would add puppy nail polish to my wish list for future pet shop splurges. "So, let me get this straight. You want me to give Kale . . . a pedicure."

"Yes. It'll be a sure pick-me-up for her. Plus"—Tammy flashed her own neon green nails at me—"then we can match. You can even add a design, like a simple flower."

"Er, maybe next time."

"Fine." She pointed at the pleather benches nearby. "I would like to watch the fun, though. Could you do the polish out here?"

"Of course. Besides, I might need you to hold her as I paint." While Tammy settled Kale on one of the benches, I excused myself to grab the nail buffer. It couldn't be too difficult, right? I'd done my own nails plenty of times before.

When I returned, Tammy held out one of Kale's paws for me to work on. I quickly made her nails smooth and rounded.

Then I picked up Tammy's nail polish. The label on it read "Electric Lime."

As I swiped on the Ghostbusters slime color, I asked Tammy, "Do you think Kale will need surgery?"

She groaned. "I'm trying to book an appointment with the Surgical Center for Canine Companions, but the top surgeon's so busy. Kale might be in a doggie wheelchair for a while."

"What a shame." I finished Kale's first paw and lifted another one. "It's strange, but all the puppies that I've seen from Russ Nolan have had some issues with their legs. Do you think it's the poor housing environment there? Or maybe something genetic?"

"I don't think it's inherited." Tammy's smooth, manicured fingers plucked a sleek iPhone from her bag. She tapped on it and showed me a picture of a dog with a gold medal around its neck. "Look at this photo of Kale's father, an award-winning stunner."

That furry face on the phone seemed very familiar.

Tammy continued, "He's a prizewinning dog from Magnus Cooper. I still don't know why someone with his good rep would work with the likes of Russ Nolan."

I moved behind the wheelchair and gently lifted one of Kale's hind paws. "Me, neither. Are you certain they partnered up?" During my own conversation with Magnus, he had sounded like he loathed being associated with Russ Nolan.

"At his crib, Russ Nolan showed me this framed picture of the sire. That's a huge reason why I even bought Kale."

I peeked at the image on her phone again and noticed a slight sheen. "What's that glossy spot?"

"A reflection of the glass, I think. Or maybe it's from the fancy photo paper. It seemed to have a slick texture."

As I swiped the last bit of bright green on Kale, I said, "I'm really surprised the two of them hit it off. They seemed so . . . different . . . in their care of animals."

"I don't know. Opposites attract? Russ Nolan's place did seem run-down, even from the porch where I met up with him. Kale looked fantabulous, though. Too bad I didn't get a chance to see her mama."

"All finished," I said, showing Tammy the polished puppy nails. She oohed at them and paid me with a crumpled fifty-dollar bill.

As Tammy headed toward the door with Kale trotting and wheeling behind her, I heard Marshmallow give a loud meow. Kale stopped, turned her head, and gave a few short barks. I wondered what that back-and-forth noise was about.

"Time to go," Tammy said to Kale. "We've got things to do today. Besides, it's almost lunchtime." She hustled her puppy out the door.

Not five minutes later, a male figure dashed into my shop. He carried two big brown paper bags in his hands. His T-shirt featured a panda wielding a skillet. "You ordered from Wok On?" the young man asked.

He spoke with a squeaky voice that I associated with a high schooler, though he seemed to be in his early twenties. Sparse black stubble ran above his upper lip, but I couldn't tell whether he'd forgotten to shave or was going for a mustache. Facial hair could be hit-or-miss for Asian guys.

He lifted the bags in the air again, snapping me out of my reverie.

"I didn't call for food delivery."

He studied the receipt stapled to one of the bags. "This is Holly-woof, right?" He proceeded to read out my address.

"That's the right contact info, but I didn't call you."

He dropped the paper bags down on the counter with a grumble. Grease started oozing from the bottom of one of the bags. I would have to pull out my cleaning supplies again to wipe down the leaking mess.

"Well, someone called this huge order in," he said. Squinting at the receipt, he pulled out his cell phone and dialed. When he put the call on speakerphone, I heard a familiar voice answer.

"Hello? Who call?" Ma. But why had she asked Wok On to deliver food here instead of to her own home?

The young man said, "I have your order of shrimp fried rice, orange chicken, General Tso's, beef and broccoli, and sweet-and-sour pork. You asked to deliver to Hollywoof, right?" Weird. Ma usually detested Americanized Chinese food. She turned her nose up at it, said the dishes weren't authentic enough.

"Of course lah," Ma said. "My daughter at store?"

I butted in to the conversation. "I'm right here, Ma. Do you want me to tell him your home address?"

"No need. You *mamak* yet?"

"No, I haven't eaten yet. But you ordered a feast." My jaw dropped as the realization dawned on me. Uh-oh. I think I knew why the delivery boy had shown up.

"Oh, really?" she said, her voice ringing with false brightness. "Maybe Cody also need take break. Eat, too."

The young man fumbled his phone. "How do you know my name?"

"I'm friends with your great-auntie. We in same mahjong club. She say you come back college, but now live with parents."

His face turned as bright red as packaged sweet-and-sour sauce. "It's only temporary," he told me. "I play bass in a band, and we'll make it big soon."

Ma pressed on with her verbal attack. "You single. Mimi, my daughter, free. Have lunch. Everyone gotta eat. Beside, already paid for." She hung up. End of discussion for her.

She'd left me alone with a wannabe musician stranger. How could I salvage this awkward situation? "Mothers," I said, rolling my eyes. Maybe the two of us could commiserate together, but Cody started backing away from me.

"Seriously?" he said. "You had your mom order takeout to get a date. You must be crazy desperate."

Marshmallow hissed from his corner and started creeping toward Cody. "And what," Marshmallow said, "you're a great catch? Boomeranging back home to your parents?"

I took a deep breath in and blew it out. "My mother thought up this scheme on her own," I told Cody. "I didn't ask her to."

Cody's eyes started watering. Was he now regretting his rude attitude? He pointed at Marshmallow and sneezed. "I'm allergic to cats."

Marshmallow inched closer, making Cody sneeze harder. "Good, because I'm allergic to jerks."

Cody backed up toward the entrance. "Can you call your cat off?"

"Sorry." I shrugged. "That cat has a mind of his own."

Cody bolted out the front door, still sneezing.

"Good riddance," I said. "But what am I going to do with all this food?"

I could stow some of it in the mini fridge in the back room, where

I kept the extra batches of my homemade dog biscuits. It'd be a tight squeeze. Ma had definitely over-ordered.

I started scrounging in the bags, intending to make myself a lunch portion. Perhaps I could save the rest of the food and eat it across the entire week. Pushing aside the napkins and disposable chopsticks, I noticed that Wok On had also provided a dozen fortune cookies.

Those wrapped goodies gave me an idea. Like Ma said, "Everyone gotta eat . . ."

CHAPTER

nine

NOT KNOWING EXACTLY which door to station myself in front of, I'd planted myself in the center of the apartment court-yard with a checkered picnic blanket beneath me. Multiple Chinese take-out containers with their reheated contents were nestled at my side, and Marshmallow lay curled near my feet. Sixty minutes had ticked by, and I was still waiting for him to arrive.

Finally, I spotted Josh slipping through the back gate near the parking spaces. His bangs swung left and right as he hauled a brief-case, looking ready to burst, over to his apartment. Unit number one, I noticed. As in "You're the one." Not that I was superstitious like Ma, but it'd be easy to remember.

I waved my arms up and down. "Josh, over here." I'd already eaten dinner, but it looked like I needed to start on my dessert now: a slice of humble pie.

He glanced at my resting spot. A small smile flickered on his face before he shut it down. Did he not want to talk to me at all after that fiasco at his office? I could only try.

"I'm having dinner alfresco tonight," I said. "There's plenty of food to share."

He put the apartment key into the lock.

"I also have fortune cookies," I said, lifting a fistful into the air.

Josh nodded and unlocked his apartment. He stepped inside, but I noticed he'd left the door open. Hope bubbled in me. A few minutes later, he reappeared without his briefcase.

"What's your favorite Americanized Chinese food?" I asked as he sat down cross-legged on the blanket about a foot away from me. "General Tso's? Sweet-and-sour pork?"

He took the take-out containers and peeked inside each one. "Orange chicken," he said. "Super breaded with barely any meat. And the orange sauce is scary fluorescent. But I still like it."

I passed him the whole container, along with a pair of disposable wooden chopsticks. "Knock yourself out."

He chewed on the ball-like pieces of chicken. "Not really warm anymore, huh?"

I stared into his eyes, those beautiful browns I could fall into (and for). "Confession," I said. "I've been sitting here for an hour waiting for you to show up. I feel terrible about barging into your workplace and surprising you with my problem the other day. And for bringing my cat."

Marshmallow bristled and tapped my foot with one sharp claw.

Josh ducked his head. "Actually, I'd just lost my first case and didn't think I had the skills to help you, so I used your cat's presence as an excuse." He turned to Marshmallow. "Sorry about that, buddy."

Marshmallow turned his head toward Josh. "About time somebody apologized to me. I was the one being carried around in a woman's purse. And don't call me '*buddy*.'"

I formally introduced the two of them by name. Josh gave Marshmallow a guy nod of recognition. Marshmallow didn't offer up his paw, but he did relax, stretching out near my feet.

"Now that we're back to speaking again . . ." I stacked a few empty take-out containers together. "Do you think you might take on my case? I could pay you in, say, fortune cookies."

He smiled, making his cute dimple wink at me.

I started blathering. "But, of course, I know you have a lot of work. I saw a huge stack of folders on your desk. And that briefcase you were carrying just now looked so heavy—"

Marshmallow swiped at my leg. "Are you trying to get him to *not* help?"

Josh crinkled his nose. "Actually, I have fewer clients ever since I lost the case. My bosses might not be too confident in my skills right now. They keep me busy filling out lots of patent applications." That load he had hauled into his apartment signaled less work?

With a frown, Josh began picking up and putting down pieces of orange chicken with his chopsticks.

"You know," I told him, "I read on a wise slip of paper that a smile uses less muscles than a frown."

His eyes widened, and he scrutinized my face. "You memorized my fortune from the other day."

I saw a loose thread on the picnic blanket and played with it. "The strip of paper made me realize you love fortune cookies. That, and the filled glass container displayed on your desk."

He chuckled, and a sparkle lit up his eyes. "You noticed? I collect fortune cookies to help encourage me. The sayings pick me up whenever I'm having a bad day. Silly, right?"

"No, it's sweet," I said.

He scooted closer to me, leaving only a few inches of space between us.

I heard a grating noise. *Hack, hack.* My gaze swiveled to Marshmallow in alarm.

Josh pointed at my cat with his pair of chopsticks. "Er, is your cat about to cough up a hairball?"

Marshmallow quieted after a few more choking sounds. "Sorry, false alarm," he said. "But I sure felt like throwing up when I saw you two flirting."

Giving Marshmallow the stink eye, I said, "I think he's back to his usual self now."

Marshmallow trained his gaze on Josh. "You know, lover boy didn't actually agree to assist yet."

"Oh," I said, turning toward Josh. "Could you possibly help me out?"

He put away his chopsticks and held out his hand, palm up. "That will be three fortune cookies, then."

"Here you go." I counted out the wrapped goodies and gave them to him.

He made sure to tuck them away in his shirt pocket.

"Aren't you going to eat one now?"

"I only crack them open when I'm having a bad day, remember?" His knee grazed mine. Was it by accident? But he didn't move away.

He continued, "But seriously, I think I can look into this matter for free."

"Pro bono? For me?" I placed my hand against my chest. He wanted to help me without charge. Did he like me? My heart fluttered.

He nodded, his bangs swishing over his eyes. He brushed them out of the way to gaze into my face. "I can justify it to my bosses because I'm required to take on at least one pro bono case a year."

His kindness in taking on my case and believing in my innocence made me melt. "Perfect." I definitely wanted Josh on my side, and free didn't hurt. I couldn't afford an attorney on my budget, no matter how cute he was.

Josh leaned toward me, and I held my breath. He'd gotten close. I could even see his dilated pupils. What would he do next?

Marshmallow yowled.

Josh shook his head, as though clearing it, and said, "Tell me why you're involved in a murder case again."

I deflated a little. Then I cleared my throat and explained my situation. I even told him about my recent interactions, like my talk with Magnus Cooper, when I'd discovered the breeder's intense dislike of Russ Nolan.

Josh's posture stiffened. "Be careful, Mimi. That guy sounds dangerous. You could have been walking right into a murderer's home."

"It turned out fine." I played with my hair. Josh looked so endearing as he displayed concern about my safety.

I continued, "Plus, knowing that Magnus Cooper hated Russ Nolan means I could be off Detective Brown's list. Other people have bigger issues with that shady breeder."

Josh nodded. "Then you'd be off the hook. Or if you can show any reasonable doubt that you could have done it."

"Too bad Marshmallow's my only alibi." I wrung my hands. "If I could prove someone else was there that night, it would help my cause. You know, I did go back to his house hoping to find something pointing to the real killer. It was sealed by the police, but if I could make my way in—"

Josh covered his ears with his hands. "I didn't hear anything about you desiring to go breaking and entering."

"There could be a missed clue lying around."

Josh peered around the courtyard and lowered his voice. "You can't go sneaking into other people's homes. The police should keep it locked up tight until they find Russ Nolan's next of kin."

"Actually, Russ Nolan didn't even own the house. He rented it. Take a look and see how dumpy it is." I used my phone to search for the address online. When I found it, I showed Josh a picture of the squat house with its peeling paint.

He took his time examining the image and mumbled his agreement. Then his lips twitched. "That's interesting."

"What?"

Josh pointed at some fine print on the housing website. "It's actually listed for rental right now. You can click on this link to make an appointment."

"The owner must have opened it back up. I could go over there, pretending to be a renter, and take a peek." I tried to grab my phone back, but Josh placed his hand on top of mine. My skin pulsed with heat.

His brown eyes bored into mine. "Don't do it. Let the police handle the investigation."

I lifted my chin. "As the prime suspect on Detective Brown's list, I'm not just going to sit around waiting for him to arrest me."

Josh left his hand on mine. "Fine, Miss Stubborn, but you don't have to go alone. I'm coming with."

I gulped. "Okay."

He removed his hand, and my head cleared enough to plan things out. We settled on a time tomorrow that worked for the both of us and made an appointment online.

My heart leaped for joy when I said good night to Josh, because I now had the chance to spend extra time with him. Never mind that this "date" involved going into a house where a man had been murdered.

I hummed while I folded the picnic blanket and carried the leftovers back to my apartment. At home, I opened a fortune cookie to celebrate. I pulled out the slip of paper and read, "Someone admires you." I nodded. That's right.

Marshmallow nudged my leg. "Hey, Cinderella. I was going to wait until you stopped humming and pretending to be in a fairy tale, but you keep on going."

"Can't help it. Josh is such a dream."

"Eh, he's okay for a two-legger. Anyway, I wanted to tell you something Kale said to me—"

My phone rang. Recognizing the caller ID, I picked up. "Pixie?"

"Hi, Mimi. I wanted to check in with you about how Hollywoof is doing."

"Everything's fine." I crumbled the fortune cookie in my hand. "No need for you to worry about your investment at all."

But Pixie could dig beyond my words. "Have you been getting the word out? Finding new customers?"

"A few, along with some browsers."

"I see." Pixie paused. "Maybe you need to spread a wider net. Did you hit it off with my friend Lauren Dalton the other day?"

I remembered the cute headband I'd perched on Sterling's head. Lauren had seemed pleased by my work. "Yes, I think so."

"How about visiting her doggie yoga class tomorrow? She'll know everyone there and can vouch for your services. You'll be sure to make some contacts."

"That sounds like an excellent idea." Lauren had shown up right before closing time when I'd first met her. "It's in the evening, right?"

"It won't conflict with your business hours. Let me arrange everything. I'll text you with the details in a few."

True to her word, Pixie soon gave me the date and location of the class. I wondered how Marshmallow would feel about being stuck in a room full of exercising dogs. When I tried to tell him the news, I found he'd already fallen asleep on the couch.

I yawned. Better get to bed myself. After all, I'd have a full day tomorrow with two important events: first, a date with a definite cutie, and then, a date with possible customers.

CHAPTER

ten

THE NEXT WORKDAY, I tried to restrain myself from watching the clock, to no avail. I still counted down the time until my lunch break and my trip with Josh to visit Russ Nolan's house. Thankfully, a few customers trickled in and kept me occupied. I recognized them as people who'd wandered in from the beach the other day and were now bringing their pets to try out the new grooming salon. One might have even come straight from the ocean side, because his pooch looked like a comical sand sculpture of a dog due to all the grains stuck in its fur.

After a few hours spent grooming animals, I managed to clear out all the customers before Josh walked through the door. The bell jingled as Josh's lean frame came in, and I couldn't help being reminded of wedding bells chiming. Josh looked like a model out of *GQ* in his crisp white Oxford shirt with pressed slacks. I glanced down at my own dirty tee and faded jeans in alarm and started wiping off the sand trails clinging to my shirt.

Josh moved in and grinned at me with his sparkling white teeth. "You ready for our special time together?"

"Let me put this sign up, and then we'll be off." I positioned the "BE BACK SOON" placard on the front door. Even though I officially closed during the lunch hour, I didn't want to tick off any new customers who didn't know.

I locked the door and had almost pulled it shut behind me when a ball of white fur sped through the gap. Safe outside on the tree-lined plaza, Marshmallow stuck his nose in the air. "You weren't considering leaving me behind, were you?"

Josh raised his eyebrows at Marshmallow.

"Guess the cat's coming along," I said.

To his credit, Josh crouched down and spoke to Marshmallow. "Welcome aboard, friend."

I whispered to Marshmallow, "You know, there is such a thing as a third wheel."

Marshmallow flicked his tail at me.

• • •

We ended up parking at the curb, squeezing in next to some garbage cans on the sidewalk in front of Russ Nolan's house. Must be trash collection day.

A few moments later, an old pickup rumbled onto the driveway. The beat-up truck carried a haul of supplies in its bed, most noticeably a long steel pole with a mesh net attached to it. Pool equipment.

The driver, a tanned man looking the color of burnt toast, got out. He wore a huge straw hat that shaded his face, and he leaned against the cab of his truck while he waited for us to come closer.

"Mimi?" he asked. "I'm Kevin, the owner of this house."

I shook his hand and proceeded to introduce both Josh and Marshmallow.

"A fine couple like you two will make great renters." He eyed Josh's expensive shirt and made a reflex action of rubbing his thumb and forefinger together. Noticing me looking, he hid his hand behind his back.

"We'd like to take a look around first," Josh said.

"Just a minute," Kevin said, as he fumbled with the lock on the door.

Meanwhile, Josh tapped the splintering floorboards of the porch with one of his polished dress shoes. "You came here by yourself?" he whispered to me, giving a small shake of his head.

I pretended to flex my muscles in response. His worry disappeared, and he gave me a lopsided grin.

When the door opened with a sharp squeal, Kevin flung his arm out in a grand gesture. "Welcome to your new next home. It even comes prefurnished."

I braced myself for a disgusting sensory assault, but it didn't seem as bad as before. Maybe Kevin had neutralized the odor using some sort of chemical spray.

He beamed, two crooked incisors giving him a crazed look. "Of course, I did some tidying up. Though I still need to get the carpet cleaned."

Marshmallow lifted his paw up and glanced down at the dirty-looking floor. "I'm not going to step into a puddle of blood by accident, am I?"

I addressed Kevin. "Why exactly did the previous tenant leave?"

His eyes shifted from left to right. "Something happened out of the blue, and he had to . . . go away."

What an understatement. Sounded like Kevin wouldn't offer up detailed information about Russ Nolan's death. Maybe he wanted to keep the murder quiet and not scare off prospective renters.

We moved over to the kitchen area, where Josh opened and closed the scarred wooden cabinets. One knob almost fell off in his hand. He also peeked into the pantry. Some foodstuffs still lined the shelves. "Anything we need to know about the property? Is it earthquake safe? In a flood zone?"

"Don't worry," Kevin said, touching one of the tarnished cabinet handles. It wobbled. "This house has withstood decades of wear and tear. I grew up in it, and it's got great bones."

Josh swiped a finger across the cracked tiled countertop. "Any deaths on the property?"

Kevin pulled off his hat, showing flattened ash-colored hair, and mopped his brow. "There hasn't been a death inside this house." He settled the hat back on his head.

Marshmallow hissed. "Liar."

Josh kept his face blank. "I see. Well, that's reassuring. Right, sweetheart?" He clasped my hand. Feeling the brush of his fingertips, I froze. Pleasure radiated from my hand to the rest of my body. Could I keep holding his hand forever?

I would've stayed in that state, but I noticed Marshmallow slinking away to the shabby living room. A ratty sofa took center court there. Intuiting Marshmallow's destination, I felt reality hit me, a cold reminder of the recent tragedy.

I cleared my throat and pointed to where Marshmallow waited before the familiar opaque sliding door. "And what's behind there, Kevin?"

Kevin made his voice sing, rising to a higher tone. "A bonus room, a wonderful addition to an already outstanding floor plan." He led us into the secret area that had previously housed the mistreated puppies.

I held my breath as we entered, and my fingers squeezed tight around Josh's hand.

Nobody else seemed fazed by the air in the room. I took a tentative breath in. No stench of excrement this time around. The soundproofing blankets had also been taken down, and the walls had been quick-coated with an uneven layer of white paint. I could smell lingering paint fumes. The lack of windows also made me feel like I was stuck in a panic room.

Marshmallow explored the rectangular space from corner to corner. His nose twitched. "Do you smell that, Mimi?"

"The paint," I said, fanning my face to get some air moving.

"And a hint of something else," Marshmallow said. "A scent that wasn't here when we came during our first visit."

I took a whiff. The paint fumes gave me a niggle of a headache, but I could sense another odor underneath the varnish. It seemed familiar, something akin to aromatherapy, but I couldn't quite place it.

But then Josh put his arm around my shoulder and steered me away. "You're looking queasy," he said.

I took a few gulps in the more open living room. "Thanks."

Kevin spoke up. "Maybe you need some fresh air." He led us to the backyard.

I hadn't gotten a good look at that area the last time I'd come. Stepping through the glass patio door, I didn't see much greenery outside. A small concrete patio and a rectangular patch of dirt made up the "yard." Dried-up leaves scattered across the back area, but they didn't belong to any tree. Maybe they'd come from the nearby thirsty-looking hedge of bushes or had blown in on a breeze.

I peered at the patch of soil again. It looked disturbed. Instead of a smooth surface, I found little mounds of dirt everywhere, no doubt made during doggie playtime.

Smack in the middle of the backyard, I noticed four small circles ground deep into the earth. Their spacing created a connect-the-dots square shape. "What are those?" I asked.

Kevin gave a slight shudder. "That's where the prior renter would come to sit and relax at night. The circles are from the legs of the chair pressing into the ground."

"Where's the chair now?" I asked.

Kevin dusted off his hands with a grimace. "I threw that thing away this morning. It's in the bin ready for the garbage truck to collect."

"Did you throw the rest of his stuff away, too?" If Kevin hadn't been a true stickler in getting the house ready to rent, I might be able to snag a few clues unnoticed by the cops.

Kevin gave me a sharp look. "How do you know the previous tenant was a man?"

"What? Oh, um, by the poor condition of the yard. A woman would have preferred a garden, put in some flowers." A stretch. I myself had a notorious black thumb. Plants were not my thing.

Josh spoke up, using a soothing tone. "I think my girlfriend wants to know whether this place comes with any extras."

Nice save. His suave lawyer manner might manage to cover the slip of my tongue.

Kevin grunted. "What you see is what you get."

"Should we tour the bedrooms now?" I asked. The place where Russ Nolan had slept could be telling.

Kevin gave a sharp shake of his head. "I'm sorry. The bedrooms are sealed. Doing popcorn ceiling removal. This tour's done now."

Had I rattled him too much by knowing the gender of Russ Nolan? Josh and I went back to the patio door, but Marshmallow daw-dled behind us. "What's Kevin doing staying in the yard?" he whispered to me.

Maybe he was waiting for us to head in first, but I peered over my shoulder to do a quick check. Kevin seemed rooted in the backyard. He stared down at the patch of ground where the chair had been and made a quick sign of the cross. Before he could catch me spying on him, I swiveled my head and focused on going inside.

We walked toward the front door as a somber group. While Josh made a few comments about different things in the house, like the LED light fixtures and the grounded electrical sockets, I barely kept up the pretense by nodding along. Kevin trailed after us, silent during Josh's entire commentary.

On the front porch, Kevin told us he could offer a deal on the rental price. When he revealed the amount, Marshmallow's fur bristled. "What? For that piece of junk?"

"That's a special price for you fine folks. A steal for this location," Kevin said.

Josh looked at me and scratched his chin. "We'll have to think on it. If we do want to pursue this further, we'll contact you through the website link."

"Yes, and thanks for the tour," I said. Maybe some politeness could calm Kevin's nerves and smooth over my awkward behavior during the tour.

Kevin cleared his throat and spat a gooey mess down on the splintered porch boards. He retreated back inside the house. Through the closed but flimsy front door, I could hear him mutter, "Waste of time. More interested in the renter than the rental."

I waited until his steps faded away before I spoke up. "Guess I'm never going to win an Oscar for best actress."

"No kidding," Josh said. He tucked a loose strand of hair behind my ear. "But I like that about you. I find honesty attractive in a woman."

A strong heat flushed across my entire body. "Really?"

"Please, no PDA," Marshmallow said, creeping off the porch. "I might cough up an actual hairball this time."

Glaring at Marshmallow, I said, "My cat's trying to make a run for it."

Passing by Kevin's pickup to return to the car, I looked at the trash cans on the curbside. Might they still be full?

The side gate of Shirl's house swung open. She pushed out her own trash bin and placed it at the curb. "Oh, fancy seeing you again," she said.

She wore another sweatshirt and lounge pants combo. Her top featured the close-up face of a grumpy cat.

Marshmallow strutted by and purred at her.

"How's my favorite kitty? Too bad I can't shake your paw right now." She gestured at the trash bin. "My hands are occupied."

I interrupted their lovefest. "It's good to see you again, Shirl. This is my boyfriend, Josh."

The word "boyfriend" had slipped out like a precious pearl from my tongue.

Josh's dimple appeared. "Nice to meet you, ma'am," he said.

Shirl patted down her poofy head of hair. "What manners you have. I guess I won't keep you from going out with your new beau, Mimi." She snuck a glance at Marshmallow. "You know, I happened to see your cat in the neighbor's backyard and was hoping you could show me some of his other tricks."

Poor Shirl. She must be lonelier than she let on, asking me for company via my cat. "I can stop by tomorrow evening after work," I said.

"I'll be free then."

Marshmallow rubbed up against her leg to say goodbye. After Shirl disappeared through her side gate, I marched over to Russ Nolan's garbage bin. Pinching my nose, I lifted the lid and peeked in.

Sure enough, a camping chair lay sprawled on top. I picked it up and itemized the junk below: a tattered constellation poster, a supersize cereal box of shredded wheat, chewed-up tennis balls, and an empty wine bottle.

I dropped the chair back down, and Josh turned to me. "Find anything interesting?"

"Not that I could see."

With a twinkle in his eye, he said, "Well, if you're done dumpster diving, we can get going."

I nodded. Taking out the antibacterial gel from my purse, I squirted down my hand.

"Let's grab some lunch," Josh said. He glanced at his watch and frowned.

Without any time for a real lunch date, we had to go to the In-N-Out drive-thru. *Kismet,* I thought, as we ordered our hamburgers served the exact same way: animal style.

"Nice choice," Josh said. "Extra spread with grilled onions."

"Great minds . . ." I said. Did that mean we were compatible in other areas besides food?

"I really like spending time with you, whether it's house-hunting or hamburgers." Josh smiled and made his dimple flash.

After we'd parted ways, his remark lingered with me all the way until closing time. I analyzed every touch he'd given me during the house visit. And I replayed the way he'd said "girlfriend" when talking about me, like he was saying something special and true.

Because of my moony mood, I lost track of time and closed up shop later than usual. When I placed Marshmallow into his carrier in the car, I took a breath to clear my mind—I would need it to prepare myself for his reaction to my next words.

"By the way, we're not heading home yet." I told him about the preplanned pit stop.

"Me and a roomful of yoga dogs?" he said. "Just terrific. I hope you don't expect me to do Gumby-like moves."

⇒ eleven ⇐

OWNWARD DOGGIE WAS located in a bland business complex. Stolid companies flanked the yoga studio; one neighbor boasted stellar tax advice, while the other offered drop-dead rates on life insurance.

I dragged Marshmallow into the doggie gym's lobby, where a peppy strawberry blonde greeted me. "Hello! Are you here to register for classes?"

"No, I'm auditing a yoga class, the one Lauren Dalton's in. Pixie St. James arranged the details."

"That's right. Unfortunately, Lauren's class is almost over, but you can sneak in." The woman spotted Marshmallow and frowned. "You know the class is for *dogs*, right?"

"Aren't you a little *pet*-ist?" Marshmallow said.

"No problem," I told the woman. "We won't disturb anyone. We'll make sure to sit in the way back and watch."

The woman directed me to the correct room. When I opened its door, I heard strains of soothing music floating in the air.

I spotted a row of folding chairs near the entrance. Indira occupied one of them. A giant duffel bag lay beneath her feet, and Ash sat on a chair beside her. The puppy rested her head against her paws.

Right after we walked in, the dogs started emitting low growls. They must have smelled Marshmallow.

Ash yipped at them. The dogs quieted down, and Marshmallow explained, "She just vouched for me."

I shuffled over to Indira and whispered, "May I sit next to you?"

She gave a nod, and I took the unoccupied chair on her left. Then Indira placed a finger to her lips and pointed to a spandex-clad woman.

The teacher, I assumed. The woman wore a leotard that clung to her every curve. She said, "Now everyone lie down and stretch across your mat."

All twenty or so women (minus one) obeyed and lay on their mats. Lauren Dalton, though, wearing a fancy leotard with crisscrossing straps, knelt. She motioned to the frowning young woman beside her, who then plopped down and pressed her face against the mat.

Most of the dogs also stretched out, though a few had to be coaxed or manually positioned. Even Kale tried as best she could while being trapped in a wheelchair. Tammy provided help by moving her paws.

"Deep breath in, and deep breath out," the instructor continued. "Be united with your dog as you ground yourselves."

I saw Lauren nodding and beaming down at Sterling, who had stretched across the mat.

The teacher continued to lead the group in a visualization exercise, something about a healing garden. My mind wandered. It didn't help that Marshmallow also distracted me by providing commentary like, "Dogs are crazy. They look like fur rugs lying there."

Finally, the teacher ended the class, but the group didn't disperse right away. They rolled up their mats with languid movements. Maybe they felt so relaxed, they had slowed down their motions.

Meanwhile, the instructor glided over to me. She clasped her hands together and bowed. "Lauren mentioned she'd have a visitor today. I hope you enjoyed the doga class."

I rubbed at my ear. "Did you say '*doga*'?"

"Oh yes, dog yoga. Surely you've heard of it. Feel free to tell any of your canine-loving friends." The teacher did a double take on seeing Marshmallow. "Although cat-oga might prove promising as well."

Marshmallow blinked at her. "Did you say 'cat toga'? Cat toga or cat yoga—both sound horrible, lady."

From beside me, Indira zipped open her duffel bag and pulled out a fanny pack.

The instructor pursed her lips and turned to my neighbor. "Indira, you know I won't be able to let you sell your bags if Ash doesn't get better. This is a doga class, after all, not an arts and crafts bazaar."

Indira strapped on the bag made of black leather with gold accents. "You don't understand. This is my livelihood."

"Yes, and this studio is my sacred space. What I say goes."

"I've already brought in the merchandise, and the ladies will be lining up to buy soon."

"Fine," the teacher said. "For today. But don't bring back the bags unless Ash feels better. I can't have you two sitting through another session and distracting the others."

"I see," Indira said, her voice pinched.

The teacher nodded and walked away.

Indira mumbled under her breath, "I paid for this class fair and square, and I intend to make it worth my while."

She glanced over at me, but I pretended to busy myself with petting Marshmallow. Did she realize I had overheard her griping?

Indira didn't have time to question me, though, since a gaggle of women approached us, with Lauren leading the way.

She came and kissed me on both cheeks. "Mimi, so good to see you." Lauren scratched the top of Marshmallow's head. "You, too, cutie."

He retreated behind my legs, planting himself underneath my chair. "Do not let any of those other women touch me."

I smiled up at Lauren. "Marshmallow's a bit shy today. So, what a wonderful class. Thanks for inviting me."

"Any friend of Pixie's is a bosom buddy of mine." She fanned herself with French-manicured hands. "Though today's asana poses made me work so hard."

The young woman standing behind her spluttered, and Lauren turned her head. She said, "Mimi, this is my assistant, Nicola."

Despite beads of perspiration spotting her forehead and dark, stringy hair, Nicola looked striking with her supermodel height and gazelle-like body. She even possessed a classic symmetrical face, except for a bulbous nose that threw off her other delicate features.

"Nice to meet you," I said to Nicola and shook her hand.

Lauren turned to the group of women behind her and addressed them. "Everyone"—she clapped her hands—"this is my dear friend, Mimi Lee. She's fab at making dogs appear spectacular. You do remember Sterling's to-die-for sweatband, right? Look no further for great grooming services."

I pulled out my stash of business cards, while Lauren stepped to the side. A long, snaking line formed before me.

While smiling and handing out my cards, I heard Lauren addressing Nicola. "I'm parched after that workout. Where's my water bottle?"

Nicola scrunched up her round nose. "Oops. I must have forgotten to bring it."

"Incompetence will not be rewarded, Nicola."

Lauren's eyes scanned the room. She spotted Tammy standing apart from the other women. I assumed Tammy didn't want to wait in line because she already had one of my business cards. Motioning to Tammy, Lauren said, "Your water, please."

Gee, the rich really did act privileged. Being a famous producer's wife must have Lauren used to people catering to her every whim. And she seemed to take full advantage of her glamorous lifestyle, like those A-list actors with special riders in their contracts: fresh-cut flowers in their trailers and only blue M&M's in their candy trays.

Tammy ambled to Lauren and passed over a stainless steel bottle.

Lauren opened the cap. Glancing at it, she wiped it off. "Been to the beach, I see." She sipped the water. "Very refreshing. Thank you."

I finished passing out my contact information. While some of the women exited the class, others stayed and browsed Indira's wares. A few even purchased a bag or two. Soon, Indira had collected a large wad of bills.

One last lady lingered over the purse selection, considering. "I don't know if I really need a bag."

"It's super functional," Indira said. "Excellent for when you're walking your dog. See how my hands are free? I have my demo bag on now to show you how great it is."

"That does sound handy." The woman examined the black and gold fanny pack Indira wore. "Funny. I used to have a purse that looked like this. It frayed, so I had to donate it."

"Well, then, you must get this one. If only for sentimental reasons."

The woman's eyes misted. "I agree. Sold."

"Like I said, this is my demo bag. Let me pull out the stuff I was able to fit inside it." Indira started taking out everything from the fanny pack. She extracted pens, spare tampons, and a mini metal flashlight.

Indira completed the sale and thanked the woman. The duffel bag looked deflated after all the purchases from the yoga ladies.

I walked out with the last remaining women: Lauren with her assistant Nicola, Tammy, and Indira. In the lobby, Tammy waved good-bye to us. Poor Kale wheeled along behind her.

"So sad about that dog." Wanting to assess the ladies' reactions, I added, "Did you hear about the recent tragic death?"

Indira gave a curt nod. "I found out from my pool boy. Life sure gives us lemons sometimes, and I speak from experience." Then she marched over to the receptionist and started talking to her in an irate manner. Marshmallow's eyes sparkled, and he followed her.

Lauren turned to me with wide eyes. "I don't know what you two are going on about."

"The breeder Russ Nolan? He died in a suspicious way," I said. "There's an open homicide investigation."

Nicola gave a small gasp but covered it with a pretend sneeze.

Lauren turned to her assistant. "Allergies are rough. I have a natural remedy I can give you—echinacea."

Nicola shuddered and refused the offer. "Just a dry throat. Nothing serious."

Lauren said to me in a loud stage whisper, "It's extremely tough when assistants bail out on you. Best to watch over them and ensure they're in good health."

Nicola turned a bright pink but kept any emotion off her face.

Lauren tapped Nicola's shoulder and said, "You know what I just thought of? Set up an appointment with Mimi to get that *thing* done for Sterling. There's a big astronomy fundraiser coming up, and he needs to feel his best."

"Of course, Mrs. Dalton." Nicola swiveled to me and whipped her phone out. We synced our calendars, eventually settling upon a weekend to fit in Sterling's appointment.

CHAPTER

twelve

AS I UNLOCKED the door to Hollywoof the following morning, I saw Marshmallow's back arch and his fur rise up. "Here comes trouble," he said.

I looked over my shoulder, and a dose of déjà vu smacked me in the face. Detective Brown made his way across the palm tree–lined plaza toward me. A scowl darkened his hard face.

He wore the same sport coat as before. However, his hair had grown a bit longer; the sandy buzz cut seemed more scraggly and unkempt today.

When he reached Hollywoof, I held the door open for him. "Um, Detective Brown, what a surprise. Did you happen to get a new pet recently and need my services?"

"Don't be ridiculous." He flashed his badge. "Told you I'd return."

I led the way forward, flipping on the lights as I went in. "So I suppose this is official business."

"You betcha. I have a few more questions for you, Miss Lee."

I retreated behind the cash register, trying to place some sort of barrier between us. "What exactly do you want to know?"

He approached me and leaned over the counter. The sudden shadow he threw across me made goose bumps crawl up my arms. "You were snooping around at Russ Nolan's house, trying to pass yourself off as a renter. Why?"

How had he found out already? Rubbing my chilly arms, I said, "I don't have to tell you anything without my lawyer present."

He snapped upright and leaned away from me. "You secured legal representation?"

Marshmallow strolled over with a swagger. "Take that, Mr. Big Cop." He even shook out his body, making a few hairs pelt the detective's pant leg.

"I can call my attorney right this minute," I said, picking up the phone next to the cash register.

"Fine." Detective Brown moved over to the sitting area and plopped down on a cream pleather bench. "I can wait for your lawyer to show up."

I dialed Josh's work number It went straight to his voice mail. Uh-oh. Sometimes he didn't check his messages until later in the day.

But I needed immediate access to him. I called his mobile number.

When Josh answered, I said, "The detective's here at my shop. Can you swing by Hollywoof?"

"Let me wrap something up with my coworker first," he said, "and then I'll be right there."

A reedy voice piped up in the background. "Come on, man. We're in the middle of an important conversation."

"It's a client. I need to give her some legal advice," Josh told his inconsiderate coworker.

"Whatever. Why is a chick really calling your cell?" the coworker said. "I know the real reason. Bras before bruhs."

"Mimi," Josh said, "I'll be over as soon as I can."

I could feel Detective Brown's eyes on me while we waited. The silence grew more oppressive with every minute that passed, as though an ancient jade burial shroud weighed down my body.

Detective Brown drummed his fingers against the swirled marble table in the waiting area. I jumped.

He stopped beating his fingers and raised his bushy eyebrows at me. "Stressed much?" A pause. "What do you do to relax, Miss Lee?"

Small talk seemed safe enough, as long as it didn't involve the actual case. "Let's see, I read on occasion." Young adult books. I pictured myself flanked by teenagers in the indie bookstores I frequented or at the local library branch. But he didn't need to know the precise details.

"Some people loosen up by drinking," he said. "You have a favorite alcoholic beverage?"

Detective Brown stared at me with such a strange fierceness that his eyes almost gleamed.

"Or perhaps you prefer to de-stress by being out in nature," he continued. "Maybe by relaxing under the night sky?"

Josh rushed in at that moment. His gaze swiveled back and forth between Detective Brown with his intense look and me behind the counter, my jaw wide open.

"You don't have to answer anything you don't want to," Josh said. He stepped around the counter and stood beside me. He placed one hand against my trembling back.

Why would Detective Brown be asking me info about my personal habits: drinking, stargazing . . . Then it clicked. In Russ Nolan's trash bin, I'd found a constellation poster, along with an empty bottle of wine. Detective Brown had wanted to connect me to Russ Nolan.

My insides seethed. "You tried to trick me into talking," I said.

Josh slipped his arm from my back and squeezed my hand once. Then he strode over to Detective Brown and handed his business card to the cop. "My client declines any further questioning."

Detective Brown took a long time staring at Josh's info. "Do you even practice criminal law?"

Josh cleared his throat. "As Mimi's attorney, I would like to know if you're exhausting the entire list of possible suspects in this investigation."

Detective Brown crumpled Josh's business card and stuffed it in his sport coat. "Don't tell me how to do my job, Mr. Akana."

Josh spread his hands out in a placating gesture. "I'm sure you're a well-respected detective. I know my client doesn't have an alibi for that night. She also made a nasty remark to the victim before he died. But do you have anything solid tying my client to Russ Nolan's murder?"

Detective Brown stared at Josh, his eyes sparking with fire.

Josh continued, "How exactly did Russ Nolan die, anyway?"

Detective Brown gave me a piercing look while he said his next words. "As you well know, Miss Lee, by a blow to his head."

I shivered. Did he really think me capable of such violence? Whacking somebody to death?

Detective Brown rubbed the back of his neck and said, "We haven't found the weapon yet, but we'll track it down soon."

Josh clenched his jaw. "You won't find it anywhere near my client."

The two men engaged in a staredown. I could almost smell the testosterone flowing out of their pores. They acted like a pair of feral dogs, and the image reminded me of an important question I'd been meaning to ask. "There is one thing I'd like to talk about, Detective Brown."

He broke the staring contest and turned to me. "Are you ready to discuss your movements the night of Russ Nolan's murder?"

"No, I want to know about the dogs."

"Dogs?" Detective Brown said, a frown on his face. ·

Marshmallow smirked from his perch near the sunny window and deadpanned, "As a non–pet owner, you may not be aware, but dogs are four-legged animals in the canine family."

"I filed a complaint about some puppies, remember? That's how I got involved in this whole mess," I said. "Where did the police place those dogs? At a local shelter?"

Detective Brown shrugged. "I don't investigate animals. I'm interested in more valuable lives—human ones. Maybe the dogs ran away. Not a trace of them at the house, anyway."

I knocked over the jar of dog biscuits on the counter and had to right it. "You mean, they weren't around when you showed up?"

"Not that I saw. And no mention of dogs in any of the initial paperwork." Detective Brown turned his attention back to Josh. "Since I can't ask any questions of your client, I guess my time here is done."

"That's right." Josh crossed his arms against his chest.

Detective Brown moved around the counter toward me. He held out his hand. "Goodbye, Miss Lee."

Not wanting to show bad manners, I grabbed it to shake. When I did so, though, he almost yanked my arm off.

"Ow."

His eyes dimmed as he mumbled, "Not that strong of a grip." In a sharper tone, he said, "I bet there's a reason you went back to the scene of the crime. Murderers often do. Better stay in town. I'm sure we'll see each other real soon."

After the detective had left, I let out a loud exhale. Josh opened his arms, and I moved into his warm embrace. "Thanks for coming over," I said.

Josh held me for a few exciting, hammering heartbeats. "You feel perfect in my arms," he murmured.

I saw Marshmallow turn his head to look out the window with a fixed stare. Maybe to avoid watching our display of affection. At least he didn't start hacking again.

Even though I wanted to remain in Josh's embrace, I disentangled myself with a sigh. "I know you have to get back to work."

"I do need to get going, but I want to see you again, Mimi—and not for business."

A jolt of excitement sparked up my spine. "I would love to."

We grinned at each other as we stretched out our goodbye, and Josh looked back at me as he dragged his feet toward the exit.

After Josh had left and my nerves had settled, I took time to reflect on my encounter with Detective Brown. I found myself replaying the cop's nonchalant attitude toward Russ Nolan's dogs. What had happened to those poor puppies? Had they really gone running off into the streets? It seemed unlikely. Plus, if they had done so, someone would've noticed.

I knew of one neighbor who might be able to answer my questions. I turned to Marshmallow and said, "Better start practicing your pet tricks."

• • •

Following through on my promise, I traveled to Shirl's home in the evening. However, I parked around the corner to avoid attracting unwanted attention. I didn't want to be spotted around Russ Nolan's home again.

We walked over to Shirl's front door, and when she opened up, I noticed she'd dressed up for the occasion. Though she still wore a long-sleeved shirt that read, "Everything I know I learned from YouTube," she'd exchanged her usual lounge pants for a more fitted style.

Shirl greeted us with a small smile on her face, and Marshmallow again offered his paw to be shaken. After gripping it, she invited us inside her home.

The house smelled like a potpourri factory, with an overwhelming dose of sandalwood and musk. Shirl possessed an enormous collection of heavy antique furniture and knickknacks. She kept her floor dirt-free by placing plastic runners everywhere.

She invited us to her sitting nook, a space containing two plush armchairs facing each other. A round doily-covered table separated the seats. "Please make yourself at home while I check a phone message. I couldn't run over to the phone in time to catch the call earlier."

Marshmallow and I made ourselves comfortable. From the sitting room, I could see Shirl enter her kitchen and fiddle with an answering machine. The message played back at a loud volume. Her doctor had called to remind her about her next checkup appointment and to ask her to get a MedicAlert bracelet.

I saw Shirl jotting down the appointment on a supersize wall calendar next to the refrigerator. When she came back to us, her eyes glittered. "So, what new tricks did you teach Emperor?"

Was her memory faltering? "I don't know if you recall, but his name is Marshmallow."

She waved away my comment with her sunspotted hand. "Like I said before, Emperor is a much more suitable moniker."

Marshmallow purred.

I bit my tongue. Apparently, Shirl's mind remained as cutting as a blade.

"Ready?" I said, clearing my throat. I waved my arms in a mystical weaving motion. "Prepare to be amazed, Shirl. Abracadabra."

Marshmallow didn't twitch one muscle. He'd make a horrible magician's assistant. "I'm not a performing bunny," he told me.

I gave Marshmallow a pleading look. "Come on," I whispered.

Marshmallow let me sweat it out for a few moments before he crept toward Shirl. "I can do another interesting trick," he said. "But you'll have to crumple up a piece of paper, Mimi."

Odd. Still, I followed his instructions. I found an old receipt lodged in my purse and wadded it up.

"Ready?" I asked Shirl.

She nodded, her gaze riveted on my cat.

"Toss the ball in the air," Marshmallow said.

I did, a slow lob to the ceiling. Marshmallow tracked it with his intense blue eyes. Then he rushed to meet it and caught the paper with his paws.

I let out a gasp, while Shirl clapped repeatedly.

She glanced over at me. "You look so surprised he could do that."

Which I shouldn't have, since I'd supposedly taught him the trick. "Well, uh, it still amazes me every time."

She nodded. "Pretty neat. Mind if I try?"

"Be my guest."

She went to retrieve the paper ball now lying at Marshmallow's feet. As she did so, a thick golden bracelet around her wrist unclasped and fell down onto the lime green shag carpet.

"Oops," she said.

I snuck a look at her jewelry. "That's a beautiful piece. I especially like the dog bone charm."

"Got it from the thrift store," Shirl said. "I expect that's why the clasp unbuckled so easily."

She fiddled with the bracelet and secured it once more to her wrist. Marshmallow was inches away from her, watching. He sat so close to Shirl, I wondered if he'd have enough time to run and grab the ball, depending on how far she tossed it.

Picking up the wadded paper, she turned to him and said, "Time to catch, Emperor."

She tossed the ball up.

Marshmallow raced for it, snatched it out of the air, and then crashed down onto the floor in a heap.

"Marvelous." Shirl smiled, the deep lines at the corner of her eyes crinkling with pleasure.

Marshmallow squashed the paper ball beneath him and sprawled across the carpet.

"I think my cat's done with playtime. He needs to rest," I told Shirl. "What if we chat while he recuperates?"

She nodded, and we settled back into the plush armchairs.

"I don't often have company," she said. "Perhaps you'd like something to drink? I've got tap water or Ensure available."

I hid my inner grimace. "Thanks, but I'm not thirsty." I jerked my thumb toward Russ Nolan's house. "Your headaches must be better now that his barking dogs are gone."

She nodded. "What a difference."

"And with your superb hearing, you must remember exactly when those dogs were removed, right?"

She rubbed at her ears, as though trying to focus on her super sense of hearing. "Hmm, they must have left . . . the same night Russ Nolan died."

I dug my fingers into the softness of my chair. "You sure about that?"

She rubbed her forehead and reflected. "Yes, because of the sudden silence. The dogs usually barked their heads off at night. I bet that's why Russ snuck off to his backyard to laze in the evenings. From my upstairs balcony, I could see him there. He fell asleep in his camping chair every night like clockwork."

She could see him from her place? Maybe Shirl had witnessed the real killer and could give me the info to prove my innocence to the police. "Did you notice anybody strange enter his house that night?"

"Like I told the police, I didn't see a thing. I fell asleep early that evening." She fiddled with her golden bracelet. Its chain links looked quite heavy, and it stretched tight against her wrist. I bet it would leave teeth marks against her skin.

I tapped the arm of my chair. "I'm really concerned about those dogs. Where could they be?"

"Who knows? Maybe the folks at ADM finally followed up on my complaint." Shirl leaned back in her own armchair and yawned. "It's getting late."

"Oh, we'd better go, then. Thanks for letting us visit."

Shirl led us to the door, and Marshmallow allowed her to stroke his forehead as a goodbye. I could feel her watching me as I stepped onto her porch.

Only after the door had closed and we'd moved onto the driveway and out of hearing range did I turn to Marshmallow. "She wanted us to leave after I started asking her questions. What could she be hiding?"

"Probably lots," Marshmallow said. "For one, that bracelet didn't come from the thrift store. I saw it up close. A stamp on it marked it as solid 24K."

I stumbled. Maybe the bracelet had been a bribe. I mean, how could Shirl not have seen or heard anything the entire night, especially when she liked keeping tabs on the neighborhood? Someone could have given her the bracelet to entice Shirl to stay quiet. But who?

CHAPTER

thirteen

ON SATURDAY, I opened up my shop for a special appointment. I hoped that I could focus on work instead of fixating about the murder.

Lauren's assistant waltzed into Hollywoof with Sterling right on time. The tiny Chihuahua looked a bit better than he had during his original visit. Though still cute as a button, he did a strange wiggle with his backside and scooted along the floor on his bottom.

Nicola, now out of yoga wear, wore a peach pantsuit. She completed her look with a giant statement necklace made of a triple layer of glittering diamond strands.

"How's Sterling?" I asked.

"Not feeling so good. That's why we're here today."

I peered at the puppy. "He doesn't look dirty to me."

"His fur is fine." Nicola dropped her gaze from mine. "But Mrs. Dalton wants Sterling to feel his brightest, starting from the inside out."

Oh no. I thought I knew what that meant.

Just then Marshmallow covered his nose with his paws. "Where is that stench coming from?"

Nicola played with the strands of her elegant necklace. "Mrs. Dalton wants his glands expressed." She looked pointedly at Sterling's rear.

As I'd suspected: emptying anal glands. This task might be the worst part of my job.

Nicola shifted her feet. "It's for a really important social event she's been invited to attend. An astronomy fundraiser with some top-name scientists. Mrs. Dalton's dressing up for the Star Wars theme. She's had her Rey outfit for over a month now."

"I understand. And don't worry—expressing glands is a routine task," I said as I took Sterling to the back room.

Once there, I made sure to put on some heavy-duty gloves for extra coverage. Then I settled the dog in the industrial-size sink for further protection. That way the stinky fluid would flush down the drain and not spray everywhere. I didn't want either my room or me smelling like sewage.

Thank goodness I hadn't worn my favorite tee today. To prepare myself for the task, I took a deep breath in and held it. I positioned my hands at the four and eight o'clock positions, found the glands, and squeezed.

A dark liquid shot out. Unfortunately, I hadn't mastered holding my breath for long periods. I inhaled, and the strong, foul odor made me stumble back.

It took more time than I'd anticipated to get all the messy liquid out. I wished I had clipped a clothespin over my nose. When I'd finished, though, Sterling looked quite relieved.

I made sure to sterilize all the surfaces, then rubbed my hands raw using scented soap and very hot water. I prettied up Sterling and took him to the front. He didn't scoot on his bottom on his way out. Instead, he did a dignified limp toward Nicola.

I pointed at his dragging leg. "He still hasn't seen the vet?"

Nicola shook her head. "Not yet. Mrs. Dalton's calendar is so full with prescheduled functions. And she always insists on Sterling being at every one of the charity galas she attends. In fact, she bought him a matching BB-8 costume for the astronomy fundraiser."

"She really should take him in to get checked. Sooner rather than later." I petted Sterling. "I know for a fact Russ Nolan kept his dogs in terrible conditions."

Nicola mumbled, "Maybe it's because I found him through the classifieds when Mrs. Dalton asked me to find her a dog."

"I'm surprised Mrs. Dalton couldn't afford a better breeder."

Nicola looked up and jutted her chin. "She thinks money makes her the queen. I can't believe she had you clean her dog's butt. Not that it should really surprise me. I've done a lot of degrading things over the past six months without any thanks."

I touched Nicola on the arm. "Is everything okay at your job?"

"Sorry, I don't mean to complain." She plucked my hand off. "I'm probably keyed up because I was supposed to have today off."

"Mrs. Dalton sounds like a tough boss."

"Yeah. That's why she deserved a lower-quality ADM pup."

"ADM?" Those initials sounded familiar. "What do those letters stand for again?"

Nicola tilted her head at me. "American Dog Makers. Sterling's certified through them. They're not as well-regulated as the famous American Kennel Club."

ADM was the agency Shirl had filed a complaint with to get rid of the barking dogs. Maybe the organization had rescued the puppies after all. Or at least they might have more info about where the dogs had ended up.

I handed Nicola the bill, and she overpaid it. Pressing the extra cash into my hands, she said, "This is for the extra dose of humility it took to complete the task."

I watched Nicola as she left with Sterling. With her obvious bitterness, I wondered if she was the type of person to spit in her employer's coffee. I realized how lucky I was to be my own boss and answer to myself.

Now that both Nicola and Shirl had mentioned ADM, I decided to research the company. I looked up the website for American Dog Makers, but no contact info existed except for a PO Box and a phone number with a Los Angeles area code. When I tried calling them, I received a message that their voice mailbox was full.

Returning to the website, I flicked through the various tabs until I found a link to upcoming events. A dog show was advertised for the following day.

As I stood staring at the screen, Marshmallow sauntered up. "Getting sucked into Candy Crush again?"

"Haha. I'm looking up details for a dog show I'll be attending."

Marshmallow shuddered. "A building full of prima donna dogs? My living nightmare."

"Well, you can stay, but I'm definitely going," I said. "It'll be a great way to get dirt on Russ Nolan."

Marshmallow cocked his head at me. "You're not worried about what Detective Brown might say if he found out?"

Hmm, maybe I should invite Josh to come along just in case. I didn't want to endanger my tenuous position with the police. But I felt like I kept interrupting Josh's work with my problems, and goodness knows my pro bono case didn't pay his bills.

I bit my lip, mulling over how I might justify the event to Detective Brown if he heard about it. "Hmm, I could always tell the detective I needed to go because of . . . grooming research." He couldn't argue with that reasoning.

• • •

The local fairground complex looked transformed when I arrived. At the entrance, a bright yellow banner decorated with paw prints flying high in the sky read, "ADM All-Breed Championship Dog Show."

Instead of the usual hubbub of vendors and rides, there were people strolling around the large space with their dogs. I noticed an open area covered in artificial turf. Someone had created an obstacle course on the fake green.

A few trainers wearing the L.A. Lakers colors of purple and gold ran alongside their dogs. They wove around the field in their sturdy sneakers, shouting encouragements to their pups and directing them toward the next obstacle on the course. The dogs themselves scampered onto ramps, squirreled through tunnels, and leaped over hurdles. Cheering spectators watched the practice runs from nearby bleachers.

I wandered around the fairgrounds before finding more activity coming from inside a large warehouse. A multitude of owners stood near various portable tables, grooming their dogs.

I searched for a sign that would point me in the right direction and breathed a sigh of relief when I spotted one that read, "Toy Breeds." Passing by different owners, I searched for someone who looked older, a person who'd been around these events for a while. I also sought somebody with an open face, an amiable breeder who wouldn't mind shooting the breeze with me.

A gentleman in his fifties with wire-rimmed glasses looked like a good candidate. He bent down near his black short-haired Chihuahua, inspecting her already glossy coat from various angles.

I went over and greeted him. "You look like you're an expert."

"Yes, miss. I'm a veteran at these conformation events."

I cocked my head at him. "What are those?"

"That's what we professionals call these dog shows."

I pointed at his beautiful dog's immaculate coat. "Do you compete often?"

"I try to make it out to most events. My dog usually wins best of breed."

I congratulated him and added, "I wonder—have you ever heard of a fellow breeder named Russ Nolan?"

He guffawed, tears springing to his eyes. He had to wipe off his spectacles with his shirtsleeve to clean them. "That arrogant newcomer. Thought his pup could beat mine."

"Russ Nolan brought his dog to a show?"

"Yeah, one of the smaller events in town. About a few months ago. Of course, he never stood a chance." The man reached behind him and brought over a wooden box filled with rosette ribbons that ran a gamut of colors. "Look at how many awards my darling has won over the years. At that last event, she placed first."

"How did Russ Nolan fare?"

"His girl didn't shine like mine. In fact, she looked downright worn-out. Quite odd at such a young age." He shook his head. "Maybe she was inbred. A shame, because that kind of pairing hurts their health."

I ran my fingers across the colorful ribbons in the box. "It's too bad not all members in this breeding association have the same caring attitude as you."

He beckoned me closer. "To be honest, I haven't seen Russ Nolan ever since then. I think I know why, too."

"What do you think happened?"

"Heard a rumor that someone important threatened to give ADM bad publicity if Russ Nolan kept his membership." Finally, this chatty older gentleman had given me a lucky break in the case. Perhaps he'd also know where Russ Nolan's puppies had gone.

Rubbing my chin, I asked, "Do the dogs get taken away if somebody loses membership?"

The man shrugged. "I've never had to think about that scenario."

"Do you know if I can meet any of the ADM staff?" I glanced around the warehouse. "Are they in this building? Or maybe at an info booth outside?"

"The officials will be too busy running the show to answer your questions. You can try headquarters, though. It's not far from here."

Great. I'd capitalize on my lucky streak and swing by the place next.

• • •

The ADM office looked more like a garage than an actual business site. The inside of the building featured exposed rafters and dangling fluorescent lights. However, the company made itself look more legit by placing a small security camera above its doorway.

I found a bored-looking teenager on the premises. He sat on a stool near a scarred worktable with a monitor on it, displaying live footage of the outside through the security camera. He didn't glance at the screen even once. Was the guy even an official ADM staff member?

He didn't acknowledge me when I entered. Instead, the scraggly young man seemed more intent on gobbling his sandwich than on doing any actual work.

I waited for him to finish his bite before speaking. "Do you work at ADM?" I'd better ask to make sure.

"High school volunteer," he said. "Got stuck doing this for my mandatory community service."

Ah, that explained the glacial service and lack of commitment.

A mustard mustache stained his upper lip. He proceeded to lick it off. "Everyone else is out at a dog show."

"Well, maybe you can help me with some information," I said. "About Russ Nolan."

He squeezed his sandwich by accident. A shot of mayonnaise flew onto his arm and splattered the worktable. He didn't bother to wipe it up.

"You recognize that name?" I edged closer to him.

The volunteer stuffed the rest of the sandwich into his mouth. He wiped the crumbs from his lips with the back of his hand. "I might have heard of him."

"What happened to the dogs he bred?"

He shrugged. "I don't know."

I leaned in close. "Russ Nolan's neighbor complained about their incessant barking to your organization. Could ADM have taken them?"

He rubbed the back of his neck and shook his head. "No rescuing is done here. We only push paperwork."

I looked him in the eye and steeled my voice. "I need to see those dogs' records."

"The files are secured." He gestured to a small metal filing cabinet underneath the mayo-marked worktable.

Perhaps the volunteer needed more motivation to allow me access. "Do you know Russ Nolan is now dead?"

His Adam's apple bobbed up and down. "No."

"He didn't just die. The man was murdered. And that paperwork could be essential to finding the killer. I have a tight connection with the lead investigator."

His face blanched, and he put his hands up in the air. "Tell your friend it wasn't my fault. Russ bribed me with cold hard cash."

"Wait. What are you talking about?" I knew the answers lay close to me, right there in the filing cabinet. I couldn't resist and reached for it.

The volunteer didn't stop me. He sat there dazed, wringing his hands, while I yanked on the drawers.

Not much security after all. The cabinet was unlocked. Rifling through the folders, I found one marked "Russ Nolan." Not caring if it got me in trouble, I took out the most recent papers and read through them, flipping past an official-looking complaint with a scrawled signature and on to the dog-breeding records.

The documents listed a batch of puppies registered to Russ Nolan, but the name of the sire was crossed out. I brought the papers up to the light and could make out the typed print beneath the slashes of ink: "Bogart."

I let out a low whistle. "So Magnus Cooper did partner with him."

The volunteer shook his head hard. "No, he didn't. Russ paid me to insert the sire on record." He looked at me with pleading eyes, with a droopy face as sad as a hound dog's. "But I didn't put in Bogart's name myself. Russ typed it. That makes me actually innocent of doctoring the papers, right?"

"Sorry. I'm not a lawyer." I pointed to Bogart's name on the sheet. "Did Magnus know about this?"

"That's why it's crossed out. I wasn't here when Magnus stormed the office. Thank goodness, because I heard he's massive." The volunteer started trembling again and almost fell off his stool. "He could probably crush my skull with his bare hands."

I returned everything back to the file cabinet. After promising the volunteer I would keep him out of the murder investigation, I left.

But the young man's comment left me with a disturbing image.

Magnus did look strong enough to smash a skull . . . and I knew that Russ Nolan had died from head trauma.

Magnus also seemed to have a huge motive. After all, Russ Nolan had faked Bogart's name in a public record, threatening Magnus's once-stellar reputation.

CHAPTER

≈ fourteen ≈

FOUND MYSELF TRAVELING to Magnus Cooper's house once
more. He seemed to be a top suspect, and I might be able to find
some evidence at his house.

Though it wasn't typical business hours, I figured he'd be in. The
man did live upstairs.

I even took Marshmallow. That way Josh couldn't complain I'd
gone alone if he ever found out. I could just picture him with a cute
worry line creasing his forehead. Though Josh had deemed Magnus as
possibly dangerous, I felt confident going in with my feisty feline.

When I arrived, though, Marshmallow shrank back. "Is this really
a good idea?"

"Come on. Are you a chicken or a cat?" I said.

"Better a live chicken than a dead cat."

Sometimes I wondered how I'd gotten roped into partnering with
my pet. Cats made for lousy backups.

Grumbling at Marshmallow, I decided to leave him on the porch below the swaying poodle sign as lookout. "If I don't come out in ten minutes, go over to Shirl's. Jump on her phone's buttons and dial 9-1-1."

"Isn't Shirl's house a long way to walk?"

I frowned. "It's two streets over that way."

"Maybe I could stay here and yowl for help."

I sighed and made sure I could easily reach my cell phone just in case. Then I rang the doorbell.

To my surprise, Zel, the assistant from the other day, opened it.

I startled. "Oh, hello. You work weekends, too?"

She offered me a tight smile. "Room and board comes with the job."

Oh-kay. I knew housing in L.A. was expensive, but did someone really need to take on a sketchy position—one that involved living with a man decades older?

After a beat, I asked, "Um, is Mr. Cooper around?"

She nodded and stepped back into the foyer with the staircase. Then she pivoted her head up toward the second floor and shouted, "Magnus, you have company."

Loud clomping sounded from upstairs. When Magnus spotted me standing in the doorway, he hesitated on the steps. A dark cloud settled on his face, but he trudged along and met me at the bottom.

"Mimi," he said. "What can I do for you?"

Maybe I should have started with something enticing to reel him in. Let him know that I already knew his secret and sympathized with him. "It's a shame that Russ Nolan cheated you by changing the rec—" I cut a quick glance at Zel and paused. Would he want his affairs spelled out in front of staff?

"Don't worry, she's family." He gestured toward his imposing desk. "You might as well come inside and have a seat."

Zel gave me a sheepish grin as she let me in. "I really am related to him. Magnus is my uncle." That explained the casual way she'd called him to come down the stairs.

I sat down while Zel traveled to the kitchen and busied herself with wiping down the sleek countertops.

Magnus sat before me at his desk, cracking his massive knuckles. "You know about ADM."

"Yes, the records for Russ Nolan's dogs wrongly pointed to Bogart as the sire."

"He muddied my name." Magnus stopped cracking his knuckles and clenched his hands into fists.

"How did you find out about those records?" I asked.

He banged a heavy fist against his desk. "A fellow breeder told me at a dog show, right after Bogart won. This envious colleague let me know Bogart wasn't so special, having mated with the likes of Russ Nolan's female dam."

Deciding to get on Magnus's good side, I shook my head. "What a mean guy to question your reputation."

He clenched his hands even harder, making the veins on his arm pop up. "It's blasphemy. Basically, he attacked the quality of my pups. Like I'd breed weak puppies with leg defects—"

"What?" I tugged at my ear. "Did you say something about the puppies and their legs? How do you know about that?"

Magnus stared at a space to the right of my head for several moments. Then he settled his gaze back on me. "Russ Nolan inbred his dogs instead of keeping them genetically diverse. That makes it easy for them to get health conditions like patella luxation."

"What exactly is that?" I leaned toward Magnus. Was that why all the Chihuahuas connected to Russ Nolan dragged their legs?

"It's when their kneecaps go out of position."

I tapped my chin. Should I ask him more? I hoped I'd gotten enough on his good side for him to feel unthreatened. "Tell me how you know about those puppies. It's not like you met them face-to-face, since Bogart didn't sire them . . ."

But then it hit me. The aromatherapy-like scent that Marshmallow had detected in the vacated puppy room at Russ Nolan's home. A familiar smell I'd also sniffed here inside Magnus's warehouse. The herbal whiff of lavender.

I blurted out my revelation. "You were there, at the house that night." I backed my chair away and peeked into the kitchen. To my relief, I saw Zel still scrubbing away. At least there would be a witness if something bad happened to me.

Magnus pierced me with his gaze.

My throat closed up, and I squeaked out my next words. "The lavender. I smelled it in the enclosed room at Russ Nolan's house. And I know you use it in your kennel to calm down the dogs."

Magnus ran his large hand over his hair, making it stand on end. "Okay, I admit it. I had to do something. Those dogs were being mistreated, in danger."

I nodded, remembering the sick sight. "All those puppies jammed together into one room, and the smell—" I pinched my nose.

"You, as an animal lover, should understand. I had to get them out of there."

It made sense. Magnus had the know-how to rescue the dogs. And the space.

Worried about those poor pooches, I had to ask. "Where are they now?" I hadn't seen any sign of the puppies the last time I'd come.

"Of course I didn't show you when I gave you the tour. They were, naturally, in the nursery. Best to keep the babies in a cozy space. I want to find owners for them soon, though. Can't afford to house the puppies forever."

"I don't understand. How did you get past Russ Nolan? I assume he wouldn't just hand the dogs over to you."

Magnus stretched his forbidding arms and placed them behind his head. "I could have easily persuaded him. When I went over, that lazy bum had fallen asleep in his chair in the yard."

"You saw him sitting outside?" Shirl had mentioned that Russ Nolan conked out in the backyard every night.

"I peeked over there. Moved those dogs as quick as I could. That deep sleeper didn't move a muscle."

Interesting. Russ Nolan had slept like the dead—unless he had actually already died.

I examined the hulking frame of Magnus once more. The man before me may very well have done the deed.

Clearing my throat, I said, "Well, I'm glad those puppies are well looked after now."

Magnus gave a curt nod. "Someone's gotta look out for the defenseless."

I made an obvious gesture of checking my phone. "Look at the time. I better get going."

He let me leave without any trouble. I almost skipped over to the front door in my haste.

On the threshold, I glanced back. Magnus sat at his desk, brooding.

He would make a likely culprit. A giant of a man, he could have easily delivered the fatal blow to Russ Nolan. And he'd confessed to taking the pups.

That sounded like two clear motives to me. Magnus could've gotten rid of Russ Nolan because the man had damaged his clean reputation. And he'd get to save the puppies, to boot.

I exited and found Marshmallow lying on the porch. Upon seeing me, he said, "Good, you're alive . . . because I'm starving."

Glad he had his priorities straight.

We went back home, and after appeasing Marshmallow's stomach, I decided it was time for me to make a very important phone call to clear my name. I made sure to enclose myself in the privacy of my bedroom so Marshmallow couldn't disturb me. I'd seen him drift into a dazed food coma state. The last thing I needed was his siren cat snores disturbing my phone conversation.

I sat down on my unkempt bed. The wrinkled comforter featuring a nature scene gave me a sense of ease as I located Detective Brown's business card and called. I got his voice mail and left a quick message stating that I had new information about the case.

Within five minutes, he called me back. "Mimi Lee," he said, "are you ready to spill?"

"In a manner of speaking. I think you should question Magnus Cooper." I traced the delicate wings of a butterfly on my faded comforter. "He only lives a few blocks from Russ Nolan."

"Yes, the other breeder. I know about him." Detective Brown's voice sounded deeper over the phone, like a cannon booming.

"Oh. Well, are you aware that he had a double motive to kill Russ Nolan?" I ticked them off on my fingers. "One, Russ Nolan muddied his reputation. And two, he wanted to save those puppies."

"Do you have actual proof of his guilt?"

I spluttered. "Have you seen the guy's arms? He could knock down Russ Nolan with one quick blow."

"Ah, but the killer didn't use his—or her—hands on the victim," Detective Brown said. "In fact, there were no knuckle marks on the victim's neck."

"Well, Magnus could've used something else to hit him. A bat, maybe?"

"You're grasping at straws, Miss Lee. You just said he only needed to use his bare hands for the crime."

I spotted a frayed seam on my comforter and picked at it. "Magnus did go over that night. He took those pups—"

Detective Brown gave an exasperated sigh. "Stop it with the dogs. Remember, I'm concerned about the humans in this investigation. And I'm pretty certain Magnus didn't do it."

"How are you so sure?"

"Because he had an alibi for the hours between eight and ten that evening, the estimated time range for Russ Nolan's death."

"Who vouched for him?" I tugged on the thread, and it spiraled out.

"His assistant."

"You mean his niece. She's a relative. Of course she would cover for him." I poked at the growing hole in my comforter and saw some stuffing pop out. "Can you really trust her word?"

"It's better than having a cat as an alibi." A brief pause. "You know, what you're doing is quite common."

"Making sure your investigation is thorough?"

"No. When a suspect starts blaming somebody else, it's a classic move. It lets us detectives know that we should take a closer look at them."

I gulped.

"Thank you for making things clear, Miss Lee." He clicked off the line.

CHAPTER

fifteen

NDIRA WALKED IN through the door of Hollywoof on Monday, looking gorgeous in her workout gear and a fawn suede fanny pack. She exuded health with her glowing brown skin, but her poor dog seemed tuckered out. Indira carried Ash in her arms like the puppy was a wounded soldier.

My voice wavered. "Are you here for grooming?" I wasn't sure I could even touch Ash before she yelped in pain.

Indira shook her head. "I need to help Ash feel better. Do you have any medical suggestions?"

"You should really ask your vet."

She kissed the top of Ash's head. "I didn't get one yet. The breeder assured me her shots were up to date, and everything seemed fine until she got this recent leg problem—"

"It's called patella luxation." I pointed to Ash's legs. "I think it's genetic. All of Russ Nolan's dogs seem to have it."

"It figures." She cradled Ash closer to her chest. "And to think I supported the guy. He so reminded me of when I was struggling, so I decided to buy one of his dogs."

I blinked at Indira's beautiful model face. "I didn't know you had to struggle."

"I'm not like the other haughty ladies around here." Indira headed toward the seating area and lay Ash down on a bench. "I started my business from scratch."

"Really?" I went over to where Indira stood. A term from my college psych class came back to me: the halo effect. The idea that attractive people succeeded without effort, were born that way. I'd assumed Indira had run in the same glitzy circle as all the other tiny dog–toting ladies.

"Surprises a lot of people." She stroked Ash, who gave a slight wag of her tail. "Ash got her name because of my Cinderella hopes. Actually, this dog has secured most of my customers. Ninety percent of my clients come from dog classes."

"Doggie yoga?"

"Others, too." She played with the zipper of her fanny pack. "There's also dog dancing, pet soccer, Mommy-and-me SUPPing..."

"What was that last thing with the initials?"

"S-U-P-P. Stand-up puppy paddleboarding," she said.

"Seriously?" I couldn't imagine Ash balancing on a board while Indira propelled across the water using a wooden paddle.

"Ash swims alongside the board and jumps on when she needs a break," Indira said. Bitterness crept into her voice. "Of course, she can't do any of that in her current state. Russ Nolan betrayed me."

"That's a strong word to use."

"I call it like I see it." Ash started whimpering, and Indira stroked her fur to soothe her. "What can I do to get Ash back to normal so she can continue serving as the company mascot?"

I looked at Ash's bent leg and grimaced. "I'm no vet, but I think she might need surgery. Especially if she's expected to do so many sports and high-energy activities."

"Surgery will cost a fortune." Indira clenched her hand into a fist. "At first I was sad when my pool boy told me about it. But maybe that jerk breeder got what he deserved."

I flinched at her comment.

"Don't look so shocked," Marshmallow said from his corner. "Do you know what I heard when I eavesdropped on her conversation after yoga? Indira walked right up to that receptionist at Downward Doggie and told her to fire the instructor. Remember, the teacher had wanted her out of class for selling goods without participating in the exercises? Talk about a dog-eat-dog world."

His turn of phrase made me pause. Should I really be taking suggestions from my biased *cat*?

On the other hand, Indira had made an aggressive maneuver. Was that how she'd built her company up so fast—through bold moves?

Indira snapped her fingers and jolted me from my thoughts. "I've got it," she said. "I can organize a doggie playdate and combine it with a purse party. That should bring in extra money for Ash's surgery."

I couldn't quite reconcile this new vicious businesswoman side of Indira with the fellow dreamer I admired who, like me, had gone after her passion. After a slight lag, I managed to reply, "Oh, yes, great idea. And you can get some good referrals to vets and surgeons at the same time."

She grabbed my arm. "You should come, too. Make sure to invite some of your posh customers."

"Uh, I could try." Thank goodness she didn't know about my sorry finances and lack of customers.

"Let me text you my address . . . once I find my cell in here. My bags are too spacious sometimes." She unzipped her fanny pack. Only after pulling out a deck of cards, a pack of chewing gum, and a mini

metal flashlight did she find her phone. She got my digits and proceeded to text me her address.

When I clicked on the map link, I noticed she lived close to The
Strand, blocks away from the beach. "Nice location. Business must be
booming."

"It's a rental," she said. "But don't tell the others." She placed the
loose items back into her fanny pack and scooped up Ash. "See you later."

I walked her over to the front door and held it open, since she was
cradling Ash in her arms. After the door had closed with a soft chime,
Marshmallow got up from his sunning spot and scooted toward me.

"Indira sounded vicious," he said. "She didn't express any sympathy whatsoever for Russ Nolan."

"But words can't really hurt people. Fists do. That's what I told
Detective Brown last night."

"Ah, the secret phone conversation behind closed bedroom doors.
You know, I didn't totally fall asleep before you went into your room."
Marshmallow twitched his nose at me. "So what's your theory about
the murderer?"

"I bet you saw Magnus Cooper from the porch. He's a giant of a
man. He could have easily crushed Russ Nolan." I tapped a finger
against my bottom lip. "The only flaw in my thinking is that I'm not
sure why he used a weapon. He wouldn't need to."

"Is that what the cop said? He probably didn't buy Magnus as the
killer."

I nodded. "Detective Brown didn't agree with me. But Magnus
had two motives. Defending his reputation and freeing the dogs. He
even confessed to me that he took the puppies."

Marshmallow chuckled. "Then there's no way he could have killed
Russ Nolan."

"Whyever not?"

"Oh, please. Kill a man and try to lead away a pack of pups at the same time? They'd be in a barking frenzy if Magnus, a stranger, stepped onto the property."

"Wouldn't Magnus, as a breeder, know how to handle the noise?"

"Puppies aren't known for their stealth. I mean, have you ever heard of a *dog* burglar?" Marshmallow flicked his tail in the air. "Besides, they're not as well-behaved as us cats. The extra time, effort, and possible ruckus . . . why would he risk it?"

"You do have a point. And Detective Brown did say Magnus had an alibi." I cocked my head at Marshmallow. "If not Magnus, then who would be top on your list of suspects?"

Marshmallow pointed his paw at the window, indicating the palm tree–lined plaza beyond. "The woman who just left. Indira is vindictive. And she's got the strength. Didn't she just tell you how many doggie-partnered sports she participated in?"

Touching the back of my head, I imagined a sharp blow there. "I still think it's got to be a guy. Statistically speaking, men commit more murders than women."

Marshmallow blinked at me. "Shirl told us Russ didn't have any guy friends, so there's only one other male we know of to investigate. That would make—"

The distinctive calendar alert from my phone beeped. I didn't remember scheduling anything important today, but my phone always alerted me fifteen minutes prior to a planned event.

I read the description: "Library Date." What did that mean?

Uh-oh. I knew I shouldn't have given Ma access to read and modify my calendar. I'd meant it as a way for her to keep virtual tabs on me—not to provide her another means of sabotaging my romantic life.

I called Ma up, and when she answered, I barreled into a monologue. "What did you set up, Ma? A library date? You know, that last time with the delivery boy was a total failure."

"*Walao!* So bad. To make up mess, need lose many times mahjong." Ma couldn't care less about my embarrassment but wanted to save face in front of the delivery boy's great-auntie.

I let her comment slide because I needed more info on this upcoming appointment. "So, who is the new guy?" I rolled my eyes as I spoke, even though I knew she couldn't see me over the phone. But maybe she could still detect my displeasure.

"Ah. Boy like dis better. Not make music. Study a lot."

"Wait, are you saying I'm having a date with a student?" I crossed my fingers. Please don't say he's in high school, Ma. "You didn't sign me up to be a tutor or anything like that, right?"

She laughed. "No, no. Letter come here for alumni program. You so busy, no time revert to university. I do for you."

I groaned. "You set me up with somebody looking for career advice? I bet he's in his teens."

"He interested meet. I make you profile very good."

I counted to ten in my head before saying, "What exactly did you put down?"

I heard pounding steps from her end. A muffled, deep voice grumbled away. Ma said, "Daddy make me go now. He *belanja* me to nice restaurant dinner. Already reserve. Bye."

She hung up on me and left me staring at my phone. I clicked on the details in my new calendar event and mapped out the location.

I couldn't bear to stand up a poor college student. Maybe I'd explain Ma's crazy intentions to him and then bail. Afterward, I could return home and unwind from her latest mess.

Marshmallow meowed at me. "Why so sour, pussycat?"

"A surprise date. Another Ma setup. That should explain it all." I jingled my car keys. "Care to watch the disaster unfold?"

"Save me a seat in the front row."

Having a cat made for the perfect wingman. All I needed to do was tuck Marshmallow in my purse and place a shawl over the top to cover his fuzzy head.

• • •

The university library looked like a solid block of gray concrete, almost prison-like in its appearance. Its sliding glass doors swished open for us. As we passed through the library sensors, Marshmallow jostled his head. I tapped my bag, and he settled back down.

"What takes up so much space in here?" Marshmallow grumbled. "I know it's not a huge wad of cash."

I shushed him.

"Nobody can hear me but you, Mimi."

I shrugged and started looking around the main room at the people sitting down at the tables. Against the far wall, an eager-looking guy in his late teens popped up from his chair like a Whac-a-Mole.

The college kid had dressed up as though for a job interview. He wore an ill-fitting blazer that stretched too tight across his broad shoulders—maybe a relic from his high school debate team.

As I got closer, he pushed up the thick glasses sliding down his nose and grinned at me. Acne scars marked his pasty face.

I said, "You're here for career advice from an alumna?"

"Uh-huh." He nodded so much that he looked like a bobblehead. "Thanks for agreeing to meet with me. My name is Cole."

"Cole, nice to meet you. Let me first clear up—"

"It's my honor to meet you, Dr. Lee." He shook my hand with a sweaty grip.

I felt my lips pucker like a preserved plum. "And what exactly am I a doctor of?"

He half chuckled. "Oh, you're funny, too. I'm an animal science major, and I want to go to vet school like you after I graduate."

With a frown, I slid into a chair at the table and set down my purse. He sank into the chair opposite me, his bright eyes following my every movement, perhaps excited about the upcoming conversation.

"Actually," I said, "I'm not a veterinarian."

"Ha. Nice joke." His wide grin faltered. "Why do you look so serious?"

I hemmed and hawed. "There was a mistake on my profile. My mother changed . . ."

His eyes bulged behind his glasses.

"Never mind. It would take too long to explain."

He examined his thumb and picked at the cuticle. "What do you actually do then?"

I sat up straighter and gave him a reassuring smile. "I'm a pet groomer."

"You make animals look good? That's, er, interesting." He looked away from me as he spoke, maybe so he didn't have to lie straight to my face.

My bag on the table moved as Marshmallow shuffled around. "Like you wouldn't believe," I said.

Cole's eyes flicked down at my bag. Had he noticed? But he continued talking. "So, what kind of stuff do you do at work?"

I thought back over Indira's visit, my sole client of the day. She hadn't asked for anything to be done. Not much there. What about before that? I told him the truth. "Most recently, I expressed the anal glands of a Chihuahua."

Cole gagged.

"Hey, vets do it, too," I said.

He sprang up from the table. "Sorry, I just remembered. I need to complete some research for a term paper. Thanks for the chat." He ran from the table to hide away in the book stacks.

"You scared him off," Marshmallow said, popping his head up. The shawl spooled on the table. "Good timing, though. I need a breather."

I heard staccato steps speeding my way. A moment later, the librarian's stern face appeared before me. "No pets allowed," she said.

I had to think quick. "Um, he's a service animal."

The librarian pressed her mouth into a thin line.

"He's my Seeing Eye cat?"

"Leave," she said, her arms crossed over her chest. She continued to glare at me as I scurried through the exit.

Outside in the balmy night air, I looked back at the concrete building. A prison vibe inside and out. I told Marshmallow, "Probably not what Ma had envisioned."

"You know, you should stop her before it gets worse."

I groaned. "You're right. But how?"

"Well, aren't you and Josh"—Marshmallow waved his paw around—"an item?"

Were we? Kevin Walker had assumed Josh and I were a couple during the rental house tour. And I'd introduced Josh to Shirl as my boyfriend. He hadn't corrected me. Plus, the last time we'd talked, he'd said he wanted to see me in a personal capacity.

I decided to text Ma before I could change my mind.

Me: Library date flopped. BTW, I actually met someone recently.

Ma: Wah! You have boyfriend. Why no tell me? Meet him can?

Me: Soon, Ma.

Ma: Fast come. Invite for Family Game Night.

We observed a family tradition of gathering to play board or card games on a regular basis. To add excitement, we competed against one another for money. At the start of the family gathering, we dropped all our spare change into a jar, and the winner would take the loot home.

The change jar might serve as a great complement to Josh's collection of fortune cookies. Fine, I texted back to Ma.

After I sent the message, I looked back over the entire text conversation, and my throat constricted. What had I done? I'd wanted freedom from Ma's outrageous setups, but Josh and I hadn't defined our relationship yet . . . I sure hoped I'd read his intentions right.

sixteen

A T JOSH'S OFFICE building, I texted him from downstairs. I figured I wouldn't be invading his actual work space if we met up in the arctic air-conditioned lobby.

Marshmallow grumbled from inside my large Hello Kitty tote. "Freezing to death isn't just an expression, Mimi. You'd better hope I have eight more lives."

I also shivered in the intense AC, but when I saw Josh come out of the brass elevator, my whole body heated up.

He approached me wearing a sleek dark blue suit, and his eyes sparkled at me. "My favorite girl turned up."

"And don't forget about the best cat in the universe," Marshmallow added in a stage whisper.

Josh hugged me hello, seeming to breathe me in through his embrace.

When he let go, I stood there dazed.

"Everything okay?" he asked.

When I continued to stay silent, Josh placed his palm against my cheek. I wanted to lean into it.

"You're at my workplace in the middle of the day," he continued.

I glanced around the polished lobby and asked, "Is there a more private place to talk?"

Josh led me around the corner to a space half-hidden by a large staircase. There, I noticed a wooden bench with a Charlie Chaplin statue sitting on it.

As we sat down, Josh said, "Even though it's not the Bradbury Building, at least we got a replica of its iconic bench."

I patted Chaplin's bowler hat and thought about the architectural wonder that used to house the statue's twin. The Bradbury Building has been the elegant backdrop for a number of movies, probably because it features Italian marble staircases, French wrought iron railings, and open-cage elevators.

Josh took my hand in his. "Did something happen with Detective Brown? Is he harassing you again?"

The cop's name splashed me like cold water. Better to tell him now. Didn't people say to spring bad news first? "Unfortunately, Detective Brown has me pretty high on his suspects list."

"Did he tell you that?" Josh clenched his jaw.

"Not in those words exactly, but when I called him—"

His grip on me tightened. "You did what?"

My face grew hot. "I found some new evidence pointing to Magnus as the culprit. I mean, the man practically confessed to me—"

"You spoke with Magnus Cooper? Please tell me it was over the phone." Josh removed his hand from mine and reached into the inner pocket of his suit jacket. He pulled out two wrapped fortune cookies, offering one to me.

I took it and said, "I saw Magnus in person, but his assistant was there at the same time. It seemed safe enough."

Josh shook his head and crushed his fortune cookie. "Tell me everything that happened."

I told him about Russ Nolan faking the sire of his puppies and muddying Magnus's reputation. And that Magnus had stolen the tiny Chihuahuas from the house.

I continued, "When I pointed those things out to Detective Brown, he didn't seem impressed. He thought I was pinning the blame on Magnus to save my own hide."

Josh slid a hand through his hair, making his bangs flip from one side to the other. "You know, anything you say to that cop could incriminate you. Please don't speak to him without me around."

I cast my eyes down and stared at my scruffy tennis shoes. "Sorry."

"It's fine. What's done is done." He opened the wrapper of his pulverized fortune cookie and picked out the slip of paper.

I peeked at it and read, "Someone with blue eyes admires you."

Marshmallow shifted in my bag beside me. "Not these baby blues."

Flattery could get me back into Josh's good graces. "I think your fortune meant to say someone with *brown* eyes admires you." Though I didn't regret getting more info from Magnus, I felt horrible that I'd distressed Josh in the process.

Josh looked deep into my admiring eyes. "It's just that I don't want anything bad happening to you."

I gave him my best hangdog imitation.

His gaze softened. "Anything else you need to let me know?"

Marshmallow wriggled in my bag. "Ooh, tell him my alternate theory about Indira as the killer."

I shushed Marshmallow, but Josh responded instead. He touched my shoulder. "I really am on your side, Mimi."

"That came out wrong," I said, tossing the fortune cookie back and forth between my hands. "I was actually talking to my noisy cat."

"Your—" He eyed my large bag, and a look of understanding dawned on his face.

"There is one more thing," I said as my heart started thumping with both nervousness and joy. "I told my mom about you, Josh."

"You did?" A goofy grin spread across his face.

I wrung my hands. "Except she assumed you were my boyfriend."

His eyes lit up. "I'd love to have that honor."

"You would?"

His voice dipped low. "Honestly, I've never met anyone like you."

"Really?" I jiggled my foot. "But we haven't known each other too long. Plus, I'm your client . . . and a murder suspect at that."

"I admit it's a bit unusual. But Mimi, I know you're innocent, and I admire you for standing up for those puppies and yourself."

I blushed, lowered my eyes, and then looked back up at his adoring face.

He held my gaze. "I'd like for us to date, so instead of just thinking about you all day, I can actually spend time with you . . . if that's what you'd like, too."

I took a deep breath. "It's official, then. We're a couple."

He raised my hand to his lips and planted a kiss on it, as though sealing the deal.

My heart fluttered.

"As much as I enjoy giving you legal advice," he said, "it'd be great to do some non-work-related activities."

I smiled at him. "Be careful what you wish for . . . because Ma's already invited you to our next Family Game Night."

He gave me a deer-in-the-headlights look, and every muscle in his body seemed to freeze.

"It'll be perfect," I said, crossing my fingers behind my back. "You'll definitely come?"

His voice came out slow and thick. "I'll try."

I gave him the date and time for game night, along with my parents' address. The fortune cookie he'd given me I decided to save for later, so it could remind me of Josh while we were apart.

When I plopped the fortune cookie into the bag, Marshmallow said, "Ow. What's with the *avalanche*?" He headbutted my side through the bag's fabric.

As I rubbed my rib cage, I heard the sound of bustling steps. My gaze swiveled to the entrance of the office building, where I glimpsed a giraffe-like man. Instead of taking the brass elevator, he headed toward the staircase behind us.

When he spotted us on the bench, the man snickered. "Bras before bruhs again?" I recognized that mocking, reedy voice.

Josh glanced at his coworker and said, "There's nothing wrong with a coffee break."

"I don't see a cup in your hands," his coworker said as he moved past us. He climbed the staircase and added under his breath, "Strike two, Akana."

After the rude coworker left, I said, "Will you get into trouble because of this?"

He shook his head. "Nah. We're required to take breaks."

After we said goodbye, I continued to reassure myself. Josh said he'd be fine.

Still, a change of scenery would clear my mind. A peaceful ocean setting sounded lovely, and I looked forward to Indira's purse party.

• • •

Indira lived in a proper beach house, a few blocks away from The Strand, a paved pathway that allowed beachgoers to bike or stroll on smooth concrete near the calming backdrop of the glistening ocean to the west. Indira's house, like a lot of homes near the beach, had a faded exterior. No doubt the constant sea breeze had scraped off the original layer of paint. What might once have been a cheerful turquoise had now been scrubbed away to a soft seafoam hue.

With space at a premium, the house didn't sprawl. Instead, it launched up in height to make the most of its lot size.

When I walked inside the house, I found Indira's lady friends gathered in the living room. I'd expected them to flaunt their wealth with some rich accessories. Maybe a pop of color from a vibrant Hermès scarf or a luxe pair of Prada shoes. Instead, they sat cross-legged on the patterned Persian rug or perched on the microsuede sofa in their swimwear: bikinis, swimdresses, tankinis, and more.

I'd opted to change out of my usual grungy work wear into a silk blouse and knee-length skirt for this special occasion. For a second, I wondered if I'd written down the wrong address. She hadn't said anything about swimming during the doggie playdate.

I had to be at the right house, though, because dogs of all shapes and sizes crowded the room. Restrained on leashes by their owners, they barked at Marshmallow's presence. He examined his paw, making his claws unsheathe. The dogs settled down a bit.

I spotted Indira coming into the room from a side hallway. She carried Ash on a tasseled pillow like a pampered princess. "Here's the star of the show. Think of how buying one purse—or five, for that matter—would make her life better."

The ladies all made clucking noises at the puppy and shook their heads. I heard murmured variations of "Poor Ash."

Indira wove her way around the large crowd. I peered at the numerous sympathetic faces around me, seeing if I recognized anyone. Not a single soul. Maybe they represented all the folks she knew outside of the doga class. In case they needed a groomer, I left a stack of business cards on the side table near the sofa.

Indira herself moved toward the couch, and some women vacated their seats to make room for Ash. After placing her dog down with care, Indira said, "I'll be right back with the merchandise."

Ash noticed the tense dog-cat situation, nodded her head at Marshmallow, and yipped. A few dogs whimpered, and Marshmallow retracted his claws. He informed me that Ash had vouched for him and even called him a special guest of the party. Marshmallow started preening before the dogs.

Indira returned and rolled a massive suitcase to the middle of the room. When she opened it, a collective gasp of awe rang out as the women saw a mountain of fanny packs inside.

"All new designs," Indira said with a bright smile.

She did brisk business. The ladies clucked their tongues at Ash and gave Indira sympathetic looks. Then they opened up their wallets.

A woman in a leopard-print bikini, though, held up the line. She pouted while holding her little terrier near the open suitcase. "Do I have to buy one?" she said. "My friend who told me about this said purchases were optional."

"Of course. No pressure." Indira tossed her head of gleaming raven locks. "But using my pool is considered an add-on."

The lady gestured to her bikini. "I bought this swimsuit just for today."

Indira pressed her full lips together. "This is a *purse* party, not a pool party. At least, not without the required price of admission." She plucked a horrid neon striped bag from the suitcase and held it in front of the woman's face. "This would go well with your skin tone."

Leopard-print lady choked and snatched up a neutral-colored fanny pack. "This one might work well as an all-purpose bag."

Indira flashed her a smile. "Lovely choice."

The woman pointed to the rear of the house. "And when exactly will the pool man be finished cleaning?"

"Shortly," Indira said. I wondered if she'd asked him to linger so she could make sure no one could access the pool without purchasing something first.

I walked over to the back of the house and peeked through the half-open French doors. Even with his back to me, the pool man looked familiar. He netted the pool, pulling out debris with smooth strokes. A wide-brimmed straw hat covered his face.

I'd seen that hat before, not so long ago. When the man walked around the curve of the pool, I could see his profile. I gasped. "Kevin Walker?" What were the chances?

A lilting voice spoke up from behind me. "Oh, he used to clean my pool, too. Everyone around here uses him."

Kevin Walker was Indira's pool boy, the one she'd mentioned after yoga class. No wonder she'd already heard about Russ Nolan's demise back then.

The woman continued, "He offers dirt-cheap prices."

I turned around to find the speaker wearing an off-the-shoulder swimsuit. She said, "Kevin's usually reliable. Except"—she frowned—"I heard through the grapevine that he bailed on a job recently. Haven't used him since I heard that."

"A shame," I said. "Why did he need to leave the job?"

"An emergency."

I narrowed my eyes. "When was this exactly?"

Her forehead scrunched. "Maybe a week or two ago. Why?"

"Just curious." Could it have been the same night Russ Nolan had been murdered? With his pool-cleaning muscles, Kevin Walker surely had the strength to knock down the breeder. Could the landlord have taken out his own tenant? Maybe over a disagreement about the rental?

Marshmallow brushed up against my leg. "I'll get more info from the dogs," he said. "Chat with some of the pool-loving pups here." Yikes. Not only was I partnering with my pet cat, but we were starting to get on the same wavelength.

I nodded before turning to watch Kevin through the French doors. As he continued fishing stuff out of the pool, I realized the pole itself could be a deadly object—maybe even the actual murder weapon. Kevin did wield it with both familiarity and force.

The musical chime of the doorbell sounded, shattering my focus. No one made a move to get it. The guests continued to sit around chatting, while Indira occupied herself with one last customer.

She saw me watching and jerked her head toward the door. As I passed her, Indira whispered a quick thanks.

I opened the door to find Lauren standing outside.

She gave a happy squeal of surprise. "You're at the purse party?"

"Indira thought I could ask a few of my grooming clients over . . . but, uh, they were all busy."

I checked out Lauren's outfit. She wore a belted shirtdress with a familiar-looking diamond necklace. "You're not going swimming dressed like that, are you?"

She shook her head. "No. Too much to do. But I heard about this party through a friend of a friend and wanted to drop off a contribution."

I took the sealed envelope she held out to me. "I'll be sure to give it to Indira."

"Tell her it's not a donation. She despises charity. Indira can use the money to cover the cost of several bags and give them away in a special raffle."

Lauren turned to go, but I touched her on the arm. "One more thing. I couldn't help but notice your lovely necklace."

She touched the glittering strands.

"In fact, I think I saw one just like it recently. Where did you buy it?"

"Oh, Mimi, you must be mistaken. This necklace is one of a kind. Most of my jewelry is custom-made."

Interesting, because I could've sworn Nicola had worn that very same necklace to my store when I'd expressed Sterling's glands. "Hmm. Has it ever gone missing?"

Lauren's eyes grew wide. "Of course not. But then again, I do have such a large collection to keep track of. Anyway, I better get going, or I'll be late to my next appointment."

While I said goodbye to Lauren, I heard a collective cheer rise from inside the house. I went back and discovered the women slathering on sunscreen. The tropical scent of coconut filled the room. From all the chatter, I picked out a few excited comments:

"Yes, he's finally done."

"Pool party is on!"

"I call dibs on the cabana."

As the women and their dogs all filed out to the pool, I located Indira and handed her the envelope. I explained Lauren's quick drop-off and her idea for a purse raffle.

Indira thanked me and then hurried outdoors. From the pool area, I could already hear the overexcited barking and heavy splashing of multiple dogs.

Marshmallow crept to my side and purred. "Guess what I found out?"

"Hopefully, a lot."

"Yes. Rich pooches love to gossip. They told me Kevin Walker bailed out to check on his rental property the same night Russ Nolan was murdered."

"That can't be a coincidence," I said.

Marshmallow swished his tail. "I think not. Kevin Walker acted 'stark raving mad' when he left the pool owner's home."

Aha. Had the man been angry enough to commit murder?

I heard the slamming of a door from outside. A car's engine rattled and caught.

"We need to go," I said. We ran out of Indira's house and chased after Kevin Walker.

CHAPTER

seventeen

B Y THE TIME Marshmallow and I rushed after Kevin Walker, he'd already gotten his pickup truck rumbling. Marshmallow and I jumped into my car, but my hands paused against the ten and two of my steering wheel.

Would I be driving straight into danger? I could almost sense Josh's concern from afar. But if I lost Kevin Walker's trail, I might miss a key breakthrough.

Detective Brown's stern and unbelieving face flashed through my mind. Since I didn't want to go to prison, I ignored my reservations and let my reckless side kick in.

Thank goodness Kevin Walker's clunker of a car took its sweet time moving down the road. We managed to follow him down several residential streets in my stealthier Prius.

After a few more turns, he parked in the driveway of another massive, spindly house. The new house, though, looked half-hidden by the thick green bulk of tall cypress trees. I wondered if the people who lived there planted them on purpose to provide shelter from prying eyes.

Deciding to block him in, I parked my Prius right behind Kevin's truck. This way he couldn't escape my questioning.

Kevin came out of his truck and slammed the door. Even through my rolled-up window, I could hear him fuming. "Why are you following— Hey, I know you. Aren't you that renter?"

I exited my car and took Marshmallow out. How could I explain myself?

Kevin pointed at Marshmallow. "It *is* you. I'd recognize that cat anywhere."

Marshmallow licked his fur. "What can I say? I'm unforgettably handsome."

Kevin glared at me. "I don't know why you're stalking me. Must I call the police again?"

The hair on the back of my neck prickled. "*Again?* So you were the one who told Detective Brown about my visit to the house. Why?"

"You asked too many questions, seemed too interested in the previous renter. The cop told me to let him know if anyone suspicious showed up."

I squared my shoulders and took a few steps closer to him. He backed against the side of his truck. "And what about you?" I said. "Heard you bailed on a client the same day Russ Nolan ended up dead."

"Are you implying that I killed him?" Kevin straightened up and moved to the rear of his truck. "I don't need to answer any of your questions, and I have work to do right now."

Marshmallow sped past me and leaped into the bed of the truck. "Don't worry, I know how to handle this." He sat smack on the pool net and trapped his paws inside the mesh.

I smirked at Kevin. "I'll call my cat off your equipment after you speak with me. I really don't want to bother you, but I need to know what happened that day."

Kevin looked back and forth between Marshmallow and me. He threw his hands up in the air. "Fine. I have a few minutes to spare. And nothing to hide. Ask away."

I pulled myself to my full petite height and held his gaze. "Were you at the house that day?"

He took off his straw hat and fiddled with it. "I was. While cleaning one of my client's pools, I heard the ladies gossiping about how Russ Nolan sold cute little dogs out of his house."

"That's when you rushed over to the house."

He stuffed his hat back on his head. "Running a business out of my mother's house was never in the rental agreement. And he'd been doing it under my nose."

"I get it. You were understandably upset."

He turned and kicked at one of the truck's tires. "When I first went over, I was hopping mad. Wanted to toss him out on the street. But then he apologized nicely to me."

"You just let it go?"

"I'm a businessman," Kevin said, giving me a lopsided smile. "Russ used his finances to smooth things over with me."

Moola. I wondered how much it had taken to smooth over the situation. The destruction of keeping a houseful—or, rather, a roomful—of dogs would cost a pretty penny. Way more than the typical security deposit would cover, I bet.

Kevin Walker did seem like a man who could be swayed by money. And even without the extra bribe, I realized it didn't make sense for him to get rid of solid rental income.

I wrinkled my nose. "What time were you at the house?"

He turned his head to the sky, seeming to stare at the pointed tops of the cypress trees. "Night had just set in. I remember turning on my headlights as I neared the house."

That would be shortly after I left the premises, when I'd seen Russ Nolan's house bleached an ominous white. "And when did you leave?"

His eyes flicked toward Marshmallow, who continued to stand his ground. In fact, my cat had his claws out and was toying with the mesh. "I spent ten minutes there, tops. Returned to my client as soon as possible to patch things up. Besides, Russ himself wanted me out fast."

I exchanged a look with Marshmallow. "Why's that?"

"The man was expecting a lady friend." Kevin gave me an exaggerated wink. "He said he'd even bought some wine for the occasion."

My mind flashed back to the discarded glass bottle I'd spotted in the trash the other day. Kevin's claim might explain why Detective Brown had dismissed my theory of a man as the killer. The cop had been focused on catching a female murderer instead.

"That's all I have to say." Kevin crossed his arms against his chest.

Of course, he could be feeding me lies to get me off his case. But I didn't have anything else to ask him.

I beckoned to Marshmallow. "Come along now."

Marshmallow took his time to get up and disentangle himself from the pool net. Then he shook his body with vigor.

We left Kevin shaking his head at all the white fur deposited over his pool equipment.

I took Kevin's story with a grain of salt. If I could get some sort of clear evidence that he'd gone back to work, I would trust his claim more.

Of course, I did have a friend who could steer me true. Pixie St. James, the wonder-*ruff*ic sponsor of Hollywoof, had connections to all the ritzy pool owners in the beach areas and beyond.

• • •

Pixie agreed to my spur-of-the-moment visit. As I drove up the wind-ing roads to Hollywood Hills, Marshmallow spoke up from the back seat. "You're lucky I don't get carsick."

I rolled down my window to let the wind rush in. "Want me to drive faster so you can really feel the breeze?"

In the rearview mirror, I noticed Marshmallow closing his eyes. "Just because I can handle winding roads doesn't mean I enjoy seeing objects whiz by me."

I slowed down the Prius. Even if I wanted to, I probably couldn't zip up the steep, curvy incline with my little car. Besides, I liked taking in the grand scenery at an unrushed pace. If I squinted into the dis-tance, I could even make out the iconic white "HOLLYWOOD" sign.

As I approached a higher altitude, I remembered why people paid big bucks to live at the top. Even the monotone color of the parched shrubs surrounding the road gleamed with wealth. Instead of looking dry, they made the hillside shine a brilliant gold. And I couldn't begin to fathom the ethereal beauty of the city lights from this vantage at night.

All of the elegant houses were barnacled to the hilltop as though by sheer willpower. Spaced tasteful distances apart, they echoed mod-ern geometric art installations. Many displayed cool rectangular edges, but I spied a pyramid structure as well.

Pixie's own oval-shaped house shone like a gem in the sunlight, polished to perfection by multiple renovations, including sparkling floor-to-ceiling glass windows to show off the view.

Pixie had grown up "privileged," as she called it. Her great-great-grandfather had passed down the family business to her. Now she took the lead as CEO of his company and had even expanded its reach across international borders. An advocate of flexible hours for all her employees, she often telecommuted.

Upon hearing my knock, Pixie flung the door open and embraced me. I caught her signature scent: a custom blend of cinnamon and cloves.

She released me from her hug and asked, "Who's this handsome fella?"

I introduced Marshmallow to her, and she scooped him up. He didn't unleash his claws as she cuddled him. Instead, he sniffed the air.

"Pumpkin spice," I whispered.

Marshmallow snuggled in Pixie's arms. "No, I think it's the comforting essence of unbridled wealth."

I choked a little, and Pixie looked at me with concern. "You must be parched. How about a drink?" She put down Marshmallow and walked through her enormous house with her typical graceful stroll.

Marshmallow's head turned this way and that. I wondered if I'd exhibited the same awestruck manner the first time I'd visited. The multiple columned hallways leading to hidden spaces and the sleek travertine floors had overwhelmed my senses back then.

With its amazing flourishes and fabulous decorations, Pixie's house reminded me of a museum. Everything in it seemed like an invaluable piece of art.

When we arrived at the kitchen, I wondered for a moment if I should stand instead of sitting down at her inlaid mother-of-pearl breakfast bar. But the fancy bar stools with their ergonomic cushions looked so comfortable. I sank down into one of them.

Pixie offered me a refreshing iced tea, infused with hand-picked herbs from her garden. Hexagonal ice cubes floated in the glass she gave me. Marshmallow even got something to drink: a bowl of volcanic filtered water.

I tried to remember if I'd seen any signs of her cute shih tzu prancing about in this labyrinth of a home. "Where's Gelato?" I asked Pixie.

No sooner had I said his name than a fluffball came springing through a doggie door leading into the back garden. He slid a little on the smooth floor in his excitement.

I crouched down to his level and greeted him. In return, he jumped up and began licking my face. "You sure are a *sweet treat.*"

Marshmallow grumbled. "A literal kiss-up, you mean."

After a prolonged patting session, Gelato seemed satisfied with my affection. The shih tzu moved on to Marshmallow.

Scrutinizing my cat, Gelato circled him several times. Then the dog wagged his tail with abandon before settling down a few inches from Marshmallow to watch him drink.

Pixie and I were finally free to chat.

"Thanks for letting me come," I said. "Knowing your full schedule, I hate bothering you."

Pixie placed her drink, a frothy pink concoction with a raspberry on the rim of the glass, on the counter and sat down beside me. "It's my pleasure," she said. "I wish we could see each other in person more often, actually. Plus, I've been meaning to check in with you about Hollywoof. Did you make some good connections at Lauren's yoga class?"

"Sure did." I swiveled my stool to face her. "I even went to a doggie pool party recently. Maybe I'll get some leads from that, too." After all, I had placed my cards on the side table.

"Pool playdates," Pixie said. She ran her finger down the stem of her glass. "We don't go to those anymore. Gelato feels too intimidated by the big dogs. Plus, after the Catalina Island mishap, he's still hesitant about being near any body of water."

I scooted off the stool and petted Gelato on his head. "You know, I'd rescue you again in a heartbeat."

He pushed his nose into my palm, and I stroked his fluffy ears.

Returning to Pixie at the counter, I said, "Even though you two aren't into pool parties anymore, you know about that crowd, right?"

She plucked the raspberry from her glass and held it poised in the air. "I keep tabs. Why?"

"For the pool party, I went to the house of Indira Patel—"

"Her name sounds familiar. Ah, I know. She designs those luxury fanny packs."

"Yes, that's her. While at her house, I saw the pool man, a Kevin Walker. Have you heard of him?"

"Walker . . ." She popped the raspberry into her mouth.

"He's really tan. Wears a straw hat about this big." I used my hands to indicate its dimensions. "Owns a rattling truck. And I heard he ran out in the middle of a pool job to check on his rental property."

Pixie snapped her fingers. "Ah, yes. Heard about that through the grapevine. People love to go on about their domestic dramas. He almost got fired on the spot, but the pool owner forgave him after he returned to finish his work and apologized."

I took a big gulp of tea and let its coolness clear my head. "When did he show up again?"

She twirled the pink liquid in her glass. "That same evening, in fact. He wound up having to clean the pool in the moonlight. The pool owner admired his tenacity. Plus, he gave her a month of free pool services. That helped his cause."

My heart sank. So Kevin hadn't been lying. He had gone to Russ Nolan's and come back quickly.

Pixie squeezed my hand. "What's all this about, anyway?"

Did she really need to know about my run-in with the law? She'd invested in Hollywoof, essentially entrusting me with a huge chunk of money. Would she find me less trustworthy if she knew the trouble I'd gotten myself into? "It's nothing," I said, draining my glass.

Pixie gave me a quizzical look.

"I'd better get going," I said.

Peeking over at Marshmallow, I no longer found him by his water bowl. Instead, he lay a few feet away, asleep on a soft mat, which seemed to be vibrating.

I nodded at my snoozing cat. "What's he napping on?"

She flicked her wrist toward him. "That's the doggie massage mat. But I guess it works on cats, too."

I tiptoed over to Marshmallow and picked him up from the luxury mat. It turned off after I retrieved him. Must be triggered by weight.

I said goodbye to Pixie and trudged over to the front door carrying Marshmallow. Wow. He really could stand to lose a few pounds.

She wedged an envelope into my cat-filled hands. "Whatever you're dealing with," she said, "it sounds like you might need a break. A night out. Here are two tickets to a local fundraiser for a nonprofit that's right up your alley."

Pixie opened the front door but paused on the threshold. "Mimi, we're friends, not just business partners. You know you can tell me anything."

I gave her a tight smile. "Maybe in the future. I think I need to deal with this on my own for now."

Pixie's concern was sweet, but I couldn't involve her. I mean, I hadn't even mentioned a word to my own family.

Which reminded me. Family night was fast approaching. I shuddered.

It was easy to tell my loved ones about good news, like my relationship with Josh, but I didn't want to let slip anything negative. They all counted on me to be the eldest, the model daughter and sister. I couldn't let them down.

As I dragged a comatose Marshmallow into the car, I pondered over the info I'd gotten from Pixie. Kevin Walker hadn't lied about returning to work on that same evening. Had he also been speaking the truth about Russ Nolan's love life?

The breeder had been expecting company, waiting for a lady visitor. Who might it have been? Could that woman have seen something important—or even have been the killer herself? I knew one nosy neighbor who might have the scoop.

CHAPTER
eighteen

DRIVING ON THE 405 the next day after work, I grumbled to Marshmallow about the traffic. "If only you qualified as a passenger, I could use the HOV lane."

In the rearview mirror, I saw him stick his nose in the air. "Yeah, cats are worth at least two humans."

"Be grateful that at least you're relaxing in the back." My hand hovered near the horn. Should I honk at the guy trying to cut in front of me?

"I'm in a caged box," Marshmallow said. "It's no spa, sister."

"I have to be your chauffeur."

He swiped at the bars of his carrier. "Drivers take you where you want to go. I didn't sign up for this jaunt."

"Aw, Shirl isn't so bad."

He didn't comment during the rest of the drive to her house.

Shirl, on the other hand, seemed enthused to see us. She led us to her sitting nook, where she'd already positioned a laptop on the doily-covered table. "You caught me in the middle of my YouTube marathon, but I can take a break to see Emperor do some live tricks."

The video was on pause, and I could hear a loud buzzing noise coming from the kitchen. "What's that sound?"

"The popcorn machine warming up. It takes a while before it gets to popping." She sat down in one of the plush chairs.

I perched on the edge of the armchair opposite her. "We won't keep you long, Shirl. Actually, I wanted to ask you again about Russ Nolan, whether you saw a lady visiting him the night he died . . ."

She crossed and uncrossed her legs. "I told you I didn't see a thing. No one visited him."

"Really? Kevin Walker told me otherwise."

She looked over her shoulder toward her neighbor's house.

"You can tell me, Shirl," I said. "I understand if you don't want to talk to the police, but I'm your friend."

Her face scrunched up. She looked like she was on the brink of deciding to confide in me. Then a series of pops burst from the kitchen. She scrambled off her seat and disappeared.

When she returned, she was carrying a giant bowl of buttered popcorn, and her face looked shuttered. "There's nothing to tell," she said.

"He didn't have a girlfriend?" She didn't respond, and I wondered if I might *butter her up*. Leaning toward the bowl, I took a big whiff. "That smells heavenly."

She pulled away the bowl of popcorn and crossed her arms over it in a protective motion. "Russ Nolan didn't have a lady friend."

That was a far cry from the statements she'd made when I first met her. "What about all those women you saw visiting his house? You even accused me of being his girlfriend before. Surely one of them could have actually taken a shine to him."

She scoffed. "Not with his cheap taste in wine."

Marshmallow spoke up. "How would she know about his drinking habits?"

If she'd seen the label on his wine bottle, it meant she'd had the opportunity for close-up observation.

Shirl watched me exchange a look with Marshmallow.

"Are you sure you don't have more to tell me?" I asked her.

She stuffed a handful of popcorn into her mouth and munched. "I've told you all I know."

Shirl unpaused the video, and the cat onscreen started tiptoeing on its hind legs.

Marshmallow shook his head. "What a joke. Cats belong on the ground. That's why we have four paws."

"Are you sure you have nothing to add?" I asked Shirl, but her eyes remained glued on the screen.

I sighed and gathered Marshmallow. "Guess we'll be on our way."

As we exited the house, I heard my phone chime out a reminder. I opened up my calendar app. Time for Family Game Night.

● ● ●

Ma and Dad had loaded the dining table with snacks. I spied bowls of dried squid, roasted broad beans, and, my personal favorite, peanut candy. Those square-shaped treats melted like sugar in my mouth, depositing peanutty goodness on my tongue. Inevitably, the delicate layers of the pastry left crumbs everywhere.

Ma fanned her hand in front of my face. "Your boyfriend is where?"

Um. I'd lost myself in dreams of peanut candy. Why hadn't he shown up yet?

"Maybe he got caught up at work," I said, grabbing a few pieces of peanut delight.

Ma traced the outline of a silver rose on her dark blue *qipao*. I'd noticed she was wearing the traditional figure-hugging dress tonight. She'd even put on makeup and opted for false eyelashes.

Dad pulled at the collar of his shiny polyester dress shirt. No doubt he'd worn it at Ma's bidding. "What's your man do again?"

"He's a lawyer," I said.

Ma squeezed Dad's hand. "Wah! Must make good money."

"A steady income," Dad added.

Alice popped her head out of the closet and said hello.

"Ooh, my favorite Lee," Marshmallow said, sprinting her way. *Gee, thanks,* I thought as he did a figure eight around her legs.

My sister grinned and patted him. Then she turned to me and said, "What kind of games does Josh like?"

"Let me ask him." When I looked at my phone, though, I realized I'd already missed a text from him. It read, Sorry. Something came up.

I blinked at my cell. Had he bailed on me in four words? Was this like a breakup text? I hadn't said so, but he must've known meeting my family would be a huge milestone. Or was that the real reason he'd failed to show up?

I pulled an Alice and locked myself in the bathroom to get some privacy, just like she had during the egg tart sympathy party we'd thrown her. Pacing around the cramped space, from sink to shower and back again, I dialed Josh's cell. No answer.

I called his office. Voice mail. Was he avoiding me on purpose? Had I pressured him too much by extending an invitation to meet my family so early in the relationship?

I sat down on the toilet and placed my head between my hands. This dating thing was harder than it looked.

A soft knock sounded at the door. "Mimi?" my sister asked.

I let her in.

Seeing my crestfallen face, Alice gave me a long hug. "What happened?"

"Josh can't make it, and he told me over text. Now he's avoiding my calls."

She placed an arm around my shoulder and led me back to the dining room. "There could be a million reasons why he couldn't come."

My parents, seated at the table, looked up at me with puzzled faces.

"Did he run into traffic?" my dad asked.

Alice tossed a sweet smile their way. "Josh is busy tonight, so we'll meet him during the next family get-together."

Ma harrumphed.

I sat down as Alice went to search the hall closet to select a game. She picked out a four-player option: Scrabble.

After we set up the board, Ma clucked as she selected her tiles from the bag. "Not show. Such a nerve."

Dad's head bent near Alice's, and I leaned in to listen. "Have you actually met this Josh fellow?" he whispered to her.

For a moment, his forehead crinkled up with worry. Maybe he was recalling the time I'd made up a pretend classmate in kindergarten. He'd learned about my immense imagination at Back to School Night when he'd talked to the teacher.

"I grew out of make-believe, Dad," I said.

He held up his hands in a gesture of surrender. "Just asking Alice a simple question." But his forehead unfurrowed.

After we organized the letters on our racks to our hearts' content, Ma patted my arm. "What about library date? College student nice, eh?"

"Ma, he came for career advice, not to improve his social life. And he was a teen. That's so wrong."

"Let's get started," Alice said as she tapped her finger on the star in the center of the board. We began to play.

Mired in misery, I could only create words related to the dismal state of my mind: "alone" and "cancel." Even Marshmallow could sense my sadness, and he sat in my lap, nudging my hand to pet him. Stroking his soft fur did calm me down.

About five minutes into the game, Marshmallow asked, "Is something up with Alice?"

Huh? I looked at my sister's face, but it only held intense concentration. She seemed focused on completing her latest word, "school."

I clapped for her. "Ooh, double word score."

She shrugged. Always so humble.

Marshmallow's gaze seemed intent on following all the letters crisscrossing one another on the board. "Did you check out her other words?"

I examined the board and tried to sort the various words by player. Dad had put down "golf" and "pal." His plays were also easy to pick out because he never made words beyond five letters. Ma had gained valuable points by using the word "family" and had even scored a proper bingo by disposing all her tiles to make "weddings." Alice must have put down "principal" and "worry."

Everyone waited for me to take my turn, but I paused the game. "Is everything okay at school, Alice?" I gestured to her words. "Did Principal Hallis threaten you again?"

Her eyes started glistening, and she sniffed. "They're not just empty threats anymore." She reached into her purse and pulled out a pink slip.

I gasped while she leaned her head against Dad's shoulder.

"How dare she?" I said.

"She *is* the boss." Alice folded the paper. "I thought the principal might be more understanding. She has a hedgehog. Aren't pet owners supposed to have a strong sense of empathy?"

"Not all animals are the same," I said.

She sighed and returned the piece of paper to its hiding place. "It hurt being the only one singled out. Not even the teacher who got hired three months ago received a slip."

Dad put his hand on her shoulder. "Princess Two, how are you holding up?"

Alice tucked her hair behind her ears. "The principal didn't give me a specific date that I need to leave by. I'm hoping to make it through the end of the school year. In the meantime, I'm just trying to love on the kids every single day I get."

I saw Ma scoot down in her chair. Soon, I felt a sharp kick to my shin. Ow. She glared at me. "Big sis *boleh.*"

I shook my head. "Not this time, Ma. Big sis no boleh. I no *can do.*"

She raised her overpowdered eyebrow at me. "Give up? Not Lee way."

So I added another task to my growing mental checklist: "Help Sister." It would rank a little below my top two priorities: "Find Killer" and "Confront Boyfriend."

We finished up Scrabble, persevering to the end, with the family drive Ma had instilled in us. Of course, Alice won the game. She usually did. But maybe this time we unconsciously let her.

As I drove back home, I thought about my top two priorities again. I didn't know where the killer lived, but I certainly knew where my so-called boyfriend did. I would go over at the crack of dawn and confront him about skipping out on Family Game Night.

CHAPTER

nineteen

I N THE CHILLY predawn, even Marshmallow with his thick fuzzy coat shivered. I clutched my thermos of hot tea and took huge gulps.

"How long will we have to wait out here?" Marshmallow asked.

"As long as it takes. I made sure to check the carport, and all the spots were filled, which means he must be home." I stood right outside of apartment number one, planning to accost Josh on his way out.

"You should have brought over some comfy chairs for us."

"At least we have this." I unrolled the yoga mat I'd taken from my place. I must've bought it when I was on a Pilates kick, but now it sat unused in my hall closet.

Marshmallow lay down on the mat. "Where's the cushioning on this thing?" he asked.

"It's for stretching and exercising, not sleeping." I tapped his paw. "Hey, maybe we can do some cat-oga while we wait."

Marshmallow yowled. "No way, sister."

At the sound of the plaintive crying, Josh's door creaked open an inch. Eek. How could he look so cute at this hour? His hair looked mussed, and he was wiping sleep from his eyes. "Mimi? Marshmallow? Are you two doing exercises in front of my unit?"

"Finally, a chance for me to escape into a place with heat." Marshmallow slipped through the open gap of the door while I steadied my voice.

"We're here to see you," I said, rolling up the mat.

He bent down. "Let me help with that."

"No thanks."

His closeness and the faint whiff of pine made me heady. Why did he always smell so good? My fingers fumbled.

"Must be a slippery mat," Josh said. "Or the cold's chilling your hands." He blew a burst of warm air across my fingertips. "Please come inside."

I finished with the mat and entered his apartment. If I had expected a messy bachelor pad, I didn't find it. No dishes were piled up in the sink. In fact, they sat in an orderly row, drying inside a bamboo rack. The place looked tidy, even ready for company.

However, the walls, with their lack of framed pictures, did scream a blinding white. But with his busy job, maybe he didn't have the time to decorate—or maybe he didn't want to damage the walls. The security deposit at our complex wasn't anything to sneeze at. The hassles of apartment living.

Josh motioned me farther in. "Have a seat anywhere. Looks like your cat snagged a place in the dining room."

"I adore your decor," Marshmallow said. He'd laid claim to a spot at the (literal) head of a fish-shaped dining table.

The chairs and table were made from solid pine (maybe that explained Josh's yummy woodsy smell). The chairs had silver cushions with a layered design that mimicked fish scales.

"Interesting table," I said, sitting down at one side.

"My parents bought it for me. Said it would remind me of home. It's the Hawaiian state fish, you know, the humuhumunukunu kuapua`a."

I stared at him for a beat. "Gesundheit."

"That's really the name of the fish."

I traced my fingers across a fin. "Do your parents live close by?"

"No, they're still on the main island."

Josh sat down beside me and stopped my fin tracing. "You didn't come here to talk about my family."

I pulled my hand away from him and sighed. "I came to talk about mine."

He hung his head. "I'm really sorry—"

I dropped my gaze and concentrated on the fish's tail, tracing its shape to keep me from crying.

"I barely had time to text you. I had to do it in secret during my review."

My head snapped up. "What do you mean?"

His face clouded. "The partners called me in for an impromptu performance meeting."

"Right before Family Game Night?" What disastrous timing.

Josh blew air out of his mouth, making his bangs fly up. "My colleague got me in trouble. Told them I was trying to sneak out early and leave for the day with my work only half-done."

I tapped against a wooden fish scale in thought. "I can probably guess who tattled. Your nosy neighbor, Mr. Bras before Bruhs."

"The very same charming fellow."

I lifted my head and locked eyes with Josh. "Why didn't you call me? I would've understood."

"The meeting went long, and I didn't want to ruin your Family Game Night."

Marshmallow gave a slow shake of his head. "Own up to it, man."

"I do understand, but I was also looking forward to introducing you to my parents and Alice," I said. Plus, it would make the Josh-and-me thing official.

A flush crept up Josh's face. "To be totally honest, I was kind of scared about meeting your whole family. I should've just shown up late. Mimi, I messed up."

A growl erupted from my stomach, and I tried to cover my tummy with my hands.

"Told you to eat breakfast," Marshmallow said.

Josh sprang from his chair and rushed to his kitchen, where I saw him retrieve a small frying pan. "Food always helps me feel better."

"I was too nervous to eat before," I whispered to Marshmallow under the sound of Josh's cooking.

"Never stops me." Marshmallow sniffed the air. "The grub doesn't smell half-bad."

Josh soon placed a breakfast plate in front of me: two eggs sunny-side up and a frown of a bacon slice. He clasped his hands together and pleaded. "Forgive me?"

"Maybe a little," I said, digging in.

He gave me a dashing smile and ran back to the kitchen. He then put out a bowl of milk for Marshmallow. "I need to apologize to you, too, because you're part of the Lee family."

Marshmallow sniffed at it and turned his nose up.

Josh scratched his head. "I thought cats liked milk."

Marshmallow pushed the bowl away with his paws. "Oh, grasshopper, you have so much to learn. I'm lactose intolerant."

I pointed at Marshmallow. "Many adult cats can't digest milk too well," I said. "They don't have the right enzyme to break it down."

"Oh." Josh sat back down with a small sigh. "Maybe it's best I stick to subjects I know, like law."

I nudged his shoulder. "How did the performance review go, anyway?"

He slid a palm down his face. "Horrible. They said I'm working at an unsatisfactory level. Claimed I lack concentration. I guess the same colleague also tattled about you dropping by the office and taking up my time with a pro bono case."

"The partners didn't like that? I thought lawyers were supposed to take on free cases." I speared the piece of bacon with my fork.

Josh sighed. "I can't assist, not technically. The bosses want me to focus on billable hours, meaning work that actually pays."

"How much time do you need to put in?"

"A typical associate bills over two thousand hours a year, but not all the time spent working is billable. So it translates to at least sixty hours a week."

I dropped my fork with a clatter. "That sounds like a lot. You really should focus on other cases, then."

He turned to me and touched my shoulder. "I'll still make time for you."

"That's very sweet of you," I said, but I knew I'd only contact Josh if I truly needed him.

"And with me being so busy, it's probably wise not to go sleuthing by yourself."

"But I'm not alone," I said. "I've got the extremely talented Marsh-mallow."

Thinking I was joking, Josh laughed.

But Marshmallow purred and said, "I am the very best."

Josh checked the kitchen clock and frowned. He said he'd need to leave soon to get in all those billable hours, so I finished my breakfast with a few big bites. Then I grabbed my mat and thermos, whistling for Marshmallow to follow me out the door.

When we got back to our place, Marshmallow spoke up. "Thanks for complimenting me back there."

"You do make a great investigative partner."

"What are you saying?" Marshmallow arched his back. "I'm the lead detective on this case."

"Ha. And who have you interrogated lately?"

Wait a minute. That gave me a light bulb idea. I needed to learn the identity of the mystery lady who'd visited Russ Nolan the night of his demise, and who could tell me about that?

Kevin Walker had left before the woman had even shown up. Russ Nolan's neighbor Shirl denied seeing anything at all that night. And Magnus hadn't spotted anyone besides the "dozing" Russ Nolan when he'd rescued the dogs.

Of course, Russ Nolan himself couldn't be contacted without a serious séance. But I could ask for info from more than spirits and two-legged eyewitnesses. There were some furry creatures who'd been on the scene as well. A talented cat who could translate dog to human-ese would come in handy right about now.

"I have just the job for you, Investigator Marshmallow," I said. "However, it may involve some breaking in ..."

• • •

After I'd finished up with my grooming clients for the day, Marshmallow and I waited until night fully blanketed the landscape. I changed into an all-black ensemble, because that's how they do it in the movies, right?

"I'll lead the way when we get there," Marshmallow said. "Humans have horrible night vision."

Reaching Oak Lane, I slid my quiet Prius in like a shadow a few houses down from Magnus Cooper's place. I could see lights gleaming from his upstairs. We crept around the perimeter trying to figure out how to access the rear yard.

A chain-link fence secured the back area, but I thought I could scale it. The patterned gaps would serve as hand- and footholds.

I moved closer to the fence, and security floodlights flashed on. I froze for a few moments, my heart thumping.

When I detected no movement from within the house, I gripped the metal wire with sweaty fingers. I'd climbed trees as a kid, but scaling the fence took longer than I'd anticipated. I huffed and puffed to get over the top, while Marshmallow flipped over it like an acrobat.

He sat waiting for me on the other side, licking his paw. "What took you so long?"

"Easy for you to say. Cats are natural gymnasts."

"Having only two legs throws you off," Marshmallow said. "Come follow me. And try not to make too much noise."

Tiptoeing after Marshmallow, I snuck over to the warehouse. I recalled Magnus saying they kept the door to it unlocked in case of fire.

I turned to Marshmallow and asked, "Did we think this through? What about the dogs? Won't they give us away with their frenzied barking?"

His eyes gleamed in the dark. "Don't worry, I've got this. Just slide the door open a crack."

I did as he requested and watched as Marshmallow crept up to the door's edge. He gave a short meow. A moment later, he received some yips back. He then made a few strong purrs, and the dogs inside grew silent.

"What did you say?" I asked him.

"Told them we're doing an official investigation. Said I'm a police cat."

"Come again?"

Marshmallow flicked a dismissive paw at the warehouse. "Dogs are so gullible."

We crept forward into the dark interior of the warehouse. I followed Marshmallow's form past stalls of quiet dogs. A few of them whimpered or panted in low tones, but none caused a ruckus.

We traveled to the very back of the warehouse, where we located the door to the nursery.

"Pull the handle," Marshmallow said. "But let me go in first."

I used my fingers to touch the door's surface, because my eyes still couldn't make out much besides outlines. When I felt a rectangular bar, I yanked on it. The door opened a foot wide, letting a soft glow of light spill out. Marshmallow darted inside.

Excited barks erupted inside the room. I looked toward the front of the building. Could they hear the noise from the main house?

Must have been too far, because no one came running to check. Finally, the barking subsided.

I saw Marshmallow's eyes glint at me from the doorway. "They're ready for you," he said.

I slipped into the nursery but left the door not quite shut. The worst situation would be getting trapped inside if there happened to be an auto-locking mechanism. No way would I be able to explain my presence to Magnus without getting hauled away in handcuffs.

The soft glow in the room I'd noticed before came from a few battery-operated night-lights. Maybe they calmed the little puppies down. A strong lavender scent permeated the air.

As I looked around the room, the nursery seemed full of furballs.

A few puppies yipped at me, while a number just circled and wagged their tails. Several adult female dogs lay watching us but didn't move toward me. Their eyes flicked back and forth between Marshmallow and me.

I couldn't believe these were the same puppies I'd seen drenched in filth before. (Although some of the dogs must have belonged to the mamas in the room, because they shared glossy coats of black and white instead of the tan of Russ Nolan's dogs.) However, all the puppies seemed well-kept and happy in this cozy space.

I walked toward a cute tan runt and reached out to pet it. One of the adult females rushed at me, growling.

"No touching," Marshmallow told me.

"Is that the mama? She has the wrong color fur."

He shook his head. "The mother of Russ Nolan's puppies isn't around. From what the puppies tell me, they got taken from their mother real young and nursed on bottles by the breeder.

"Also," Marshmallow said, "I told the mama dogs you'd stay near the exit. That way you're not a threat to the little ones."

"Fine." I backed up and leaned against the doorframe. "Have at it, Marshmallow."

It was strange watching Marshmallow interview the puppies. His meowing got drowned out by a chorus of energetic jumping and barking.

"Maybe I should speak with them separately." Marshmallow tried to get the dogs to line up, but they all huddled together.

"You could talk to just one of them," I said.

"Okay. I'll pick the oldest, the ringleader." He singled out the biggest of the tan pups.

After a flurry of back-and-forth exchanges, Marshmallow translated for me. "This is Tigre, the most coherent of the bunch. He says they never saw a lady in the house. When Magnus came to free them, nobody else was around."

"And where exactly was Russ Nolan during the rescue?" I had to make sure I'd gotten an accurate accounting from Magnus.

Marshmallow relayed my question, and Tigre gave a few growls. The runt I'd tried to touch in the beginning also whimpered.

"Russ Nolan was outside sleeping in a chair," Marshmallow said. "In fact, little Sparky here tried to check on the breeder. Thankfully, the man slept through the rescue."

"So Magnus took them out the front?" I said. "That was risky."

"Easier than crossing paths with an irate Russ Nolan." Marshmallow meowed at Tigre again, who responded right away.

Marshmallow nodded at me. "Yes, they went through the front, though it took a while. Little Sparky was slow to leave Russ Nolan's side."

"And there was definitely no sign of a woman in the whole house?"

Marshmallow asked Tigre, but a few other dogs added their sharp barks to the discussion.

"Interesting," Marshmallow told me. "No woman was seen, but the puppies sensed he'd had a visitor that night. Let me get the full story."

Marshmallow turned to Tigre, who gathered all the dogs in the litter together. They each gave a few barks in an uncoordinated doggie chorus.

Marshmallow turned back to me and provided a summary. "This is what they know: Russ Nolan had company over, because they heard the clinking of glass."

I nodded. "He probably uncorked his bottle of wine."

"Also, they heard a lady walking around with clattering steps. Maybe high heels? The doorbell rang after that—"

My eyes widened. "Did he have three visitors in one night? Magnus, the mystery lady, and someone else?"

"The visitor who rang the doorbell smelled like musty potpourri."

"Shirl," I said. "It has to be." Why had she kept mum, then? What had she witnessed that had made her go silent?

Marshmallow continued, "However, the potpourri visitor soon left. Minutes passed, and the dogs heard angry voices in the house. The lady click-clacked away and slammed the front door."

"Anything after that?"

"Russ Nolan's heavy tread clomped throughout the house. Then he settled outside."

"And nothing afterward?"

"No, at least not within the confines of the house. And with all the excitement and the late hour, the dogs started dozing off."

Hmm. Had someone crept back in while the dogs had been sleeping? Could it have been the mystery lady, maybe come back with a vengeance? After all, there had been raised voices. Who was she, anyway?

I tapped my foot on the nursery floor. "The puppies don't know anything about the lady in heels?"

Marshmallow addressed the dogs. One of them gave a small squeak in reply.

Prodding the puppy forward, Marshmallow said, "This little lass remembers the woman had a familiar orange scent. The smell still lingered in the air when they left with Magnus."

"Where did she recognize it from?"

"She'd smelled it before on one of the customers who'd dropped by the house."

"When exactly?"

Marshmallow turned to the puppy and interrogated her. His

whiskers twitched as he faced me. "Interesting. This lady must have come within the past month to adopt. And only three puppies were chosen this last round."

I counted the number off on my fingers, trying to match each puppy with a new owner. I gasped. My recent Chihuahua customers accounted for all of the purchases. "Three. That would make the owners . . . Lauren, Indira, or Tammy."

"Exactly." Marshmallow swished his tail.

"Can the little puppy describe the woman any further?"

Marshmallow shook his head, and I noticed the little dog had retreated to blend in with the rest of the pack. "I asked her already. She said all humans look the same to her, what with their long stilt legs."

"All right, then." I smiled at each of the dogs in turn and pulled out the stash of dog biscuits I'd brought along. Placing the treats down, I said, "Thanks for all your help."

Marshmallow and I slipped out. At the main house, all the lights had been turned off. The building stood tall and silent. We scrambled over the fence again, and I grinned in the dark. Nobody had suspected a thing.

CHAPTER

twenty

A HEARTY POUNDING AT my door startled me from a deep sleep. I glanced at my alarm clock. Six in the morning. Maybe the visitor would go away. I shut my eyes. The knocking persisted.

Finally, I flung off my covers, sending a startled Marshmallow flying.

He flipped, landed on all fours, and glared at me. "Why'd you do that?"

"Someone rude won't quit trying to break down my door." I yawned. "Hey, didn't I buy you a kitty bed?"

"It was too cramped for me." He stretched out to his full length, taking over a good amount of my floor space.

I stepped over his sprawled form and made my way to the front door. Upon opening it, I found myself staring at none other than Detective Brown.

He barked out his words. "Good morning, Miss Lee."

I rubbed the sleep from my eyes. "Why are you on my doorstep so early in the morning, Detective?"

"I'm here to take a look around your place."

"Excuse me?"

He fished inside the pocket of his dark gray sport coat. Was that the same jacket he'd worn the other day? Maybe he had a whole collection of them to avoid doing laundry. He pulled out a document and waved it in my face. "Obtained a search warrant."

Reading through the legalese, I realized it was an official order. My mind woke up pretty fast after that. I gulped, stepped to the side, and allowed him to enter. "And what exactly will you be searching for?"

He walked in with his clunky shoes. I flinched but decided this wasn't the best time to tell him about my no-shoes rule. He stopped in the center of my apartment and spread out his hands in an encompassing sweep. "By all means, Miss Lee, tell me where to start looking."

"There's nowhere to look. Nothing incriminating for you to find." I stood my ground, hands on my hips, knowing that the fuzzy bunny slippers I wore tempered my serious glare.

"We'll see about that." Detective Brown started searching high and low, peering into dark corners. He shifted my furniture and unearthed masses of dust balls, making him sneeze.

Serves him right. I asked, "Why am I your prime target, Detective?"

He turned, and I swore his eyes twinkled at me. "New evidence came up and pointed to you."

I gaped at him. "But that's impossible."

He again reached into his jacket pocket. This time he produced a clear bag with a crinkled piece of paper. With all the stuff he kept in there, I wondered if he had some kind of magician's coat. "Does this look familiar to you?"

He smoothed it through the plastic protection and came closer.

After giving it a brief glance, I said, "Looks like a standard receipt."

His index finger pointed to the top of the paper.

Looking closer, I read the words: "Patron name: Lee, Mimi."

I recoiled from the receipt. "Where did you find that?" One of my old library slips. I felt relieved that at least it didn't list any questionable materials.

"This paper was discovered near the scene of the crime."

"That's weird." Had I dropped it when I'd gotten a tour of the house from Kevin Walker?

Detective Brown tucked the evidence bag back into his pocket. "A neighbor found it stuck in the slats of her adjoining fence. Must have blown over from Russ Nolan's backyard."

A neighbor? I felt my breath quicken. Did he mean Shirl?

Detective Brown patted his bulging pocket with satisfaction. "Good thing she spotted it. She'd marked it for her recycling bin and was about to throw it out when she saw the unfamiliar name and gave me a call."

Marshmallow let out a low growl. "I think that's the same receipt from when we played catch."

Ah, the wadded-up ball I'd used for the game.

"You know, I visited Shirl at her house the other day," I said. "Must have dropped it by accident then."

Detective Brown shook his head. "Nice try. She found it the morning after the murder."

My hands shook. Shirl had framed me.

Detective Brown donned some gloves and continued to poke around my apartment. He messed up my sofa cushions while looking under them. After peeking into closed cupboards, he left them ajar.

Why had Shirl thrown me under the bus? Well, she had acted jittery the other day when I'd questioned her about the mystery lady. Had she felt threatened somehow by my snooping?

I followed Detective Brown's progress. He hadn't collected a single item yet. "There must be something dangerous I can find here," he murmured.

Recalling my previous conversation with the detective at Hollywoof, I wondered if he was searching for the murder weapon. Did he think he'd find something that could cause head trauma in my apartment?

He pulled everything out of my hall closet and left the items scattered across the floor. Nothing there except my huge jumble of shoes. And the folded yoga mat.

Good thing I didn't own any heavy-duty exercise equipment. Something like a pair of dumbbells might have given Detective Brown cause to pull out his handcuffs.

Did I have anything at all in my possession that could inflict a head injury? On my nightstand, I remembered I had piled up several books—in a twist of irony, all checked out from the library.

However, I harbored a partiality for mass-market paperbacks. Thank goodness I didn't own something like a hardcover of *Crime and Punishment*. Light and compact, paperbacks barely weighed down my hands while I read them. They would be too flimsy to impart heavy damage.

Detective Brown didn't take too long to finish looking around my tiny apartment. In the end, he confiscated one thing: my favorite mug.

A sky blue piece of pottery, it read, "Stay PAWsitive." I doubted anyone could've used *a cup* as a weapon.

"Done?" I asked as Detective Brown cradled the mug in his gloved hands.

"I suppose so," he said, grumbling.

"FYI, that mug is already compromised—has a big crack. Hard to fix, unless you know *kintsugi*."

He gave me a puzzled look but deposited it into an evidence bag. "I'm getting this analyzed by the lab ASAP."

"Knock yourself out."

Too late I thought about my choice of words. The cop blinked at me.

After he left, I started panicking. Detective Brown had searched my home. He'd manage to wrangle approval for a warrant. That meant he was actively building a case against me and trying to speed up my arrest.

I took a deep breath and dialed up Josh. Immediately, I got his voice mail. I left a vague message about a legal emergency.

Why wasn't he answering? I shoved all the moved furniture back into place.

Maybe Josh didn't have good reception. I stuffed items back into the hall closet, repositioned spices in the cupboard, and straightened my stack of paperbacks before resolving to text him. I had to at least try to reach him again.

Me: Detective Brown searched my place.

A delay of a few seconds and then a ping.

Josh: Stuck in court. Sorry, phone was on vibrate. Did he have a warrant?

Me: Yes, and I think he was looking for a weapon.

Josh: He confiscate anything?

Me: My favorite mug. But I don't think you can harm anyone with a cup.

Josh: Sorry, Mimi. Must have been traumatic. Don't need to work late tonight. Can I swing by?

I pondered my response, shuffling through some unopened mail I'd left on my messy kitchen table. It would be nice to have Josh come by, but I'd prefer a different setting than the emotional land mine of my searched-over apartment.

Also, I realized I didn't want to just talk about legal stuff. Wouldn't it be great to get away from it all? To immerse myself in a different environment? When I found the fundraiser invitation Pixie had given me in the pile of mail, I smiled. Perfect.

Me: Pick me up after work? There's a special charity event I'd like to attend. And wear your finest.

• • •

My own fanciest attire consisted of a little black dress. I'd succumbed to the myth of the LBD as a staple item in every adult woman's wardrobe and had impulse-bought the A-line with a swingy skirt in college.

When Josh showed up, he was wearing a sleek suit that looked tailored to his toned frame. He gave a low whistle and said, "You look stunning."

I sparkled. My grin must have stretched from ear to ear.

We drove to the charity gala in his car, a polished black Lexus with leather seats. While navigating, he asked, "So what is the event for?"

I reread the invitation on the cream cardstock with embossed lettering. "A fundraiser for a company called PetTwin."

"Interesting name. Wonder what they're about . . ."

When we arrived, I double-checked the address to make sure we'd ended up at the right location. I hadn't realized the event would be held at a performing arts center.

We made our way to the lobby and saw empty tables draped in crisp white fabric arranged throughout the vast space. A stream of people flowed from the lobby and through a pair of open double doors. I assumed the entryway led to the stage.

As we also approached the doors, an usher wearing a bow tie urged us forward. "It's about to begin."

Josh and I sat in velvet seats near the back as the lights started to dim. A large screen descended from the rafters. I heard the whir of a projector, and a beam shot forward in the dark. When Josh snuck his hand over the armrest to hold mine as a commercial played on-screen, I had to muffle my soft sigh.

PetTwin's advertisement described them as a high-tech company specializing in apps that matched rescued animals with potential owners by using personality quizzes and interactive profiles. The commercial ended with short testimonials from a number of local shelters that had embraced the technology with gusto.

Then the screen retracted, and a spotlight beamed right at the center of the stage. A woman with long red hair, like a real-life Ariel, climbed up the steps to the stage and stood at the podium. Speaking into the microphone, she said in a brassy voice, "I'm Stacy, the founder of Pet-Twin. Thank for you coming to support us and purchasing tickets to this event. I hope you enjoy the delicious appetizers." She motioned to the lobby with a flutter of her fingers. "You'll find a few tablets near your place settings so you can explore our apps firsthand. Rest assured that our company is on the cutting edge of the newest innovations, including 4-D pet meet-ups. We again are grateful for your generosity."

Everyone applauded her short speech and beelined out of the auditorium and back into the lobby. At our assigned table, I swept Pixie's name card into my clutch. Nobody would be any the wiser that she'd given me her spot.

I glanced at the other name placards at the table and recognized one of them: Lauren Dalton. At least I would know someone at the table.

Too bad Lauren hadn't arrived yet. A couple sat down and started making small talk with Josh. Then others came and immediately grabbed the tablets lying around to check out PetTwin. Peeking at their screens, I saw them flip through adorable photos of cats, dogs, bunnies, and more. Only when they'd started their personality questionnaires did Lauren and her husband show up.

I studied Mr. Dalton. For a famous Hollywood producer, I'd expected someone more glamorous. Instead, I discovered a squat and bald man, his head too large for his frame. In fact, its size looked like it could throw off his balance.

I greeted Lauren with a hug and shook hands with her husband. Then I turned to my dashing boyfriend and introduced Josh to the Daltons.

In no time at all, the men started talking about their favorite sports teams, and I turned my attention to Lauren. "What a lovely outfit," I said. She did look nice, even though she wore an atypical understated look: a simple burgundy sheath.

"Actually," she said, smoothing her dress, "I feel awkward not having some kind of costume like I usually do at charity functions. But my dear hubby wanted a low-key fashion statement. Plus, dressing up isn't as much fun without Sterling to match me, and they won't allow pets in the theater."

A waiter with a tray passed by and offered us flutes of champagne.

As Lauren sipped her bubbly, I asked, "How's your puppy doing? Are his legs any better?"

She clinked her glass with mine. "Sterling's feeling great. It's a cause for celebration. He's so much better after going to his acupuncturist."

I managed to swallow my sip through sheer willpower. "They have specialists for dogs?"

"Of course. Pet acupuncture. I think his sessions have resulted in nothing short of a miracle."

The waitstaff approached our table again. This time, they offered a selection of small bites. Each appetizer featured unique ingredients: green chile and artichoke bread, fruit and coconut spring rolls, and ricotta fritters.

I took a spring roll, and Lauren reached for a fritter with an elegant motion. In her simple dress, she really did look different than her usual decked-out self. Hmm. Something else was missing beyond a typical fancy costume—

"Oh, you're not wearing any jewelry," I said.

She chewed her appetizer and dabbed her mouth with a cloth napkin. "We were running late. I really wanted to wear something special, like my bone bracelet, only I don't know where it's gone."

I dropped my half-eaten spring roll, and it tumbled onto the floor. "It's not actually made from bones, right?"

"No, silly." She encircled her tiny wrist with her index finger and thumb. "It's a golden bracelet with a bone pendant."

I knocked my glass over. "Oops." Using my napkin, I dabbed at the growing wet circle on the fancy tablecloth.

I'd recently seen a bracelet just like the one she'd described—on Shirl's arm. Could Lauren have bribed Russ Nolan's neighbor into staying quiet? Had she been the mystery woman who'd gone over to his place and dropped her bracelet there by accident?

I needed to find out more about Lauren's movements on that night. Did she have an alibi for the hours between eight and ten? If only I could find someone with access to Lauren's schedule without alerting the woman herself.

But I did know somebody who could get those details. I whipped out my phone and asked, "Oh, Nicola left something at the shop the other day. Could I get her number?"

Lauren studied me with a calm intensity, her eyes looking like deep pools of indigo. "I have a better idea, Mimi. Bring the item by my place. Nicola always comes over every morning at six sharp to make me a breakfast smoothie."

"That's early. Maybe I could set up a different time with her directly?" I didn't want my conversation to be under Lauren's watchful eye.

Clutching my arm, she said, "You must come. I insist."

She waited for me to nod before she eased her grip. Then she gave me her home address in Hollywood.

I looked over at Lauren's husband. At that early hour, Mr. Dalton should be home as well. And Nicola would be there. I'd be safe enough. But just in case, I planned on bringing spunky Marshmallow along. Thank goodness I'd never trimmed his dagger-like claws.

CHAPTER

twenty-one

A S I'D EXPECTED once I'd seen her Hollywood zip code, every-thing at Lauren's mansion appeared over-the-top. I'd gone mid-way up the long winding drive to her house when an attendant flagged me down and asked if I wanted to use the car elevator. I didn't know how such a thing even functioned, so I declined.

Instead, I parked on the side, near some sculpted yew trees. On the front steps, I spotted a male figure waiting. Mr. Dalton stood with a roller suitcase propped near his feet.

I strode up to him and said, "Hello again. I'm Mimi Lee, and this is my cat Marshmallow."

Seeing his confusion, I added, "We met last night at the PetTwin fundraiser, remember?"

"Oh, right." He rubbed the top of his bald head and said, "I can never keep track of the faces and names from the charity events my wife makes me attend."

"Lauren forces you to go?"

"Sometimes. But it's an even trade. I also ask her to go to my press events once in a while."

I imagined the glitz and glamour of those parties. "Those must be exciting."

"Not to her. She bailed on my last one after twenty minutes, but at least she shows her face to humor me."

Sounded like a double standard. As evidenced by last night, Lauren required her husband to attend the entirety of a charity extravaganza but had bailed on his press event after putting in a brief appearance. Unless she'd had a good reason to leave.

Mr. Dalton glanced at his phone and continued, "My chauffeur is so slow. I may need to replace him."

That gave me more time to find out about Lauren's character. "Did she feel ill at your last event?"

"Bored, more like." He gripped the handle of his suitcase. "Lauren even dragged her assistant there to accompany her. The poor girl had a prior engagement scheduled for that evening and almost missed it."

I saw his limo snaking its way over. "When was your shindig?"

He gave me a date—the same day as Russ Nolan's murder. My heartbeat raced, and I heard internal thrumming in my ears.

The car pulled up, and Mr. Dalton nodded at me before getting into the limo.

I walked up the front steps and stood for a few moments, staring at the giant pair of carved oak doors at the entrance. Why had Lauren left the party early? If she had stayed, she'd have a solid alibi.

Taking a deep breath, I pressed the doorbell. Lauren opened the door and greeted me with kisses on both of my cheeks. Inside the entryway, I noticed a monstrosity of a sparkling chandelier with knifelike crystal shards.

After I'd said hello, she led me and Marshmallow through her maze of a house. I realized that every light fixture in the home, not just in the foyer, was a draping crystal chandelier.

Her huge kitchen seemed more utilitarian than fancy. It had multiple marble islands for meal prep. Gleaming pots and pans hung from an overhead rack.

Nicola stood at a table slicing apples. She paused for a moment and waved at me.

Lauren touched my arm. "I told Nicola you'd be coming over to return something to her. What'd she leave behind again?"

I coughed, giving myself time to think, and tapped my purse. "An engraved pen. I'll give it to her later. She looks busy."

Nicola maneuvered to a fridge located about twenty feet away from us. From its pull handle, I realized it was a walk-in unit. She wandered into the large refrigerator and came back carrying a robust bunch of kale.

Marshmallow yawned and curled up in a sunny spot in the kitchen under a large skylight. "It's too early for me." He groaned and closed his eyes.

I leaned against the empty island where Lauren stood, her polished nails resting against its cold marble surface.

"I saw Mr. Dalton outside," I said. "He looked like he was going on a trip."

She drummed her fingers, making a tap-tapping beat. "Needs to be on location for a film."

"He must go to some amazing places. How often do you travel with him?"

"Never, nowadays. He says I'm a distraction on the set. Plus, I learned early on that we never got to sightsee because he has to work such long hours." Loneliness. Could that be the reason she'd visited Russ Nolan?

She stopped drumming her fingers. "It's been like this for years."

"Sounds like you two have also developed a system for attending public activities. He goes to your charities, and you go to his press events."

She splayed her polished nails and examined the immaculate curved tips. "I hate those things. All flash without purpose. Not like my charities, which actually help those in need."

"Media extravaganzas do seem superficial when compared to your fundraisers. Are you ever able to leave a press event early?"

"Actually, I did the last time."

"Ooh, where'd you go when you played hooky?"

"Nowhere exciting. I had to run an errand."

"In the evening?"

She didn't answer. Instead, in a louder tone, she addressed Nicola. "Use only the leaves. I don't want even the hint of a stem in my smoothie."

Lauren didn't want to talk about her marriage anymore. But perhaps her assistant could provide me with some extra info. "I think Nicola might need my help," I said.

Lauren nodded and lowered her voice, "Yes, please. You can make sure she does it right."

I crossed the expansive kitchen to arrive at Nicola's side and helped her separate the kale leaves from the stalks. Then Nicola retrieved the cutting board she had used for the apples along with a wicked-looking chef's knife.

"Is working in the house normal for your position?" I asked.

She grunted at me. With strong thwacks, she chopped the kale into small green pieces.

I looked over at Lauren, who'd pulled out her phone and was staring at it, mesmerized.

Lowering my voice, I said, "Is this a happy home?"

Nicola dumped the apples and kale into a blender. Then she retrieved a jar of local organic honey and plopped in a few teaspoonfuls.

When she plugged in the blender, I realized it'd be a great time to ask her more pointed questions under the noise of the whirring. She'd probably tell me the ugly truth. After all, there was no love lost between Nicola and her employer.

Nicola hit the start button. As I watched the ingredients mixing, I asked, "How's their marriage?"

"I'm not paid to involve myself with their couple dynamics."

I tried a different tack. "As her assistant, you must be familiar with Lauren's jewelry. Last night she mentioned this bracelet she loves with a dog bone pendant on it."

Nicola bit her lip.

"I think I saw it," I said.

"You did?" Nicola's eyes grew wide. "Mrs. Dalton said she misplaced it, but I thought it might have been stolen. Did you find it being hawked on eBay?"

I shook my head.

"Well, where did you—"

Lauren called for her breakfast smoothie, so Nicola had to fill up a glass of gleaming green and bring it over to her boss.

Lauren placed her phone down and sipped. She sucked her teeth. "A tad too sweet. Did you use the green apples?"

Nicola twisted her hands together. "You ran out of those. I had to substitute with Galas."

"I see." Lauren raised her eyebrows at her assistant. "Guess this will have to do."

Nicola returned and placed an arm around my shoulder. "Mimi wanted to check out your costume closet. I mentioned your wonderful Rey outfit to her during Sterling's last grooming appointment. May I show it to her?"

Lauren smiled at me, specks of green dotting her teeth. "I can tell you about all the fascinating details of my wonderful collection."

Nicola shook her head. "Please finish your smoothie, Mrs. Dalton. You know, time is tight this morning with the acupuncture appointment coming up."

"You're right. I'll catch you two in a little bit," Lauren said, waving us off.

As Nicola marched me through the intricate hallways, I asked, "Do you happen to know where Lauren went the night of Mr. Dalton's last press event? She had to leave early."

"That's easy enough to find out. I have her calendar on my phone." Nicola stopped walking and looked straight into my eyes. "If I tell you where she went, you'll give me more details about the jewelry, right?"

I nodded.

She checked her phone and said, "Looks like Mrs. Dalton met up with a friend. Somebody with the initials 'A.D.M.' is listed for that night."

Those three letters in combination meant something entirely different to me. Not a person, but a company's name. I knew I'd have to follow up with them later.

We continued walking and finally reached the costume arena—because it wasn't what I would call a closet. The size of half my apartment, the room was surrounded by glass on all but one side. Only the back wall was opaque, because it held three sections filled with items: shoes, clothes, and accessories.

I spun around, feeling like I was stuck in a giant fishbowl. Seeing me scrutinize the glass, Nicola said, "I picked this place so we could talk without being surprised by Mrs. Dalton."

Even though I hadn't really wanted a clothing tour, I got distracted by the extensive rear wall and gaped at the amazing display there.

Nicola snapped her fingers. "Now can you tell me more about the bracelet?"

I turned my attention back to her. "Sorry—it's such a huge collection."

"Please describe the bracelet you saw." She cleared her throat. "Of course, Mrs. Dalton will be so relieved to hear you located it."

"The piece looked heavy, maybe 24K gold. And, of course, it had a bone charm."

She nodded. "Yes, that sure sounds like it."

I stepped over to the clothes and touched the Rey outfit with its long robe. Would Lauren wear this costume only once? What an extravagance. And all her jewelry reflected her rich taste as well. "Do you think Lauren might have left the bracelet at Russ Nolan's?"

Nicola frowned at me. "But she never even met the man."

"Well, I heard Russ had a lady guest over one night. That, combined with the bracelet . . ."

"You think that he and—" Nicola clapped her hand over her mouth.

"Yes, Russ and Lauren must have met up," I said.

She shook her head, hard. "You've got it all backward. Russ *was* interested in someone—me. We set up a time to go stargazing. I actually borrowed the dog bone bracelet for that night."

I crinkled my nose. "You did?"

"But it went missing. Only I didn't realize until the next day." She searched my face. "Are you sure Russ didn't sell the bracelet?"

"I don't think so. The last I saw, it was on the wrist of his neighbor."

"The old lady who wears the YouTube sweaters and big pants?"

"That's right," I said, though I knew Shirl wouldn't have appreciated Nicola's description.

Nicola reached into her pocket and pulled out a box of orange Tic Tacs. "Excuse me. I chomp on these to calm down." She popped one in her mouth.

I smelled citrus. Aha. The bright-colored candies explained the scent the dogs had noticed that night and confirmed Nicola's date story.

"Tell me about your stargazing night," I said.

She crunched the Tic Tac in her mouth. "In one word, *horrible*. Shirl interrupted our start of a romantic evening. She came over to complain about the barking."

That sounded like Shirl's MO. But why hadn't the neighbor told me about Nicola being there? Instead, she'd thrown me under the bus and gotten Detective Brown to search my entire apartment.

Nicola rubbed her wrist and said, "I borrowed Mrs. Dalton's bracelet that night, but its clasp was loose. Russ commented on how the bracelet kept coming undone. I knew I should've picked something else, but it was super cute."

Sounded like Nicola had taken Lauren's jewelry, just as she'd done with the three-layered diamond necklace. "Maybe it fell off your wrist by accident, and Shirl picked it up," I said.

Nicola swallowed hard. "Russ really didn't take it? I thought maybe his invitation to watch the stars had been a ruse in the end to steal the jewelry. He had previously complimented me on my fine taste."

"Did you witness anything odd that night?"

In a pinched voice, Nicola said, "Russ did get a strange call. He sounded downright secretive over the phone, and I started suspecting he might have been two-timing me."

"Why'd you think that?" Although I was surprised Russ Nolan had anyone, including Nicola, clamoring for him.

"I heard him say her name."

"Do you remember it?"

"Like I'd forget. Kell."

"Huh." I stepped closer to Nicola. "Think back. What were his exact words on the phone?"

Her breath quickened. "I only heard the snippet from his side. 'This is not a good time, Kell.'"

She looked so defeated. "Perhaps that meant something different than what you think it does," I said, squeezing her hand.

Her eyes misted. "Are you saying he *wasn't* seeing someone else at the same time? That maybe he had been attracted to me?"

Love was strange. Who knew which people would hit it off? Guilt washed over me as I recalled how I'd sprung the news of Russ's death to the small group of women after doga class. If I'd known about Nicola's relationship with Russ back then, I would've broached the topic with more gentleness.

All of a sudden, Nicola swiped at her eyes with her sleeve. She sprang over to the wall and grabbed Rey's staff. Then she started swinging it around in practiced slashes.

I heard clapping from behind me. Turning, I saw Lauren standing in the doorway with Sterling. "What a wonderful demonstration. Nicola does take regular shaolin classes, and it shows."

Nicola wielded the staff like a kung fu master. Watching her deadly swinging, a new suspicion surfaced. Could Nicola have delivered the fatal blow to Russ Nolan? She had thought he'd been two-timing her that night. Might the murder have been a crime of passion?

Lauren stepped over to me and air-kissed my cheeks. "I have to take Sterling to his acupuncturist now, but I wanted to say bye before I left."

I looked down at her little dog. "He does look a lot better."

"Those needles are pure magic, I tell you. Anyway, gotta run. Nicola, please show Mimi out."

As Lauren exited with her puppy, Nicola put away the staff. Then we returned to the kitchen, where I prodded Marshmallow awake.

"Already?" he said, stretching.

"Yep, and we've got things to do."

*   *   *

The first item on my to-do list was to see why Lauren had gone to an appointment at ADM after she left the press event. I tried calling the office to save me driving time.

Nobody picked up, and I couldn't leave a message in their full voice mailbox. I figured I could swing by the headquarters before opening up shop.

I made my way over to ADM and found the same volunteer lounging at the scarred desk. A cold slice of pizza sagged in his hand. Pepperoni for breakfast?

"My bosses are doing a staff meeting over coffee," he said. This business certainly didn't run a tight ship. On the other hand, I didn't blame the supervisors for wanting to get out of the stuffy garage-like atmosphere. Or for needing a caffeine pick-me-up this early in the day.

"Okay, so you can help me," I said. "A friend of mine visited here, and I need to know more about that evening."

He gave me a blank stare.

The situation felt similar to guiding a lazy dog in obedience class. "Could you take a look at the appointment calendar?" I asked.

He chewed his pizza with his mouth open, and I watched red sauce splatter his chin. This human trainee lacked the cuteness of a pup, though. "We don't have a planner or anything like that."

"I just need to figure out what time she came by that night and how long she stayed for. She needs the timing to, er, expense her mileage for tax purposes." I hoped the kid didn't know anything about the IRS. "Don't you keep some type of record?"

"Nope." He finished up his slice of pizza.

I pointed over his shoulder at the closed-circuit TV monitoring the outside premises. "What about that camera? Doesn't it record images? There should be videos available."

He swiveled to the monitor. "Maybe I can find some footage, but what's in it for me?"

With irritation, I slid a twenty onto the worktable next to him. American Dog Makers should be paying *me* as I trained this youth in customer service. However, the teen seemed willing to help after receiving my hard-earned money. He pulled up some videos on the computer.

When we found the right footage, I examined its time stamp. Lauren had entered the building at eight thirty in the evening and left at nine thirty.

"That's pretty late to have an appointment," I said.

"I recognize that lady," the volunteer said. "She's some hotshot producer's wife, so the top brass made an exception for her. She wanted to file a written complaint about the breeder of her new puppy."

Now I remembered the formal document with a scrawled signature I'd seen in Russ Nolan's folder. What the fellow dog show competitor had said also floated back to me, about how somebody with pull had threatened to give ADM bad publicity. The facts matched. Lauren Dalton had used her connections to take membership away from Russ Nolan.

But if Lauren had been at ADM headquarters for an hour during that time frame—and Detective Brown had said the death occurred between eight and ten—she wouldn't have been able to travel all the way to Russ Nolan's house to commit the murder. I scratched her off my suspects list.

I reflected on the phone conversation Nicola had overheard. Who had Russ Nolan gotten the call from? Someone named Kell.

Or perhaps he hadn't been saying "Not a good time, Kell," but "Not a good time. Kale . . ." Instead of talking to someone named Kell, maybe he'd been referencing another name during his conversation.

In Russ Nolan's circle of friends, how many people had one of those unisex names? Or rather, how many dogs were called that? I knew where to find Kale's owner, because she was the local elementary school's PTA president. All I needed to do was peek at the school calendar to find her next scheduled meeting.

• • •

I arrived late to the PTA meeting and hid in the back. Sitting at the rear of Armstrong Academy's cafeteria reminded me of my elementary school days.

The wooden sectional tables with wheels were pushed off to the side, jammed against walls filled with student artwork. The smell of microwaved pizza wafted in the air.

Marshmallow sat under my folding chair, scrunched down in my Hello Kitty bag. Nevertheless, his protruding fur tickled my ankles. I shifted my feet as I listened to the meeting.

Onstage, Tammy stood addressing the dozen or so folks who had shown up. Everyone else besides me sat in the first two rows to pay better attention to her speech.

Despite Tammy's glittery short-sleeved top, she had a serious expression on her face. I tuned in to the last half of her sentence. ". . . a new fundraiser," she said, lifting up a cardboard box.

A man with a bald patch on the back of his head spoke up in a loud bellow. "Is that *candy* we're selling?"

"It's chocolate," Tammy said. "Rich in antioxidants."

A woman gasped. "But not dark chocolate—it's *milk*. What's the cacao content?"

Tammy shrugged. "This is what I could get on the fly."

Another woman waved her maroon-manicured hand in the air, and Tammy called on her. "I don't understand. I thought we were doing a dog show fundraiser. My kids were ecstatic about your original idea."

Tammy shuffled some index cards in her hands before speaking. "We ran into some difficulty securing the right kind of performance dogs."

"Didn't you say you could rent some cute Chihuahuas and have them trained in no time?" Maroon Nails said.

Tammy fanned her face with the index cards. "No time left for any more questions. Sorry, we have to go over our budget this evening, so I'm turning the stage over to our treasurer."

A lady wearing a peach chiffon dress and pearls stepped onto the stage and swapped places with Tammy. I didn't bother listening to the numbers and percentages she spouted.

My mind remained on the school fundraiser Tammy had mentioned. The old one involving dogs. Had Tammy wanted to use Russ Nolan's pups for it?

After the meeting adjourned, I waited for all the parents to leave before heading over to Tammy. She continued to look down at the index cards in her hands. I wasn't sure if she was analyzing the speech she'd given or merely avoiding an onslaught of questions from upset PTA parents.

I tapped her on the shoulder. "Hi, Tammy."

She startled. "Mimi? What are you doing here?"

I thought of the first school-related thing I knew and babbled. "Um, my sister's a teacher. But she's at a different place . . . er, for now."

Her eyes focused on me. "I see. She needs a job."

"Well, she did just get a pink slip." My thoughts strayed to my sister. Poor Alice. She loved her job. And although I wanted to help her fight to keep her position at Roosevelt Elementary, maybe it wouldn't be a bad idea to have a reserve plan.

"Sometimes the school will retract those . . . but I'm besties with the principal here. Your sister can mention my name as a reference."

It'd be a great backup for Alice. "That would be a lifesaver. Thank you so much."

Then I refocused on the murder case. I took a deep breath and gambled on my next words. "One more thing. I happened to be talking with Lauren's assistant. She mentioned you had a phone conversation with Russ Nolan about Kale."

She crinkled the card in her hand. "Well, that's not surprising. I complained to him about Kale's health."

I gestured to the stage where she'd spoken during the meeting. "Were you working with him for that doggie fundraiser you spoke of?"

Tammy sighed and slipped the index cards into her distinctive metal-studded bag. "I tried to, and it would have been the event of the year. Kids and puppies—what could be better? Russ Nolan promised me top-notch dogs and even sold me on the idea by showing me Kale, who seemed in prime health at the time . . ."

"So did you confront Russ about your dog's medical condition?"

"Yes." She stood up and folded her chair with a snap. "I even asked whether I could return Kale."

I collapsed a nearby chair. "What did he say?"

"No refunds."

We took the chairs to the back and placed them in the storage rack. "That's rough," I said.

"I canceled the dog show when I discovered Kale's poor health. Even if I couldn't give the puppy back, I thought Russ Nolan would help with some of the medical bills at least."

"And he wouldn't?"

We put away more chairs.

"Didn't do a single thing for me. So I filed a lawsuit to get him to pay up." Tammy's eyes clouded. "I actually went over to his house to tell him . . ."

"Oh. The day we met." I remembered her showing up in her sleek SUV as I stared at the police-sealed house.

She cast her gaze at the floor. "Sadly, it was too late by then. And, of course, now I'll never get a penny to help pay for the surgery."

"Sorry, Tammy."

"No matter. I will rise up." She flung her metal-studded bag over her shoulder and held out a box of chocolates to me. "Want a bar? It's to better kids' education."

"Okay." I paid for two dollars' worth of charity.

Tammy strode out the door, her chin lifted high.

"Poor Tammy and Kale," I said to Marshmallow. "And she sure needs that surgery."

"She was in a lot of pain," Marshmallow said. "Told me about it when I met her in the shop that first time." I remembered their back-and-forth barking and meowing.

"I hope she gets better soon."

We walked back to the Prius, and Marshmallow paused near my car's rear tire. He looked up at me. "I believe Kale's feeling a little better. Through the doggie grapevine at the pool party, I heard that Tammy gave her special shots to numb the pain."

I shook my head. "Will that really be enough to fix the leg problem?" Poor Kale—and the rest of her siblings. They all deserved better than to deal with bad health problems caused by an unscrupulous breeder.

CHAPTER

twenty-two

A S I UNLOCKED my shop the next morning, the phone was ringing off the hook. I let it go to voice mail. The caller didn't leave a message, but then the phone rang again.

I hesitated to pick up. Could Detective Brown have somehow concocted a solid scenario that involved my favorite mug as the murder weapon?

Better to face the music now than later. I took a deep breath and picked up the phone. A male voice—but not the one I was expecting—spoke.

"Magnus?" I said.

"Mimi. Good thing your shop's listed on Yelp."

What would make him want to call me? "Do you need my professional grooming services?"

"I need to see you, that's for sure. If you want to bring along supplies, feel free."

I didn't have to check my wide-open calendar to know I was available. "When did you want to come over here—wait, did you say '*bring along*'?"

"Yes, you can stop by my place right now."

"This very minute?" I'd barely opened the store.

He cleared his throat. "As soon as possible. You can come with your tools and clean these *dog biscuit crumbs* off my puppies."

Uh-oh. Magnus knew I'd snuck onto his property.

I fumbled the phone. It clattered against the countertop.

When I retrieved it again, I heard Magnus say, "Everything okay over there?"

"Fine. I'll be at your place soon."

Should I call up Josh to let him know where I'd be, just in case? But then he'd ask me probing questions, and given his lawyer skills, I'd probably confess to sneaking into the warehouse.

If Josh had been unenthusiastic about my peeking into Russ Nolan's police-sealed house before, I doubt he'd be pleased to learn I'd actually trespassed now. I decided to let sleeping dogs lie. Instead, I screwed up my courage and took my very awake cat with me as I headed to Magnus Cooper's house.

When Marshmallow and I approached his front door, a cool breeze raised goose bumps on my arms. Having grown up with temperate SoCal weather, anything under seventy degrees felt nippy to me.

I rang the bell while Marshmallow stood sentry beside me. Magnus opened the door, and his face looked set like stone.

Lifting my basket of grooming supplies to chest level, I shielded myself.

Magnus didn't invite me in. He crossed his arms, blocked the doorway, and said, "What were you doing in the nursery?"

Should I tell him about the doggie eyewitnesses? Maybe if I could put a more believable spin on it . . . "I thought the dogs might have ex-tra evidence in regards to Russ Nolan's death."

Magnus glared at me. "I washed them clean of his filth. There shouldn't be anything tainting them from that house. Why are you so interested in Russ Nolan anyway?"

I sighed. "The detective on the case has me pegged for the murder."

Magnus guffawed. "Why would he think a slip of a girl like you could be a threat?"

"I don't know. And I'm really sorry about visiting the puppies without your permission." Holding my grooming supplies out, I said, "Please, let me make it up to you. I can groom your dogs."

He uncrossed his arms but didn't move.

"Must I do everything around here?" Marshmallow said. Purring, he sidled up to Magnus and did a dramatic shiver.

Magnus blinked at my cat for a moment. Then he stepped aside and waved us in. "Come inside, but only so your cute kitten can warm up."

"Thank you so much." I rubbed my arms and entered. In the photo area, I noticed Zel trying to catch two puppies running around.

Rushing over to the pen, I said, "Let me help you. I can also groom their fur. Sometimes the brushing calms them down."

She gave me a frazzled smile and said, "All yours, Mimi."

After I set my basket of supplies down, the puppies circled me out of curiosity. Speaking in a calm voice, I crouched down to their level. As I stroked them, they started acting more at ease. I massaged their little bodies and smoothed their fur with gentle motions.

Magnus nodded from the sidelines, and his niece seemed amazed by my dog-whispering skills.

"All done," I said when I'd both tamed and groomed the dogs.

"Wow," Zel said. "Can you also help me ready them for a photo shoot?"

She pulled out an Eiffel Tower backdrop. Then we positioned the dogs. The girl we dressed in a tulle skirt, while the boy wore a beret on his head. In between them, Zel laid down a velvet pillow with fake plastic rings attached to it.

"Aw," I said, as Magnus grabbed his Nikon. He started snapping pictures of the mock doggie proposal.

At the end of the picture-taking, Magnus turned to me and gave a thumbs-up. I'd gotten back into his good graces.

Marshmallow, in the meantime, had gotten bored and started wandering around the house. Out of the corner of my eye, I saw him leap onto the top shelf of a bookcase. He perched there, peering at a framed photo.

"Take a look at this," he said, tapping it with his paw. Of course, the frame toppled right over.

"Oops." I hurried to Marshmallow's side and righted it while he jumped off the tall bookcase. Maybe Marshmallow wanted to distance himself from his guilt.

I examined the frame with care. No cracks in the glass or dents on the metal border. Then I noticed the actual picture and did a double take. "Is this Bogart?" In the shot, Magnus's pride sire was dressed in a fancy bow tie, a glass of bubbly at his side.

Magnus came over to survey the photo. Then he turned to Marshmallow, who'd positioned his paws beneath his face and was looking up with wide innocent eyes. "It's okay," Magnus said. "I have tons of these postcards lying around."

"Postcards? What do you mean?" I said.

Magnus took me to a spinning rack set on a side table. "We don't just print calendars. We do postcards, greeting cards, and all sorts of stationery. Bogart is one of our top stars."

I spun the card carousel and spied a familiar picture. Bogart with a gold medal draped around his neck. The same photo Tammy had shown me when she'd talked about Kale's birth father. "Could Russ Nolan have bought one of these?"

"If so, not from me personally. But he could've ordered online or walked in and purchased one from my niece."

Zel glanced my way. "What does this Russ Nolan look like?"

I described Russ Nolan to her, including his distinctive stubble beard.

"Nobody came in looking like that. Maybe he ordered online. I can go through our records." She turned to Magnus. "Can you take care of the puppies while I check?"

"Sure. I should let the puppies rest anyway. They're probably tired." Magnus whisked them away to the warehouse while Zel sat down at the computer.

After some clicking, she pulled up a detailed spreadsheet. "Could this be him?"

She pointed to an "R. Nolan," who had ordered several postcards a few months back. A familiar address appeared next to his name.

Soon, I heard Magnus's heavy tread returning, and I spoke to him. "Looks like Russ Nolan did order some postcards."

Magnus chuckled. "Maybe he wanted to see what high-quality Chihuahuas look like."

"If only." I shook my head. "One of my customers told me he used them as headshots to advertise the prized sire of his pups."

Magnus banged his fist against the desk, making the computer keyboard jostle. "Not only did that man change the breeding records— he even used my own photos against me."

The quality of the postcard prints was such that I'd mistaken them for real photographs at first glance. I bet Tammy had been likewise bamboozled.

How had she felt after realizing she'd been hoodwinked? Mad enough to commit murder? At least angry enough to have filed a lawsuit.

I left Magnus and Zel peering at their computer, the two of them grousing about copyright and how to insert watermarks on their pictures.

"Great detecting," I told Marshmallow once we'd gotten outside. "Now to get more info on that lawsuit..."

We strolled through the neighborhood while I made a quick phone call to my favorite lawyer. Josh picked up on the first ring.

Had he been waiting for a call from me? My nerves sparked.

"Mimi," he said. "It's so good to hear from you."

I loved the smile in his voice, and even though he couldn't see it, I grinned right back at him. "Sorry to bother you at work."

He half chuckled. "How else would you get ahold of me? I feel like I'm even sleeping here nowadays."

"That bad, huh?" I shuffled my feet along the sidewalk.

"Actually, yeah." He lowered his voice. "Someone was let go yesterday, and they're talking about more cuts soon."

"I guess your firm needs clients, just like my grooming business."

"That, or a giant infusion of cash."

"Ah, rich clients, then, not money-sucking pro bono ones like me."

"So this isn't a social call?"

"I wish." Spying a scraggly weed growing in the crack of the pavement, I toed it with my sneaker. "Do you happen to have access to legal documents?"

"What do you mean?"

I stomped on the weed. "One of the puppy owners filed a lawsuit against Russ Nolan. Her first name's Tammy. Do you think you can follow up on it?"

He gave a loud exhale. "It'll take some digging around, but I have a few friends at clerks' offices. Once I locate the right courthouse, I can give you more details."

"Thanks, Josh. I really appreciate it."

"Sure. But don't hold your breath. I'm juggling quite a bit over here."

I lifted my shoe. The weed sprang up, undamaged.

My phone vibrated as I got another call. Seeing the ID, I groaned. "Josh, I'm going have to hang up."

We said goodbye, and I switched over to the new caller. "Detective Brown," I said, "how may I help you?"

The detective didn't waste any time with chitchat. "I hear dispatch mentioning a disturbance in Russ Nolan's old neighborhood. Are you involved?"

"What? No!"

My tone of indignation must have appeased him. "Better not see your name mentioned in the report," he said. "I've half a mind to drive down there, but I'm currently on assignment elsewhere."

"This doesn't involve me, Detective."

His voice turned gruff. "See that you stay out of trouble, Miss Lee."

I hung up, wondering about the disturbance he'd mentioned.

Marshmallow glanced at me. "What's up, pussycat?"

"There's something happening at Russ Nolan's right now."

"Interesting." Marshmallow purred like he'd gotten hold of some rich cream. "That's not too far from here, right?"

"We could take a quick look . . ."

He nodded. "Curiosity never killed *this* cat."

We hopped in the Prius and drove over to the other neighborhood, and I noticed a police car sitting in front of Shirl's house. I eased my own car past her home and parked a bit down from Russ Nolan's place.

We took cover from the convenient shadow cast by a large PODS container near Russ Nolan's house and checked out the commotion next door. Shirl stood in her doorway, brandishing a rolled-up newspaper in a furious motion. Meanwhile, a policewoman in the driveway was chatting up a young woman I recognized as Nicola.

I leaned toward them to catch their conversation. Nicola brushed off her white power suit. "It's all right, Officer. My friend and I just had a misunderstanding."

The policewoman glanced back and forth between Shirl and Nicola. Between the professional-looking young lady in a sleek bun and the older, grumpy woman in an oversize sweater and drawstring pants, I knew which party the law would side with. "Please have a more agreeable conversation," the officer said, "using quieter voices."

"Yes, ma'am," Nicola said, while Shirl grunted.

Taking their responses as assent, the policewoman left.

Neither Nicola nor Shirl spotted Marshmallow or me in our hiding spot. Besides, they seemed quite preoccupied with glaring at each other.

Despite her previous assurance to the cop, Nicola started speaking to Shirl in a screeching tone. "How dare you steal the bracelet." She marched toward Shirl, who stood unwavering on her front porch.

Shirl began rapping her newspaper tube against her hand like a nightstick. "Don't mess with me, missy."

"I'm not trying to," Nicola said. "Give me the bracelet, and I'll leave you alone. I won't even report the theft."

Shirl frowned, the worry lines on her face creasing even more. "You *lost* the jewelry, so finders keepers. Besides, I need a bracelet."

"It fell off my wrist by accident. The clasp was loose."

Shirl shrugged. "You should take better care of your stuff."

Nicola shrank before her and clasped her hands together. "Please give it back."

Shirl rolled up the sleeve of her sweater. The gold bracelet glittered on her arm. "I don't think so. It's quite pretty. Plus, I'm an animal lover, so the bone pendant fits me."

Marshmallow commented, "A cat's claw would have looked better."

At that point, Nicola tried to grab the bracelet, but Shirl dodged her. The older lady still had quick reflexes.

"Why do you even want it?" Shirl asked. "You don't need a trinket from that slimy Russ Nolan. Do you know he didn't waste a minute after you left that night? He had another woman come by soon after."

Nicola staggered like she'd been slapped. "That's a lie."

"Believe it or not, but I'm telling you what I saw."

"Actually, it wasn't a present from Russ." Nicola took a deep breath. "I might get into big trouble for losing it . . . because the bracelet belongs to my boss."

Shirl eyed Nicola's formal suit with distaste. "Then I'm sure your boss will have an expensive insurance policy to cover the loss." She slammed the door in Nicola's face.

Nicola remained on the porch, her hands clenched at her sides. A minute later, I heard the loud blare of TV from within the house.

I walked over and placed an arm on Nicola's shoulder. "Are you all right?"

She turned to me and blinked. "Mimi? Why are you here?"

"Oh, I was nearby . . . completing some mobile grooming work."

She clapped her hand over her mouth. "What? Was I so loud that you could hear me down the street?"

"No. Marshmallow and I just happened to be strolling around the neighborhood after I finished my job. Let me walk you back to your car. You can't hang around here much longer."

Nicola's face crumpled. "I don't know what I'm going to do."

I looked around the street. "What kind of car do you drive, anyway?"

She moved with leaden steps away from Shirl's house. "I took an Uber. My clunker broke down a week ago, and I can't afford a new one."

"Well, where do you need to go? I can take you there." I doubted Nicola would be fine if left alone. Her face looked drained of color, and she seemed ready to collapse in a heap on the sidewalk.

"I already called in sick today. Thought I could sort this matter out quickly. I figured the neighbor would be more understanding."

Ha. If only she knew how Shirl had sold me out to Detective Brown.

"We could go grab a cup of coffee," I said. "I'll make the time."

She closed her eyes. "Just take me home."

"Okay, I'll see you safely to your place, then."

• • •

Nicola lived in a cramped apartment on the second floor of a sprawling complex. When I climbed the staircase, it creaked beneath my feet. Rust flaked off every time I touched the tottering handrail. Beside me, Marshmallow complained about the lack of elevators.

Inside Nicola's one-bedroom apartment, I felt claustrophobic. It seemed more like a studio that someone had sectioned into two lopsided parts by throwing up a random wall.

However, she'd decorated the space with strings of twinkling lights in an attempt to create a cheerier atmosphere. It didn't work.

In the main room, Nicola had jammed an upholstered armchair into one corner. She curled up in it, and Marshmallow positioned himself under her feet like a furry footrest.

I stood before her while she moaned. "What was I thinking?" she said. "I wasted my time going there."

Marshmallow wiggled out from under her legs and climbed into her lap. Nicola started petting his soft fur, and it seemed to help her. "I didn't get back the bracelet like I'd planned on."

"Yeah, Shirl is one tough cookie."

Nicola's mouth dropped open, and she placed Marshmallow on the floor. "Oh no. Where are my manners? I'm a horrible hostess."

She went to the tiny alcove she called a kitchen and rummaged through her cabinets.

"I don't need anything, Nicola. Really. Come back and relax."

"I'll find something for you. Have a seat while I look."

Besides the breakfast counter near the kitchen with two wobbly-looking wooden stools, the only furniture in the apartment appeared to be the armchair Nicola had vacated. I perched on its armrest in case she wanted to return and reclaim her seat.

Nicola managed to find a bag of cookies and arranged some on a plate for me. She bustled over and said, "Go ahead and eat."

Out of politeness, I took one. The cookie tasted odd. How long had she kept that bag in the pantry?

She saw my tentative chewing. "I forgot to tell you. They're gluten-free." Her eyes misted.

"Are you okay, Nicola?"

She took a cookie and stared at it. "Russ was sensitive to gluten, too. Besides the stargazing, we had allergies in common."

"You miss him, huh?"

She placed her uneaten cookie back on the plate. "Whatever. It doesn't matter. I didn't even know him that long. And the fact that he had another woman over ..."

"Shirl could've been saying that to get a rise out of you."

Marshmallow blinked at me. "Do you really believe that?"

I shrugged.

"You know Shirl better than me," Nicola said, leaning in close. The plate of cookies threatened to fall on my lap. "You could talk her into giving the bracelet back."

"Er . . ." I didn't really want to go against Shirl again. Last time hadn't turned out so well.

Nicola's lip quivered. "What if Mrs. Dalton thinks I stole it? I was only borrowing it, but she wouldn't understand. She'd probably fire me on the spot."

Being in Los Angeles, the lifestyle of the rich and famous seemed so close you could touch it, and Nicola had. The temptation to want more could be intense—not that I'd ever pretended to exude wealth.

But I knew what it was like to struggle and be at the bottom of the totem pole. I'd done my fair share of demeaning pet duties for sure. The worst was when I was a designated pooper scooper. I hadn't even been allowed to walk the dog. Instead, I had followed the owner around with a plastic bag.

"Please," Nicola said. "I need Mrs. Dalton on my side. She has the ear of her husband, and she can be my way into the movie industry."

"Say what?"

"The assistant job is a temporary gig. Once I get Mr. Dalton's attention, then I can land a juicy role."

I could almost see the stars glittering in her eyes. Did I really want to be the one to destroy her naive dream?

And who knew—maybe her ploy could work. After all, I'd gotten a big break after I'd rescued Gelato. This *was* Hollywood, where happy endings were crafted.

I sighed. "Okay, I'll do my best to get it back." Of course, I didn't have a clue about how I would do so, but I tacked retrieving the bracelet onto my growing list of difficulties. It would pair well with getting Detective Brown off my case and redeeming Josh in my family's eyes.

CHAPTER

⇒ twenty-three ⇐

AT HOLLYWOOF, MY only tasks for the remainder of the day involved two easy paw-trimming appointments with customers who'd picked up my card at Indira's pool party. Still, after experiencing Nicola and Shirl's catfight in the morning, I felt exhausted when closing time came.

While driving home in the evening, I wondered what edible items I might zap in the microwave for a quick dinner. Or maybe I could pop open a can. Couldn't Marshmallow and I just share some sardines?

Imagine my surprise when I saw a bouquet of roses resting on my doormat. Luscious red blossoms burst above clear cellophane wrapping. A note lay tucked between the bright fragrant petals:

Mimi,
You're invited for dinner tonight. Come by when you get home.

Josh

P.S. Sorry about the messy lawyer handwriting.

JENNIFER J. CHOW ·

I picked up the bundle of roses and buried my face in them. Their lush smell made me feel super cherished.

Marshmallow tapped the bottom edge of the apartment door with his paw. "Whenever you're done daydreaming..."

I unlocked it and let him inside. As I searched for a flower vase, I hummed.

Huh. It didn't look like I had any proper floral containers, so I made do with an empty gallon-size can of soy sauce I'd gotten from the bulk store.

I filled up a bowl of food for Marshmallow and said, "You're on your own tonight. I've got a hot date."

"Make it back before your curfew," Marshmallow mumbled.

I patted him on his head. "Don't be jealous." Then I bolted into my room to change into a nicer pair of jeans and a ruffled top.

My heart beat fast as I headed over to unit number one and rapped on the door. Josh opened up after several knocks. He'd dressed down from the fancy attire he'd worn for the charity event, but he still looked casual cute.

He wore a slouchy flannel shirt so soft I wanted to snuggle up against it. I breathed in his usual delicious scent of pine and earthy goodness.

His apartment looked dimmer than I remembered. On second glance, I realized he'd turned off all the lights. In their stead, he'd scattered lit candles.

On the fish-shaped dining table, he'd set up a silver candelabra. Tall white candlesticks dripped layers of wax down their sides.

I turned to Josh. "How long have you been waiting for me to arrive?"

"All my life," he quipped, giving me a lopsided grin.

"Oh, is that what's for dinner?"

He gave me a blank look.

"Cheese?" I laughed at my own joke. "But seriously, isn't dinner cold by now?"

"I thought of that." With a gentle touch on my back, Josh maneuvered me over to the humuhumunukunukuapua`a table, set for two.

I fiddled with the fancy cloth napkin and tested the weight of the heavy porcelain plate before me while Josh brought over the food. "Poke and Spam musubi," he said. "Already cold."

I oohed over the dishes. The poke featured fresh ahi tuna, gleaming tender and pink. The Spam musubi was tucked into tight rolls. Though I didn't prefer eating processed meat, I liked the savory combo of roasted seaweed, rice, and Spam.

After a few bites, Josh ran his hand through his hair. "I do need to share a bit of news with you first. Then the rest of the night can be about us."

I nodded for him to continue. Besides, my mouth was too full of Spam to speak.

"I went to the courthouse and looked at the records."

Swallowing, I said, "What did you discover?"

"I didn't get to the fine details, but here's a quick summary: Tammy sued Russ Nolan, claiming he'd sold her a defective animal. She even got her vet to sign something certifying the puppy's poor medical condition."

I picked up another roll of musubi. "What was the name of the vet?"

"Dr. Exi."

"Huh." I bit into the seaweed and swallowed. "Thanks for tracking down that info for me."

He smiled, the flickering candlelight making his face appear to glow even brighter with happiness. "I love helping you."

Really? I felt my own joyous flame rise up inside me.

Over dinner, we continued to chat about the small and big issues in our lives. I talked about Hollywoof and my family—whom he still needed to win over because of his Family Game Night absence. He spoke about his upcoming court dates, the thankless job of filing paperwork, and the absurdities of office politics. I didn't mind listening. I liked him sharing about his daily struggles and triumphs.

When the hour grew late and my eyes started drooping, he walked me back to my apartment. In the soft moonlight, he gave me a sweet kiss on the lips, and I floated like my very own shining star in the sky. Luminescent, I crawled into bed.

· · ·

When morning came, I didn't want to open my eyes. I wanted to linger in sweet dreamland. Or at least relive last night's tender moments.

But then I started having trouble breathing. Was I having a heart attack? Twenty-five seemed too young to have a major cardiac problem without any prior symptoms.

I checked my heartbeat—and felt fur instead. My eyes flew open. "Marshmallow! I told you not to sleep on my bed."

"Sorry, not sorry," he said as I sat up, rubbing my chest.

"Thought I was having a heart attack back there. I panicked about needing to see a doctor."

My words echoed something Josh had told me the night before. I realized how I could further the goal of clearing my name, but I might need to twist Marshmallow's paw to do so.

I left Marshmallow dozing on my bed while I snuck out to the living room and made a quick phone call. Due to a cancellation, I managed to snag an appointment with Dr. Exi, Tammy's vet.

At the vet's office, I surveyed the jungle-themed waiting room. The receptionist sat behind a curved desk with strategically placed stuffed wild animals. After only a short wait, we were directed to an examination room.

The small space housed a sink, a computer station, and a centralized table. Photos of pet patients were pinned to large corkboards hung on the walls. Dr. Exi appeared to take on all sorts of animals: dogs, cats, lizards, frogs, and more.

I placed Marshmallow down on the table in the middle of the room.

"Tell me why we're here again," he said.

"I need info from Dr. Exi. He's the vet who gave evidence to support Tammy's lawsuit."

"And I'm the guinea pig?"

"No, you're the extremely helpful cat. Who, truth be told, does need a checkup."

"I get it. I'm the decoy."

The door clicked open, and we both focused our attention on the man entering. Dr. Exi wore powder blue scrubs and gave us a sharp grin. He possessed straightened Hollywood teeth, but I almost expected a pair of fangs to jut from his gums. His sallow skin and dark, inky hair made me think of Transylvania. Maybe that's why I got an opening so easily: Pets—or their owners—were scared of him.

The veterinarian introduced himself and extended his hand to me.

I grasped it, relieved to find that his body temperature seemed normal. "Mimi Lee," I said. "Exi's a unique surname."

"I get that a lot." His voice droned, like he'd explained it a million times before. "The immigration officers couldn't understand my grandfather's accent, so now I'm stuck with Exi."

"Come to think of it, I've heard your name mentioned by one of my grooming customers. Tammy? She owns a cute Chihuahua named Kale."

He gritted his teeth. "Yes, the PTA president. She practically controls Armstrong Academy, my son's school." No love lost between Dr. Exi and Tammy, then.

Moving over to the table, Dr. Exi said, "And who do we have here?"

"My wonderful cat, Marshmallow. My sister gave him to me. She picked him up from a rescue shelter."

"A fine specimen," Dr. Exi said.

Marshmallow purred at the praise.

"Maybe a tad heavy, though?" I placed my hand against my heart in remembrance of his weight.

Marshmallow stiffened on the table. "Hey, that's all fur."

"Let's see," Dr. Exi said, placing Marshmallow on a scale.

Marshmallow glanced at the numbers. "That's normal, right?"

Dr. Exi rubbed his pointy chin. "A little heavier than I'd like. He's not called Marshmallow because of his food choices, right?"

Marshmallow glared at me. "I hate that name."

"He eats healthy cat food," I said.

The vet placed Marshmallow back on the table and examined my cat's eyes and ears. As he jotted down notes, I tried to steer the conversation back to Tammy. "So, while I was grooming poor Kale, I noticed something wrong with her legs . . ."

Dr. Exi shook his head. "Unfortunately, a genetic condition. It was so bad I prescribed some ketamine injections."

Dr. Exi then whipped out a thermometer and approached Marshmallow's rear.

Uh-oh.

Marshmallow hissed and gave me a death glare. "This exam is now officially a pain in the butt."

"Normal temp," Dr. Exi said. "Your cat's as fit as a fiddle besides the weight. You can pick up some information about balanced diets outside. We have brochures stocked in the waiting area."

I cuddled Marshmallow. "You were a superstar."

"Hope all that prodding was worth it," he grumbled, shifting his bottom on the table.

Dr. Exi scratched his head. "One thing I was wondering. Has your cat been microchipped?"

"I'm not sure."

"I couldn't quite tell due to his, er, heft."

"I'll have to check with my sister," I said and thanked Dr. Exi for his time. Then we returned to the waiting room.

"Do we really need to pick up a brochure?" Marshmallow asked as we stood near the wall display of glossy pamphlets. Scanning the titles, I located the one about eating a balanced diet. Another brochure caught my attention because of the variety of animals gracing its cover: ferrets, mini pigs, and hedgehogs. The title read, "Do You Want an Exotic Pet?"

I skimmed through its text. Aha. I knew how to help Alice and where I'd be going during my lunch break.

CHAPTER

twenty-four

I SHOWED UP AT Roosevelt Elementary and marched right over to the principal's office. As a deliberate choice on my part, I entered without knocking.

Principal Hallis looked up from her paperwork. She frowned at me, making ugly lines appear around her mouth.

Before she could speak, I said, "You gave my sister a pink slip, and I heard those can be retracted."

She steepled her hands. "I'll probably let her finish out the year since I hate disrupting schedules. However, I don't think we'll have the resources available for her to return next term."

I planted my palms smack down on the edge of her desk. "Alice was the only teacher you gave a slip to. And she's not even the newest staff member hired at this school."

She shrugged. "Alice has the wrong personality for this institution. She's too cheerful."

I huffed. "She teaches *kindergarteners*. Those kids are all about smiles and fun."

Principal Hallis tsked. "The children are here for their education."

I straightened upright and picked up her framed photo of the hedgehog. "You're as prickly as your pet."

That made her smile, a slow, saber-toothed grin.

I pointed at the picture. "How about we make a deal?"

She crossed her arms and leaned away from me. "What could you possibly have to offer me? Do you think you might *groom* my hedgehog in exchange for letting your sister stay?"

I plopped the frame back onto the desk. "You don't seem like someone who would appreciate kindness as a bargaining chip. I have another deal in mind. How about I don't report you to the authorities?"

She narrowed her eyes at me. "I'm not following."

Whipping out the exotic pets brochure I'd taken from the vet's office, I flipped it to a specific page. Pointing at the text, I said, "Hedgehog pets are illegal in California."

She drew in a sharp breath. "Nobody told me that when I moved states."

I tapped my head and repeated something I'd heard from Josh before. "As the saying goes, 'Ignorance of the law is no excuse.'"

Her nostrils flared. "Fine. I'll keep your sister on."

"I thought you'd come around." I left without shutting her door.

The receptionist raised her eyebrows at me in the school office. "Everything okay?"

"Yes, I had a lovely chat with Principal Hallis."

I tossed the pet brochure into the recycling bin. The receptionist's eyes flicked toward the glossy paper. I gave her a little wave as I proceeded outside into the golden sunshine.

• • •

Five minutes after I returned from my successful visit with the principal, Indira showed up at Hollywoof. Even Marshmallow didn't have time to settle into his prime real estate spot by the window. He remained sitting at my side as she walked in.

Marshmallow made a choking sound. "What is she wearing?"

Indira flashed me a brilliant smile. "Like my new look?"

I assumed she wasn't referring to the moisture-wicking clothes she had on. She wore something strange across her chest. "Is that a giant fabric pocket?"

Ash popped her head up from the holder as Indira nodded. "It's the prototype for my new puppy pouch. What do you think?"

I touched the stretchy fabric. "It's got a nice feel."

"Lycra," she said, "but I'm thinking about using other materials in the future."

I peeked at Ash. "She looks very comfy in there."

"That's the whole point. Plus, renting a doggie wheelchair would cost a fortune."

I stroked Ash's soft head. "Thanks for coming by, Indira. How can I pretty her up today?"

"Oh, she doesn't need anything done." Indira moved over to a wall rack and examined the leashes there. "I'm here to discuss a business proposal with you."

I drew alongside Indira and stared at the merchandise. "Meaning?"

"Imagine," she said with a flourish of her hands, "a beautiful display of handmade puppy pouches."

I did have some extra wall space I could cover with new goods. "Go on."

"It's a win-win. I supply the products, and you sell them. We'll do an eighty-twenty split . . . in my favor, as the creator."

"What about fifty-fifty instead?"

"Sixty-forty, final offer."

"Uh, maybe," I said. "But who would buy them? People like walking their dogs and getting exercise."

"Not owners with pampered pups who like to tote them around. And"—she rubbed the tip of Ash's ear—"not people with injured dogs."

I gazed into the puppy's warm brown eyes. Ash didn't whimper, but it was hard to tell how she felt. "Is Ash doing all right? Did you save up enough money for her surgery yet?"

"I did." She tossed her hair. "The pool party was a smashing hit."

I bet Lauren's extra donation had tipped the scales. "Did you set up an appointment for the procedure, then?"

"I've interviewed all the surgeons within a five-mile radius. I'm looking for the best deal. Know what's funny? I ran into Tammy at one of them."

"Oh, really?"

"Yeah, at the Surgical Center for Canine Companions. She seemed to be having a heated discussion with the receptionist."

"Did she see you?"

Indira harrumphed. "She avoided me. When I greeted her, she put on a pair of giant sunglasses and walked right past me. She actually sniffed as she walked by, like she couldn't stand my presence."

"How odd."

Indira shrugged. "Wouldn't be the first time I was given the brush-off by the rich."

"Don't you run with the same crowd? I thought you took those fancy classes, like at Downward Doggie?"

"None of the others are nice to me, except Lauren. Even with my fancy house, I'm not good enough for the lot of them. Not old-money rich enough." She tugged at a lock of her hair. "The worst people are the ones who marry up, like Tammy. At least I worked hard to get to where I am. I didn't need to trap a wealthy man."

"Having your own business is tough," I said, gesturing to my shop. "I mean, look how many customers I have strolling through the doors."

"Don't let them take you down," Indira said. "Keep at it."

"Thanks." I lifted my chin. We sisters in business really should support each other. "And I'll take ten puppy pouches to start."

"Deal," she said, shaking my hand. "I'll swing by when I have them all sewn."

"Looking forward to it."

I watched Indira leave with her usual poise.

"That's moxie," I said to Marshmallow. "She succeeded on her own terms."

"You can do it, too," he said. "I've seen you at work. Great grooming."

My heart melted. "You do have a sweet side, Marshmallow."

"Yeah, well. It must take mad skills to make even *dogs* look somewhat presentable." Then he crept over to his usual spot and curled up for a nap.

CHAPTER
twenty-five

JOSH AND I agreed to do an evening video chat to keep in touch as his work continued to spiral out of control. We'd never get to connect otherwise, despite living in the same complex. His schedule had flipped to extreme hours; he left early in the morning and returned super late at night. Besides breakfast, he ate all his meals at his desk.

On-screen, he shifted the fast-food bag out of the camera's eye, but not before I caught the distinctive yellow arrow and red lettering.

"In-N-Out?" I said.

He gave me a sheepish grin. "Good food at a low price point."

"Maybe you need to eat on a budget. With the hours you're putting in, you're probably making below minimum wage."

"Tell me about it. I don't have the heart to do the actual calculations." He edged his bag back into the frame and opened it. "Hope you don't mind," he said. "I'm famished."

I lifted up my own microwaved burrito in camaraderie. "Here's to a romantic dinner."

He chewed on a fry. "I confess. I grab In-N-Out sometimes because it reminds me of our first date."

"Yeah, we're really living it up with our dining exploits."

Josh creased the top of the white take-out bag. "I swear we'll go on a proper date when I get some free time. And, um, after I secure approval."

"From whom?" I bit into my burrito. The steaming cheese almost burned my tongue.

"Your family, of course. I still need to redeem myself in their eyes." He ducked away from the screen, and I heard some private munching.

I used the time to take a few big bites of burrito myself. Then I said, "Don't worry. You've got a second chance, because Family Game Night is coming around again."

His head came back into view. "Really? Let me block out the date now. Can you give me the lowdown of what goes on during the game night?"

I took a few slow bites, chewing as I thought. "Okay, here's the deal. We enjoy playing the games, but that's really secondary to the snacks. Getting together is probably an excuse to chow down."

"Oh, is it a potluck?"

"No." I looked at the ceiling. "Actually, Ma and Dad always provide the food. Alice and I show up to eat and play."

"Huh." He threw a few fries into his mouth.

Was he wondering how spoiled we Lee sisters were? Maybe I should impress him with my latest selfless feat. "Speaking of Alice, guess what? I got her job back."

"That's wonderful. Did the school get extra funding?"

"Nope. I outwitted the principal." I proceeded to tell Josh about her illegal hedgehog and my threat.

He plugged his ears with his fingers. "I'm not hearing this. I don't want to know about people breaking the law, even in small ways. And I can't condone blackmailing."

I sighed. "I'm usually Miss Nice, but sometimes that works against me. I mean, look at the mess I'm in from merely placing a call to the police to help out little puppies."

Josh rubbed the back of his neck. "You know, I still haven't read through that entire lawsuit yet. But Tammy's name did crop up in a different context."

"How so?"

"My clerk friend told me about a divorce filing he ran across . . . for Tammy and her husband."

"Oh no." I left the last bites of my burrito untouched.

"It's too bad when marriages split," Josh said. Ooh, he was a romantic.

I wondered how Tammy felt about the separation. Was it a marriage based on money, like Indira had suggested? Or had Tammy believed in the fairy tale—only to have it shattered?

Indira said Tammy had brushed her off at the surgeon's office. Was it due to the haughty attitude of the entitled? Or did the oversized sunglasses, sniffles, and brittle attitude mask a broken heart?

"Maybe I should see how Tammy's doing," I said.

"You're sweet," Josh said. "Too late to check on her now, though."

"Right, but I have an idea where I might find her in the morning."

We said goodbye and blew kisses to each other.

Afterward, I checked Armstrong Academy's online calendar. Though the school offered an e-blast, parents must have also enjoyed having duplicate paper copies, because tomorrow's activity involved stuffing folders.

• • •

When I waltzed into the cafeteria, I saw flyers positioned on the long tables. They were stacked in separate neon-colored piles. Three ladies led the paper charge—two collated while the third stuffed the papers into student folders. I didn't recognize any of the women.

The lady with the folders looked up and squinted at me. "You look familiar. Soo Yi, right?" She enunciated her words. "Welcome to America."

I suppressed a groan. The woman seemed to have me confused with an immigrant mother. Must be that all Asians looked the same to her.

Although . . . could I use her confusion to my advantage? At least she'd welcomed me into the group. I didn't correct the woman, waiting to see how things would unfold. She soon waved me over to sit down and help stuff papers.

I copied her movements, wondering how much English my immigrant doppelgänger knew. I ventured forth a word: "Tam-my?"

The women paused in their actions and gave one another snide looks. The collating lady said, "Tammy is sick."

The other women snorted, and a firestorm of gossip erupted. They probably thought my "foreignness" meant I wouldn't be able to understand their rapid chatter:

"I knew it would come to this. She hasn't worn her wedding band in months."

"That was quick. Didn't they get married last spring? At least she'll come out all right. He must make a fortune."

"Didn't you hear? He drew up an ironclad prenup."

"What an idiotic idea she had for a fundraiser. A pet show?"

"That dog was probably the last straw. Rumor has it the pup destroyed his wallet."

The last lady lowered her voice and muttered, "And I, for one, can't wait for her PTA presidency to end."

With that final statement, we finished organizing the papers and folders. The other women set out to deliver the packets to the designated classrooms while I digested everything I'd heard.

Sounded like Tammy had been experiencing marriage woes for a while now and Kale had pushed things over the edge. With all that she had going on, I was surprised Tammy had gathered the mental energy to show up at the surgical center. It must have been important—and I wondered about the heated discussion Indira had witnessed.

CHAPTER

twenty-six

FROM HOLLYWOOF, I made the phone call to the Surgical Center for Canine Companions. As I waited for the line to ring, I grabbed a microfiber cloth and started cleaning around the store.

After the tenth ring, a woman picked up and said, "SCCC, can you please hold?"

"Sure." The place must get busy. Why didn't more of those local pet owners make their way over to my shop? I dusted the TV screen with extra vigor.

When the hold Muzak ended, the woman said, "Thanks for waiting. How may I help you today?"

"I need to confirm an appointment, but I can't remember the date. It's a surgery for my Chihuahua, Kale."

"Let me look that up for you, ma'am." A pause. "I'm reading the notes in the computer system. We will be able to issue you a refund—"

I fumbled the phone. "Excuse me?" The kerfuffle at the center. Tammy must have been trying to get her money back.

"We realize that it's a stressful time for you, given your difficult *personal situation.*"

"Oh. Thanks for understanding."

"Certainly. However, when we called your home number . . ." She clucked her tongue. "We got your, um, husband on the line. He insisted on keeping the surgery and paid for it out of his own pocket, mentioning how much his daughter adores Kale."

"I see."

"Well, glad we cleared that up." Her voice burbled on. "Kale's set for the nineteenth, then. Two in the afternoon. We'll be sure to give you a reminder call the day before."

The woman hung up. Was Tammy in so much emotional distress that she hadn't wanted to go through with helping Kale? Not that I blamed her. Taking care of a recovering puppy during major life changes could only add extra stress.

I relayed my thoughts to Marshmallow. He didn't say anything, but he twitched his whiskers at me.

• • •

After two shampoo appointments in the morning, my customer before lunchtime wanted to get her Havanese braided. Twisting the dog's locks, I remembered the fun I'd had creating plaits in my little sister's hair. The repetitive motion reminded me of happy childhood times.

The client also seemed pleased with the results. She gave me a large tip and took several business cards, promising to recommend me to her friends.

As I started to close down for lunch, someone burst into my shop. Maybe I could stay open a little bit longer. I did need the business.

But when I looked beyond my first impression of disheveled hair and a rumpled outfit, I realized I recognized the newcomer. "Nicola?"

She looked a mess and so unlike her usual sleek self. In her arms, she carried Sterling. "I came as quick as I could. You have to help me, Mimi."

I saw her red-rimmed eyes and knew she'd been crying. "Is it the puppy?"

"No." She gripped Sterling so tight, even that patient puppy whimpered. I extracted him from her arms and set him down on the ground. He wagged his tail at me.

I guided Nicola over to the nearby bench to rest. "What's going on?"

She stuttered. "Mrs. Dalton found out that the bracelet is missing."

"Oh no. How did she react?"

Nicola covered her eyes with her palms. "She's going to fire me if I don't bring it back by tomorrow."

"Did you tell her where it is?"

"No." She removed her hands from her face. "I did admit to borrowing it, but I said I couldn't locate it in my home."

"I can't believe Lauren realized so soon. Your boss told me she had such a massive collection she could barely keep track of it."

"She wouldn't have noticed, but"—Lauren pointed at Sterling's neck—"she put that on him today and wanted to match. She told me to take Sterling so I could *remember* what the bracelet looked like and find it ASAP." The dog wore a gold-plated collar with a bone pendant, a larger version of the bracelet.

"Uh-oh."

Nicola looked at me, clasping her hands together. "Please. You said you would help me."

So I had. Why had I made such a rash promise? How could I get the bracelet from Shirl? She didn't have any weak points, unless . . . That angle just might work.

"Come on, everyone," I said. "Time for a road trip."

CHAPTER
twenty-seven

O N OUR WAY to Shirl's house, Nicola sat shotgun, though she was too distraught to take over the requisite navigational duties. Marshmallow and Sterling sat in the rear, chatting with each other. My cat summarized their conversation, saying that Sterling felt a lot better, thanks to his acupuncturist.

When we got to the neighborhood, I noticed a flurry of activity at Russ Nolan's house. Both the main door and the side gate stood wide open. A gardener's pickup truck sat parked at the curb in front.

"Time to get that bracelet," I said, unlocking the car doors.

Nicola wouldn't budge. Instead, she stared out her passenger's side window and gulped in deep breaths. "I don't think I can do it."

Should I wait out her sudden panic attack? But she seemed to get more frightened by the minute. "Fine," I said. "Why don't you stay here? Maybe it won't take me too long."

Nicola's breathing slowed down to a normal rhythm. I rolled down the windows and then handed her the keys.

I took Marshmallow and Sterling out of the car. Marshmallow matched my stride, while I carried the tiny pup over to Shirl's home and rang the doorbell.

I heard slow, halting steps from inside. Then the door swung open.

"Why are you here, Mimi?" Shirl's gaze flickered over to the two animals before it settled back on me.

Without preamble, I said, "Could you give the bracelet back to that young woman, Nicola? She's going to get fired from her job because of the missing jewelry."

Shirl grimaced at me. "Why should I care? That girl has no respect for her elders. She caused such a ruckus the cops had to come."

"You don't have to return it for Nicola's sake. But you might want to show kindness to the real owner of the bracelet." I lifted up Sterling for Shirl to inspect, and the little dog cocked his head at her. "See this Chihuahua?"

"I admit that dog's pretty cute, but what's the puppy got to do with anything?"

"The owner's bracelet matches his collar." I pointed out the gold-plated loop around Sterling's neck. "Right down to the whimsical bone pendant."

She reached out and touched the collar, and Sterling licked her arm before she could pull away. Shirl smiled at him. "You know me well. I won't do it for the girl. Or her boss. But for this little guy, I will."

I waited for Shirl to slip the bracelet off her wrist, but she said, "Come inside for a moment."

The musty scent of potpourri assaulted my nose as I edged into her house. As a precaution, I remained hovering near the entryway in case she decided to play a trick on me. Sterling and Marshmallow stayed by my side as I watched Shirl go over to her doily-covered table. I saw the bracelet lying there.

"The clasp is broken anyway," Shirl said. "It wouldn't have lasted long."

Once she'd handed the jewelry over, I said, "Thanks for returning it. You've got a good heart."

She gave a noncommittal grunt. "I stayed mum when the police investigated, all for nothing. I don't even get to keep it anymore."

I opened my palm, admiring the gold chain as it shimmered in the sunlight. "So that's why you didn't say anything to the police in the beginning. You thought they might make you give the bracelet back to its rightful owner."

"Doctor's order was to get an ID bracelet in case something happens to me, since I live alone. It was a pretty find, though I didn't have time to get it engraved with my health conditions."

I then remembered the phone message I'd overheard on my prior home visit, about her needing a medical bracelet. "And is this somehow related to why you threw me under the bus to the police? You gave them my old library slip as evidence."

"Sorry," Shirl said. "You noticed the bracelet too much, and I didn't want it getting reported as a theft."

"Since you're returning the jewelry, can you retract your statement to Detective Brown? He's really on my case and trying to tie me to Russ Nolan's death."

She nodded. "All right, I'll try."

I slipped the bracelet into the inner pocket of my purse. "One more thing. Did you really see another lady go over to Russ Nolan's house after Nicola left?"

Her forehead crinkled. "I did see a female figure stop by the backyard later that night. She leaned over Russ, who was sitting in his chair like usual. But it could've been his date again."

A leaf blower started whirring from next door. "What's going on over there?" I asked. "I saw a pickup truck parked near Russ Nolan's old house."

"Extra work is being done on it. Think there's a new renter on the way. I've seen several vans coming and going."

"So someone is finally moving in?"

"Any day now," Shirl said. "I haven't met them, but the new neighbor can't be worse than the previous two."

I thanked Shirl and showed myself and the animals out. When we got closer to the Prius, I noticed something strange that stopped me in my tracks. The car windows were rolled down, but Nicola wasn't in the vehicle.

Where could she have gone? Looking around the street, my eyes strayed to Russ Nolan's house and the nearby storage unit. I'd seen the container the last time we were here. In fact, I'd hidden in its shadow to eavesdrop on the strident conversation between Shirl and Nicola. I should've known then that someone would be moving in soon.

Glancing at the open side gate of the house, I wondered if it might be my last chance to explore the crime scene. Besides, I didn't want to stand around waiting for Nicola any longer. Who knew when she'd come back?

Marshmallow saw me gazing at the gate. "Way ahead of you, sister," he said before sprinting through the side entry.

I smiled. We made a pretty solid detecting team.

Then, cradling Sterling in my arms, I ran after Marshmallow. In the yard, two startled gardeners stared at me. The one carrying a leaf blower turned it off. He'd already driven a pile of shriveled-up leaves to the back of the fence. The other set a huge bag of grass seed on the small concrete patio.

"Cat," I said, tilting my head toward Marshmallow, who stood on the back fence like a tightrope walker.

The gardeners nodded and continued with their business. Pretending to be recovering from the sprint, I took in deep breaths while surveying the yard. It remained the same wasteland as when Josh and I had pretended to be renters. Remembering that he'd called me his girlfriend on this very plot of dull dirt, I stood dazed for a few moments.

Marshmallow meowed at me. As I moved toward him with unhurried steps, I noticed the gardener who'd carried the grass seed retrieve a till and start loosening the soil. *Click.* It hit something. I stopped walking toward the back fence and watched him.

After digging in the dirt, the gardener retrieved a buried tennis ball. He tossed it to the side. As he tilled his way to the center of the yard, his tool snagged on another item.

He added the new object to the discard pile. At that point, Sterling jumped out of my arms and rushed over to the unearthed treasures. I followed him as the puppy scurried over to the latest addition.

I examined the new item, a clear cylindrical object about an inch long. It looked like nothing short of a cheap pen cap.

Sterling starting acting frenzied. He crouched down closer, and his nose touched the plastic. Would he eat it? A horrific image of Sterling choking flashed through my mind. I snatched the pen cap away and pocketed it.

All of a sudden, a banging came from within the house, like the frantic opening and closing of doors. Was the renter inside even now? I waited for someone to bust me for being on their private property, but nobody appeared.

Best not to take any more chances, though. I walked over to Marshmallow, cupped my hands, and called out, "Come here, kitty."

He didn't budge from his spot on the fence until the gardener finished tilling all of the dirt. Then he leaped with an elegant bound and followed me over to Sterling, who remained near the junk pile. The puppy had started chewing on the ratty tennis ball.

I pulled it out of his mouth after some struggle. Sterling would definitely need a bath when we got back. As we piled out through the side gate, I heard a *thump-thump* sound from the front porch.

I spied an older gentleman watching me, Marshmallow, and Sterling exit the yard. Thankfully, he looked like a friendly grandpa, all laugh lines and a sunny smile. He wore a long-sleeved shirt and suspenders, and the cap perched on his silver hair completed his newsboy look.

"Quite a troop you have," he said, pointing at us with his brass cane. That must have been what had made the thumping noise I'd heard.

"They're a handful," I said, my thumb jerking over to the backyard. "Natural explorers. And quick, too."

"It's my fault," the man said. "I left everything open while I went to eat lunch. The yard gate for the gardeners, and the house to air out since the carpets just got steamed."

He leaned on his cane. "I'm Henry, by the way. Do you live nearby?"

"A pleasure to meet you. My name's Mimi," I said. "But I'm just visiting."

"A shame you're not close by. I want to get to know my neighbors in these original California Craftsman homes."

"Come again?" I peered at the run-down houses around me.

He pointed out the different architectural features. "See those beautiful gabled roofs? And the beams made from local redwood? These houses are a slice of history, and they're the perfect compact size." He eyed the taller house next door. "Well, most of them are small."

"Shirl lives there. Actually, she might be around your age." I paused. "Just don't go over to borrow a cup of sugar."

"I wouldn't dream of it." He gave me a wink. "I'm the kind of person who brings treats to everyone else when I move into a neighborhood."

"Then the two of you just might get along."

After I'd said goodbye to Henry, I peered at my car. I was relieved to see Nicola seated back on the passenger's side.

I headed over and said, "Where have you been?"

"Oh, I went for a walk. Had to get some fresh air."

Her cheeks did look flushed . . . But was the scarlet color from exercise?

CHAPTER
twenty-eight

BACK AT HOLLYWOOF, I reached into my purse and handed over the bracelet to Nicola. "Like I promised," I told her.

She breathed a sigh of relief. "Now everything will work out perfectly."

I left her dreaming about her movie star future as I hustled Sterling into the back for a much-needed bath. In the sink, he seemed to luxuriate in the suds.

What a difference acupuncture had made. He didn't yelp at me or tremble in pain. Though his knee still didn't slip into the exact correct position, I could massage him in the bath without a struggle.

I dried his fur to silky smooth and gave him a quick cuddle. "I'm so glad for you, Sterling."

He himself did a circle dance of happiness on the grooming table. Then, sniffing at me, he moved closer and nudged my jeans. He started to yip and didn't stop.

Not understanding what he wanted, I called for Marshmallow. My cat sauntered in with slow strides, not bothering to walk any faster. "What's up, doc?"

"Sterling's worked up about something."

Marshmallow spoke with Sterling and then turned to stare at my pants. "There's something in your pocket he wants to see."

I checked my jeans and pulled out the plastic cap I'd confiscated. I'd forgotten I had stashed it in my pocket. Bending over to Sterling, I asked, "Do you know what this is, boy?"

Marshmallow translated for me, but Sterling didn't have a clue.

"Why's he so frantic, then?" I asked.

"He's excited because, he said, whatever it is, it smells like Sparky."

I walked back to Nicola still reflecting on Sterling's strange comment. When she saw him, Nicola clapped her hands in delight. "He looks so handsome. You've really saved me, Mimi."

I gave Nicola a perfunctory wave as she left. My fingers reached for the piece of plastic I'd pocketed. I felt its contours. It didn't seem like a good toy for dogs. Where would Sparky even have gotten the thing? Well, I could solve the mystery by asking the little guy himself.

I called Magnus Cooper and asked if I could visit. To my surprise, he seemed excited to hear from me. "Mimi," he said, "you won't believe what happened after you groomed the puppies for the Eiffel Tower photo shoot. My sales tripled. That's never happened before, and it's all because of you. I meant to call and tell you, but we've been so busy catching up on the additional orders."

"That's wonderful." Somebody out there did appreciate my work.

"Can you come and do it again? I'll make sure to give you a piece of the financial pie."

I checked the time. "How about after I close up shop tonight? And do you think it'd be possible for me to groom a specific dog, the littlest of Russ Nolan's Chihuahuas?"

"Anything you want," he said. "I'll see you soon."

· · ·

When I went over to Magnus Cooper's house, I noticed he'd left the front door unlocked. Marshmallow and I arrived to find Sparky sitting in the penned area.

Magnus stood with his back to me and spoke to the puppy. "Now, what scene should I set up for you?" He lifted his camera and appeared to frame the shot.

"Right behind you, Magnus," I said. He turned, and I held up my supplies kit.

"Great. You can start grooming while I select a good backdrop. I'll return soon with some props."

Marshmallow watched while I worked—not that there was much for me to do. Sparky already looked so cute with his wide brown eyes and diminutive size. I did add some extra sheen to his coat with a brief coconut oil massage of his fur.

After making sure neither Magnus nor Zel was around, I showed Sparky the plastic object.

He cocked his head at me and barked twice.

"Sparky's wondering how you got that," Marshmallow translated.

The tiny Chihuahua nudged my hand with his nose and whimpered.

"It smells like his owner," Marshmallow added. "And something else . . ."

I petted Sparky while he and Marshmallow hashed out the details. The two looked almost comical as they nodded and tilted their heads to listen to each other.

Marshmallow summarized for me. "Sparky found that weird object wedged behind Russ Nolan's back in the camping chair. Wanting his master to wake up and play with him, Sparky buried the plastic toy in the yard. But when Sparky nudged Russ Nolan, the man never woke up. Then Sparky was called in from the yard, and he had to leave with the other dogs."

Poor Sparky. He harbored love for his master, not realizing what terrible conditions he'd grown up in. He'd had no comparison . . . until coming to this new place.

All of a sudden, Marshmallow hissed. "Put it away, Mimi. Magnus is coming back."

I tucked the cap into my pocket as Magnus returned with a blue backdrop. Fluffy clouds were painted on the canvas. I watched Magnus set up a floor fan and plug it in.

"Give me a hand with his costume," he said. "Zel's out tonight with a few friends, and I need your help." What a one-eighty from his prior suspicious attitude. Before, Josh had been worried about me even stepping into this home, and now, Magnus welcomed me with open arms.

It took a serious collaborative effort for us to squeeze Sparky into a muscle-enhanced superhero outfit. Magnus positioned the dog at just the right spot so that when the fan blew, the breeze made the cape billow.

"Perfect," I said.

Sparky looked the part of a superhero pup, and he'd acted like one in real life. He'd found something the police had missed. An item lodged in the crevice of Russ Nolan's chair. Maybe a significant clue to the crime—and to the killer's identity.

CHAPTER

twenty-nine

I N THE EARLY morning, I brought over a pink bakery box of dough-nuts to the police station. An assorted mix of a dozen scrumptious flavors: sprinkled, jelly, chocolate, and more unique, delectable toppings, like salted caramel.

I'd expected the police station to be extra exciting. Maybe some flashing sirens and criminals being led around in handcuffs. Perhaps I'd come at a quiet hour.

Even Detective Brown's desk seemed ordinary when compared with my overactive imaginings. No bags of evidence littered the top of it. Only boring paperwork cluttered the surface, and old coffee rings stained the wood.

Detective Brown rubbed his bloodshot eyes and said, "Why are you bothering me at work, Miss Lee?"

"I've brought you a peace offering." I placed the doughnuts down and opened the box a crack to let the smell of maple flavor the air.

"Do you think I'm a walking cliché?" He pointed at his taut stomach. "I like to work out."

"No, Detective. I thought it'd be a nice gestu—"

"Spit it out, Miss Lee. What's the point of your unexpected visit?"

I pulled out a Ziploc bag with the plastic cap look-alike secured inside. "I have new evidence."

Detective Brown stared at the item. A glimmer of recognition seemed to light up his eyes, but then he shook his head. "You think this is somehow connected to the Russ Nolan case?"

"I do. I found it buried in his backyard."

He coughed. "And what were you doing at his house?"

"Um. You see, my cat escaped, and I had to chase him into the yard."

He shook his head. "Why do you think that little piece of plastic is so vital?"

"The dog I had with me—one of Russ Nolan's puppies—started barking like mad when he saw it."

Detective Brown blinked his weary eyes at me. "You're basing your theory on some noises from an animal? And you haven't told me why you were in that neighborhood to begin with. I know you don't live around there."

I closed the lid of the doughnut box to stifle its distracting heavenly scent. If I didn't, I might be tempted to snatch one before any of the cops did. "I happened to be visiting my friend Shirl. She's the neighbor."

He gave me a hard stare. "The same old lady who gave me a receipt incriminating you as the killer?"

"It's a complicated relationship."

He rapped his fist against his cluttered desk. "You two must be somewhat on polite terms, though, because she ended up retracting her statement."

I couldn't help smiling.

Detective Brown continued, "The old lady wasn't certain of her memory anymore. Blamed it on her age. Said maybe she'd found the slip of paper after the murder, perhaps around the time you took your rental tour."

"That's more like the truth. So does this mean you're looking elsewhere for suspects now? You can start with this." I wiggled the baggie in my hand.

A deep frown stretched across his face. "Your piece of trash doesn't prove anything. Maybe it's a pen cap."

It did sort of look like one. However, it was too wide and long for a typical ballpoint. "Can't you get the lab to examine it just in case it proves helpful?"

Detective Brown sighed. "You told me you got it from the yard, and I assume you handled it plenty. Even if it is connected to the crime, which is doubtful, you've contaminated things, so it can't be used as evidence."

Ugh. It's not like I'd expected to make a discovery that day. So what if I'd held it? It's not like a normal citizen carried around a pair of tweezers and gloves with them everywhere they went.

Seeing the frustrated look on my face, Detective Brown said, "Tough luck, Miss Lee."

His phone started ringing, and he moved to answer it. He waved me away with one hand. If he wouldn't appreciate the baked goods I'd brought, then I'd keep them myself. When I inched toward the doughnuts, he placed his palm down on the pink box in a possessive manner.

I left the station in slow motion. I knew Detective Brown wasn't in my corner. Glancing at him speaking on the phone, though, I realized he looked swamped with other matters to move against me—for now.

• • •

I went to Hollywoof to open up shop and found Indira standing outside waiting for me. She lifted the giant cardboard box in her hands. "The puppy pouches are all done," she said. "I'm here to drop them off."

We went inside the store, and she showed me her hard work. Even Marshmallow seemed impressed by the beautiful designs she'd made.

"Though I wouldn't be caught dead being carried in a sling," he said. "The indignity."

I marveled at the designs done in various shades, ranging from psychedelic colors to calming pastel tones. "Great job, Indira."

She beamed at me. "I've already sold a few. Last week, the Downward Doggie moms were only too happy to purchase some."

"Are you still going to that doga class?" I said. "I remember you and the instructor didn't see eye to eye on you selling your bags there."

Indira's mouth twitched. "Fortunately for me, they let her go. Too many complaints from the students."

Marshmallow caught my eye. "Remember to not get on Indira's bad side."

I placed her bags on the hooks in the wall. "Did people like the carriers?"

Indira said, "The women at yoga gushed about the ability to carry their prized pooches around town, into stores, and at the airport using my fabulous holders."

I checked the price tag on one of them and had to stifle a gasp. For the amount they'd paid, they'd better be gushing with excitement.

Indira smoothed the fabric of the bags, making them hang just so. She tucked all the price tags out of sight and continued, "Actually, I'm surprised Tammy didn't buy one. Her poor dog practically swept the floor when she was walking in. Really, she should've stayed home with the poor pup, but she insisted on peddling candy bars. Chocolate is a *horrible* choice for an exercise and dog class."

"I feel for Kale," I said. "I bet your carrier could help her."

Indira sniffed. "Tammy made sorry excuses for not buying. Said she'd hold off because the surgery would be happening soon. Odd story about that, by the way. She said someone had impersonated her over the phone with the surgical center."

I gulped. "Well, thanks for coming, Indira. Make sure to say hi to Ash for me."

CHAPTER
thirty

LOST IN MY thoughts as I watched Indira leave, I didn't process the phone ringing near the cash register. Marshmallow finally said, "Mimi, you gonna answer that?"

Then I registered the buzzing noise, walked over to the counter, and picked it up.

"Thank the heavens," said a female voice on the other end. "I thought you might've gone on lunch break already."

"Nicola?" I said. "Did everything turn out okay?"

"No." She gave a small hiccup. "Mrs. Dalton fired me."

"What? But you returned her bracelet."

"Too late. She said she'd been thinking things over. Because I broke her trust by borrowing the jewelry in the first place, she let me go."

"But doesn't she need you to run her schedule? All those charity events . . ."

"She canceled everything this week except for the doga class to-morrow evening." Nicola's voice cracked. "She said the peaceful visu-alizations might help her recover from the emotional turmoil I put her through."

I glanced at the clock. "Do you want me to drive over to your place right now?"

She almost screamed at me. "No, don't. I mean, my place is a mess."

"I don't mind. You should see my apartment."

"We can meet up . . . but let's do the coffee shop around the corner from my place. I need to get out anyway."

"Fine," I said. "Give me the name, and I'll look up the directions."

When Marshmallow and I arrived at Cup O' Joe, I saw Nicola al-ready seated at an outside table. She wore a faded T-shirt and hadn't bothered to comb her hair. Instead, she'd pulled it up into a greasy-looking ponytail.

She didn't wave at me, or even look up, when I sat down across from her at the aluminum table. Even when Marshmallow meowed from near her feet, she ignored him.

"Tell you what," I said, signaling to a waiter. "I'll treat you to lunch today."

The man came over with a notepad in his hand.

"A whole wheat bagel with cream cheese and lox for me," I said.

Nicola didn't even glance at the waiter as he continued to stand there.

"Do you want the same?" I asked her.

"What?" She blinked at me.

The waiter repeated my order, and Nicola blanched. "No, I can't eat that. Gluten allergies."

"We have a wonderful potato bread toast," the waiter said.

"Sure, I'll take that."

The waiter whisked away with our orders.

I scratched my head. "What exactly is gluten again?"

In a dry voice, like she'd repeated the facts a thousand times before, Nicola said, "It's a substance found in cereal grains, especially wheat. Gives dough that elastic feel."

Russ Nolan and Nicola had bonded over their wheat-free food choices. My mind flashed back to the full trash bin I'd rummaged through in front of his house. Its contents didn't appear to make sense in light of this detail. "Let me see if I have this right. Russ Nolan couldn't eat wheat of any kind?"

She shivered. "He'd break into horrible hives. I myself get stomach cramps from gluten."

But I remembered seeing a giant box of cereal in his trash. "Do you know if he kept shredded wheat in his home?"

She gave me an odd look. "No, why would he?" Then she hung her head and mumbled, "Let's not talk about Russ anymore. It makes me sad."

The waiter returned with our food. "Bon appétit, ladies."

I smeared cream cheese over my bagel and layered on the smoked salmon lox. "What would you like to talk about, then?"

She stared at her potato bread toast with its side tray of various jams and jellies. "Work, maybe? I need to land a new job."

I gestured around the café. "Have you considered waiting tables? Or being a barista?"

She moaned. "I'm tired of fetching for other people."

"You'd have a flexible schedule, though." I bit into my bagel, relishing the filling combination. "Might be helpful for an actress."

"You've got a nice work situation," Nicola said. "You're able to close up shop and enjoy lunch in the warm sunshine. You get to make your own hours and—oh." She started spreading blueberry jam on her toast.

"Looks like you got your appetite back."

"Well, I just thought of the perfect solution." She pointed at me with the end of her butter knife. "I can work at Hollywoof. You probably need an extra pair of hands at your store."

I put my loaded bagel down. "Er, I don't really have enough business to take on extra staff."

"No?" A tear slid down the corner of her eye.

I hesitated. In her moment of distress, I thought of Alice and how devastated my sister had felt when she'd been given a pink slip. Besides, Hollywoof's financial circumstances might change in the future. I softened my response. "Well, let me think on it."

"I can provide you my résumé after I update it." She finished her toast with hearty bites and smiled at me.

Marshmallow piped up. "Are you sure that's wise, Mimi? Didn't Nicola disappear on us while we talked with Shirl? She never explained what that was all about."

I stopped eating and called the waiter over so I could pay the bill. Marshmallow was right. Maybe I could ghost Nicola and not actually follow up with her about any sort of employment.

Plus, I realized that Nicola had steered our conversation away from Russ Nolan. Had she changed the topic to avoid her grief—or something else?

When we returned to Hollywoof, I was glad to focus on some simple grooming duties for the rest of the day. I also looked forward to an evening surrounded by people who I could truly trust . . . during Family Game Night.

Josh decided to drive Marshmallow and me over to my parents' house. It'd make a better show of unity and might also earn him brownie points for escorting me there.

From the back seat, Marshmallow complimented Josh's car. "Smooth ride," he said. "You should upgrade *your* vehicle, Mimi."

I turned around and gave him a long glare. Out of the corner of my eye, I noticed a brown grocery bag on the floor tucked behind the driver's seat. "What's in there, Josh?"

He flashed me a brilliant smile. "You'll see soon enough."

When we arrived at my parents' house, Josh couldn't find any open spots on the street. He ended up parking on the driveway.

We walked to the front door with Josh's right hand holding mine. In his left, he carried the mysterious grocery bag.

When my parents opened the door, I noticed they'd dressed *not* to impress this time around. No doubt they wanted to give him a message about missing the last Family Game Night.

Ma wore a weathered blouse and slacks, the only nod to her heritage a printed batik scarf wrapped around her neck. Dad wore a comfortable but tattered undershirt. Thank goodness he'd put on regular shorts and not boxers.

In slow, careful English (the kind she used for perfect strangers and people she disliked), Ma said, "You are the boyfriend." She looked him up and down with a scrunched nose, probably categorizing all the flaws she found with his outer appearance.

Dad gripped Josh's hand in a stiff handshake. "About time we met."

When I walked inside the house, I noticed the poor food spread right away. On the table, instead of our usual delicious comfort foods, my parents had put out some odd-flavored snacks: vinegar-soaked peanuts, licorice watermelon seeds, and durian candies. It looked like food trial by fire.

Only Alice greeted Josh with a sweet hug. "Welcome," she said. "And since you're the guest of honor, you can pick tonight's game."

"Okay. Also, I brought everyone a snack." He opened up the grocery bag and pulled out a large two-gallon Ziploc. At first glance, it looked like it was full of Chex Mix.

On closer inspection, though, I realized it had an interesting added ingredient: seasoned seaweed. "Me first," I said, opening the bag and grabbing a handful. The winning combination tasted both sweet and salty. "This stuff is addictive."

He ducked his head. "I baked the batch myself. It's *furikake* snack mix."

"I call dibs," I said, taking the bag and adding it to the snack pile on the table.

Dad brought over an empty plastic jug, one that had previously housed mango jelly snacks. "Pennies go in here, and winner takes all."

We took turns dropping in our loose change. Then Alice directed Josh to the hall closet to select a game.

He returned with Clue. Ugh. We were horrible at figuring out the right suspect. No wonder I had problems doing it in real life.

Whenever we played the board game, it took exhaustive multiple rounds for anyone to win. Ma also always lost. She gave Josh a quick glare before examining the cards she'd been given.

Dad said, "Want to try a snack, Josh?"

Josh looked over the variety spread on the table. Unable to decide which to eat first, his hand hovered above them all.

Ma pushed the plate of candies toward him. "Durian," she said, again in her careful English. "It is called the king of the Malaysian fruit."

"Are those the spiky things I see in the produce section of Asian markets?" Josh asked.

"Yup," I said. The fruit smelled rotten and didn't taste much better. But he'd find out for himself soon enough.

Popping the candy in, he quickly covered his mouth with one hand.

Alice and I exchanged alarmed glances. He wouldn't spit it out onto the table, right?

Josh managed to swallow it down whole before saying, "Very distinctive flavor. May I have a glass of water?"

Alice hurried to grab him a drink. After he'd swallowed half the water, we began to play in earnest.

Everyone started guessing a mix of suspects, weapons, and rooms. Josh must have been using a more logical method, because he kept crossing items off his list and narrowing down the identity.

The rest of us probably made random combinations. During the game, Dad scratched his head a lot. Alice squinted at her paper with a frown. Ma scowled, her face getting redder by the minute. I chewed on the tip of my writing pen.

Josh finally sat back and grinned. Noticing the faces around him, though, he stopped short of venturing a winning guess. Instead, he seemed to try to help us by asking specific combinations. Still, we all continued to look puzzled.

Marshmallow whispered, "Do you need my help, Mimi?"

I shook my head.

Josh cleared his throat. Eyebrows waggling, he made a pointed guess. We went around the circle, and nobody had those exact cards.

Oh. Had he given away the actual answer? I waited, uncertain.

Ma also mulled over the combination in her head. Then, with a gleam in her eye, she decided to make the formal accusation using Josh's answers—and won.

Clutching the money jar, she jingled the coins inside. "I am the winner for once."

Dad gave Josh a head nod and tried some of the furikake snack mix. "Tasty." Pointing to Alice and me, he said, "Maybe you other kids should pull your weight and bring snacks over, too."

Alice shrugged and put the game away in the closet. When she returned, she gave us a glowing smile. "By the way, I have some good news. Principal Hallis told me not to worry about the pink slip. I can keep my job."

Josh nudged my shoulder. Congratulations flew all around, and everyone seemed in high spirits at the end of the night.

Alice hugged us (and cuddled Marshmallow) goodbye. When we left, my parents embraced me and shook hands with Josh.

Then they stood in the doorway, watching us while I placed Marshmallow in the back of the car. Josh waited until I'd finished and then opened the passenger's side door for me. As I got in, I saw Dad give him a thumbs-up.

Josh started the engine, and Ma began shouting from the doorstep.

"What's she saying?" he asked me.

I rolled down my window.

Ma flapped her hands in an urgent manner.

Josh peeked over at me. "Is she saying, 'Go, Stan'? Did she mix up my name with an old boyfriend of yours?"

"No." I laughed. "She's saying, 'Gostan.' Like 'go astern'? She wants to tell you the street is clear and you should back up now."

"Interesting," Josh said and started reversing. Ma beamed.

We drove down the street, and Josh said, "How did Family Game Night go? Do you think they like me?"

"You've definitely won them over, what with bringing the snack mix and letting Ma take the money jar." I paused. "Ma approves for certain."

"What makes you say that?"

I smirked. "She started using her Manglish on you."

CHAPTER

thirty-one

MY PERSONAL LIFE seemed to be on the upswing. Alice had job stability now, and my parents approved of Josh.

I hoped I would get a lucky break in the Russ Nolan case as well. Detective Brown might have been too distracted to give me immediate grief, but like a bloodhound, he wouldn't stop unless I provided him with other quarry. So I decided to return to the scene of the crime.

As we parked in the familiar neighborhood, Marshmallow groaned. "Not again, Mimi. We probably haunt this place more than Russ Nolan's own ghost."

I shushed him and said, "I'm still looking for answers."

We walked up to the humble-looking house. Though the porch still creaked, the new renter had added a lounge chair and a potted plant in a stand to make the home look more inviting.

Henry, once more decked out in his newsboy outfit, opened the door and beamed at us. "Visiting the neighborhood again?"

"We happened to be close by."

He looked at Marshmallow and spoke. "No more running into people's yards, I hope."

"Thankfully not," I said.

Henry hooked his fingers under his suspenders. "Quite a few pet owners must live nearby. I saw a young woman pass by a few minutes ago with two pups. They looked just like the one you had the other day."

"Chihuahuas are a popular breed. How are you settling in here?" I gestured at the chair on the porch and said, "You've been adding some nice touches."

"Inside as well." He shuffled to the side, and I peeked past him.

"The place looks great," I said, and it did. The house appeared more organized than before. Even the carpet seemed fluffy after the recent steaming. "I'm curious. Did the previous tenant leave behind anything in the house?"

"The house came furnished, not that it matters much to me. I'm a simple guy. A place to lay down my head is all I need."

I coughed. "Did you happen to get a stocked pantry? Some owners do that as a courtesy." After my tour, I already knew the answer. Would he see through my ruse?

Henry looked behind him, as though using his X-ray vision to peer through the kitchen cabinets. "Actually, yes."

"That's great." I patted Marshmallow's tummy. "Poor guy's hungry. Do you have any canned tuna? Or maybe cereal?"

He cocked his head at me. "I think there's rice and beans."

"No cereal? I'm surprised. It's usually a basic staple."

"I said the same thing to Kevin, the owner. He told me the previous tenant didn't eat cereal, so he hadn't bothered to purchase any."

"Well, it couldn't hurt for me to ask." I stroked Marshmallow. "But as you can tell, he won't be starving to death anytime soon."

Marshmallow narrowed his eyes at me. I smiled back at him.

So it turned out that Russ Nolan didn't eat cereal. This made the empty shredded wheat box from the trash bin appear even more out of place.

Marshmallow poked his head in the doorway and sniffed the air.

"Do you smell something?" I asked Marshmallow.

"That's cute," Henry said. "I hear pet owners sometimes talk to their animals like they can understand them."

I'd forgotten the old man was listening. "Oh, yeah." I nodded. "Marshmallow looks so intelligent, you know."

"I *am* intelligent," Marshmallow said. He swiveled his head back and forth and took a deeper whiff. "I definitely smell orange. The same citrus scent I've noticed on . . ."

I also sniffed the air. "Nicola," I mouthed.

Henry peered at my lips. "What was that? I didn't turn up my hearing aids. You'll have to speak louder."

Actually, I did smell something. But not oranges. "Flowers?" I asked.

Henry adjusted the cap on his head. "Yes. Actually, I was about to go next door when you came by."

"Really?"

He nodded, shuffled around the corner, and reappeared with an enormous bouquet of lilacs. "I'm looking forward to meeting my neighbors, starting with the girl next door."

"We won't keep you, then." I made to leave, but Marshmallow curled up on the lounge chair outside. "Oh, I'm gonna stay to watch this," he said.

Henry noticed Marshmallow's reluctance to move. "Sit for a spell if you wish."

"Good luck," I said as Henry grabbed his cane and moved with care over to the home next door.

From the edge of the porch, we could spy on Shirl's house without being seen. Henry shuffled up her driveway, and I turned to Marshmallow.

"Did you really smell orange?" I asked him.

"The same smell as her breath mints."

"She must have come in the house recently."

"Perhaps when we went to see Shirl to retrieve the bracelet . . ."

Aha. When we had finished talking with Shirl, we hadn't been able to find Nicola. She had told me she'd "taken a walk." Had she strolled inside Russ Nolan's house? And for what?

Marshmallow flicked his paw toward the house next door. "Show's about to start, Mimi."

Henry used the bottom of his cane to knock on Shirl's door. Then he stood up straight, clutching the bouquet in his hand.

The door flew open, and Shirl said, "I'm not buying whatever it is you're selling."

Henry didn't flinch at her harsh words but presented his bouquet. "These are for you, miss."

Shirl took a step back. Then she grabbed the flowers as though she thought Henry would reconsider his offer. She brought them up to her nose and spoke above the fragrant arrangement. "Who are you?"

"I'm your new next-door neighbor, Henry." He pointed our way, and I ducked out of sight.

"The new renter, huh? I'm glad you're not here to borrow something from me."

I came out of hiding to watch them interact.

"No, I'm here to be of service to my neighbors." Henry gave a charming little bow.

Shirl looked like she felt a mix of emotions, a feeling somewhere between startled and amused.

"I look forward to seeing more of you," Henry said.

She nodded and closed the door, but with a gentle click.

From the lounge chair, Marshmallow yawned. "What a letdown. I thought maybe she'd slam it in his face."

"See," I said, pointing to Henry as he started coming back in his slow gait. A big smile spread across his face. "That's what happens when you're nice to others, Marshmallow."

When Henry returned, he paused on the porch and huffed. "A gem of a woman."

Marshmallow gave a soft hiss.

"Shirl is definitely an original," I said. "Thanks for letting us take a breather."

"Any time, and feel free to visit again when you're in the area."

"I would love to." Given his bowing ways, I almost wanted to curtsy for him. I decided to shake his hand instead.

As Marshmallow and I started heading back to the car, I spied the dog walker Henry had mentioned before. On closer look, though, I recognized the woman half-running down the sidewalk.

Instead of walking her two dogs, though, she seemed to be dragging one by the leash and holding the other limp puppy in her arms.

I rushed to meet her. "Zel," I said. "What's the matter?"

CHAPTER

thirty-two

MAGNUS'S NIECE STRUGGLED to maintain control of both puppies at the same time. I took hold of the leash of the healthy dog. Little Sparky lay in her arms, and the other dog was Tigre, leader of the Chihuahua pack.

Sparky wiggled in her arms and gave a sharp bark.

"He feels a stabbing pain near his knee," Marshmallow told me. His eyes locked onto the pup.

Zel's eyes glistened with moisture. "I was taking the two of them for a walk, but then the tiny guy yelped in pain. He started dragging his leg."

"It's the genetic knee problem getting worse," I said.

"Can you give me a good referral?" Zel asked. "You must have medical contacts in your line of work."

"Stay," I told Tigre. Then I let go of his leash and searched through the contacts on my phone. "Dr. Exi might be able to help."

"Please call right now," Zel said.

I dialed the vet's office. After telling them it was an urgent matter, I managed to squeeze in an appointment for the late afternoon.

"May I borrow Sparky for the day?" I said. "I can take him to the vet for you. It's near Hollywoof."

"Sparky, huh?" Zel stroked the top of the puppy's head. "What a fun name. And it would help us if you took him. Let me just double-check with my uncle."

She texted him and got quick approval.

I motioned to Tigre. "Do any of the other dogs feel poorly, Zel?"

"I don't think so . . . at least not in the same way."

"Given Russ Nolan's track record," I said, "it may only be a matter of time."

Zel frowned. "Uncle Magnus and I have only ever dealt with healthy dogs. Would people be willing to take on these sick puppies?"

I peered into Sparky's soulful eyes. "I'd like to think so. In the meantime, though, we still must help them somehow."

She nodded and handed the tiny Chihuahua over to me.

Back at Hollywoof, while I waited for the time to pass until the vet appointment, I paced the store. I was grateful, though, to know that Marshmallow could voice Sparky's every need. I lent the tiny Chihuahua the softest dog pillow bed I could find. Marshmallow even gave Sparky his coveted sunny spot before the window to better rest.

After I wrapped up with a few clients and it came time to see Dr. Exi, I grabbed one of Indira's designs. I did feel pretty stylish strapping Sparky to my chest in a glittering golden pouch.

At the vet's office, they took us to the examination room right away.

Dr. Exi tutted while he examined Sparky. "It's not terrible, but I am out of ketamine and need to special order some to numb his pain. By the way, your pouch is an excellent idea. Puts less stress on his bones."

"Sparky isn't the only puppy I've seen with this problem," I said. "In fact, Russ Nolan bred a lot of Chihuahuas who have the same genetic issues, and they all need help."

Dr. Exi's face somehow grew paler than usual. "You need medicine for a lot of puppies? That won't be cheap."

I wondered if Magnus might cover the cost. But he'd indicated that he didn't want to keep the puppies too long, so I doubted that he'd be interested in making such a huge financial investment.

As an animal lover, if I had the money, I would do it in a heartbeat. But I didn't have the extra resources. I needed to find a person with a big heart *and* a big purse. Someone invested in charitable efforts who could really feel for the puppies' plight.

A name popped up in my head: Lauren Dalton. And, though I didn't know her entire schedule, I knew exactly where she'd be tonight.

• • •

I made sure to get to Downward Doggie early. With Marshmallow by my side and Sparky cuddled in my puppy pouch, I marched into the yoga studio with confidence. A few familiar-looking ladies came and greeted me as I waited for Lauren to show up.

When a frazzled Lauren finally arrived, she walked Sterling in. The dog seemed healthy, but Lauren looked out of sorts without Nicola around. She kept pulling on her spandex outfit, seeming uncomfortable in the clingy fabric.

On seeing me there, she did a double take. "Mimi, have you adopted a new dog?"

"Oh no. I'm borrowing Sparky for the day. Actually, I have a favor I wanted to ask you. I know you're a very giving woman and a fellow pet lover."

Out of the corner of my eye, I noticed Tammy and a few other doggie moms walk into the classroom.

"This is one of Russ Nolan's puppies," I said. "He apparently bred
quite a number of them. Though somebody is taking care of the aban-
doned Chihuahuas for now, he can't for much longer. And the puppies
are all starting to have knee problems."

Lauren let out a small gasp. "Those poor babies."

"You love dogs and . . ." According to Nicola, Lauren had the time,
since she'd canceled a few charity events. She might not be super generous toward assistants, based on her treatment of Nicola, but maybe
she'd be on board to help the pups. "The vet I spoke with said he could
give them ketamine, but it's too expensive for me to fund. Would you
take on these puppies out of your generous nature?"

"You mean, pay for their medication?" She pursed her lips. "I'm not
sure I can endure unnatural chemicals flooding their delicate bodies."

"But what other option is there?"

Marshmallow touched my leg with his paw. "How about asking
her for something she actually believes in?"

I gave him a puzzled look and saw his eyes flicker to Sterling.

"I've got another idea," I said. "Acupuncture has worked wonders
for Sterling. Maybe you could connect the puppies with your special-
ist? Help them through a more natural method."

Her eyes lit up. "Sterling's acupuncturist is so good. I absolutely
trust her work, and I've been wanting to send her more business."

"If we stabilize their health right now, maybe the puppies will
have a better chance of getting adopted."

She tapped her lip with a polished nail. "Class is about to begin.
Let's talk more afterward. By the way, do you think your doggie will
be able to participate?"

I looked down at Sparky, nestled in the gold pouch. "He's sleeping right now. Maybe when Sparky feels better—after some acupuncture."

Excusing myself, I went to the back, where I saw Tammy already seated. Kale, looking listless, was slumped at her feet.

I greeted her, but Tammy seemed lost in thought. Deciding to give her a few minutes of peace, I watched the yoga-ing puppies and their owners. I saw ladies on their backs trying to balance doggies on their upturned palms and bent knees.

Then I turned to Tammy again. "How is Kale doing?" I asked.

She didn't answer me, and I nudged Marshmallow with my foot. I knew he could get answers. Marshmallow snuck over to Kale and me-owed at her. The puppy whimpered back.

"Not doing so good," Marshmallow said. "She can't wait for the surgery to happen."

I turned to Tammy and raised my voice to get her attention. "You don't want to stay home tonight? Kale looks very weak."

Tammy fidgeted with the handle of her metal-studded bag. "I needed to get out of the house."

Of course she did. Being in the middle of a divorce situation must make for a dreadful living arrangement. And despite her cropped tanks and bling sandals, Tammy couldn't actually turn back time to the sweeter beginning of her romance.

Nodding at Marshmallow, Tammy asked, "Who's your vet?"

Without thinking, I said, "Dr. Exi."

"Oh."

Indira entered then, the last of the ladies to arrive. She rolled in a large suitcase, with no doubt a ton of merchandise inside.

Spying my soft doggie carrier, which matched her own, she gave me a smile and sat down next to me. "Who have you got in there?"

"Sparky."

"Huh. He looks a lot like Ash." Her own little pooch popped up from her white silk pouch.

I shrugged. "Yeah, well . . ."

"Thanks for wearing my design. Did you adopt him?"

"Um, it's a short-term foster," I said. Really temporary. One day only.

Marshmallow jumped onto a chair near Indira and looked at Ash, and they started chatting away.

Indira covered her ears. "An off-key dog and cat choir."

"Who said cats and dogs don't get along?"

Their duet stopped short, and Marshmallow sprang onto my lap. I startled. The chair wobbled but stayed put.

Marshmallow gave me an intense stare. "Guess what I just found out? Ash saw what was in the cereal box the day Indira became her new owner. She said Russ Nolan kept stacks of rectangular green paper in it—printed with large numbers and people's faces."

CHAPTER
thirty-three

ASH MUST HAVE spied stacks of money. Wads of cash stuffed into an empty cereal box. In fact, hadn't Russ Nolan paid Kevin Walker with money on hand to compensate for the undisclosed dog breeding activity? And bribed the volunteer at American Dog Makers with moola, too?

Pure and simple greed could be a clear motive to kill off the breeder. Who would have known about the cash stash? At least Indira. Or one of the other recent buyers.

Indira, Nicola, and Tammy. Any of them could have done it, and two of those ladies sat by my side at this very moment. Nicola and Indira could have used the extra inflow of cash to ease their money struggles. Tammy was married to Mr. Moneybags, but she might've done the deed out of a sense of justice for her injured dog.

I turned to Tammy, who sat staring at the floor. She seemed a million miles away. "Excuse me, Tammy?"

She continued to look down. Using her right hand, she traced the pale space on her left ring finger. The wedding band she had worn left a tan line there.

Kale inched closer to Tammy, perhaps feeling her sorrow. I needed to secure Tammy's attention and assess how much anger she'd harbored toward Russ Nolan.

Stroking Kale's ears, I asked, "Whatever happened to your lawsuit?"

Tammy whipped her head up. "How'd you hear about my divorce?"

Josh had told me about her separation, but . . . "I meant the one you filed against Russ Nolan."

"Oh that." She flopped her hand in the air. "It got dismissed."

But of course. After all, the man had died. The lawsuit couldn't go through after a death.

What would Tammy gain if she killed Russ Nolan? She'd have lost any chance of a legal battle and getting justice served.

Tammy seemed to gaze past me. "Why would he do this to me? I gave up the entire last year to take care of *his* child. And we even had another baby together." She pointed at Kale.

I sensed that neither being a devoted stepmother nor forced bonding over a *fur baby* could have kept her marriage intact. I really felt for Tammy, who'd taken caregiving duties to the extreme and dropped everything to head up the PTA to fulfill a supermom role. "I'm sorry," I told her.

Tammy dropped her head in her hands. I couldn't help but think of an ostrich, one who hid in the sand to avoid the dangerous world beyond it.

Since Tammy seemed indisposed at the moment, I focused on Indira. She'd created a pyramid of fanny packs on one chair. On another, she draped a colorful display of her puppy pouches.

"All the bags look beautiful," I said. "How's business?"

"Booming." She indicated the new carriers. "These are a big hit for me. Customers want multiple designs to match their varying moods—and extras, in case little Fido has an accident in one of them."

"Good for you, Indira." I rubbed my own golden puppy pouch. "This has been great for carrying a dog that can't walk. Speaking of which, how is Ash feeling these days? When's the surgery?"

She hemmed and hawed. Then she rearranged the pile of carriers, repositioning a silver bag with sparkling glitter to make it the centerpiece. "I'm still debating the pros and cons of each surgeon."

"Don't you want to help her as soon as possible?" The people at the surgical center seemed to think Kale needed an operation pronto. Wouldn't time be a major factor for Indira's dog as well?

"Ash is doing fine being carried around everywhere. I can hold off a little longer. Besides, it makes natural marketing sense and piques customer interest to see a puppy enjoying my carrier."

Indira always paid attention to the bottom line. As a result, she did seem to be enjoying a lot of success with her new pooch pouches, a line first inspired by Ash's medical condition.

I wondered how exactly Indira had obtained the capital to launch a new product when earlier she'd needed money to secure a surgery for Ash. Could it be from a dubious source like Russ Nolan's loose cash? Maybe I could weasel an answer out of her, but I'd need to do it in a more private setting.

I pretended to admire the gleaming silver carrier at the center of the pile she'd reorganized. "Can we set up another time to talk, Indira? I think I need your expertise to sell more of your pouches at my store."

"Sure, I can do that." Then she focused on the instructor, who'd started bowing to her students. "Finally. Class is over, and a shopping spree is about to begin." Indira rubbed her hands together with glee.

Soon, a swarm of women surrounded her. A few ladies also greeted

Tammy, forcing her to come out of her depressed state. She spoke to them in a robotic manner.

Meanwhile, I snuck off to chat with Lauren at the other end of the room. While I was getting information about the acupuncturist, maybe I could also get a few leads on Nicola.

I found Lauren rolling her shoulders. "Give me a moment," she said. "I'm still recovering from class."

"Take your time." Despite Lauren's exercise attire, Nicola had been the one to take the brunt of the workouts in past sessions.

I snuck a glance at Sterling to see how he had fared. He seemed in the prime of health and even wagged his tail at me.

Lauren finished stretching and pulled out her phone. She fired off a text and said, "Sent a message to her. Sometimes the acupuncturist gets busy with clients and takes a while to respond."

"While I have you here, Lauren, I'm curious about your experience with Nicola."

"Why do you need to know about my ex-assistant?"

I could feed Lauren half of the truth. "She asked me to give her a job."

"Well, Nicola was okay taking care of Sterling. She's young and capable, I'll give her that. It's why I hired her in the first place." She looked straight into my eyes. "But I have to warn you . . . Are you dating?"

"Yes, but I don't see the connect—"

"Make sure she stays away from your man. That's the real problem with her. She started small by wearing my jewelry. The next thing I know, she would've tried taking over my marriage."

I thought about the decidedly unhandsome Mr. Dalton. And also about Nicola's prior avid interest in Russ Nolan. "Are you sure about that?"

"She was always trying to chat up my husband. Once, I even

caught her giving him a photo of herself. Maybe she wanted to lure him with her youthful looks."

"A photo?" Why would Nicola do that? I snapped my fingers. "Actually, I think I know what she was trying to do. She wanted to *work* with your husband, not anything more sinister."

"Come again?"

"Nicola told me she's an aspiring actress. The assistant position with you wasn't meant to be for the long term."

"Can that be? Let me check something." Lauren tapped away at her phone. "I found Nicola listed on IMDb. Maybe I did sack her without real cause."

"Do you think you might rehire her?"

"It's too late. I already put out feelers and have interviews lined up. Anyway, I would want someone permanent. And maybe a lot older—and uglier—just to be on the safe side."

"One more question, Lauren. It's about Nicola's personality." If Nicola had gotten rid of Russ Nolan, it might have been for money, but a crime of passion seemed likelier. "Did she have a dark side? Maybe some sort of instability?"

"I don't think so. In fact, she seemed particularly cheery after Sterling arrived in our lives . . . although her happy attitude plummeted recently."

"When?"

Lauren opened up her calendar app. "Around this date. I remember because Nicola called in sick, but she sounded depressed more than anything else. I had to scramble to get a substitute."

I looked at the date and did a quick intake of breath. She'd called in sick the day after Russ Nolan had died. Why? Had she felt sad about their date going awry—or remorse over taking his life?

Lauren's phone pinged, and she read the new text. "My acupunc-

---

turist's blocked out a time for us to come by tomorrow morning. And don't worry. I'll pay for their first acupuncture session. Those poor darlings..."

"You're too kind," I said.

Her eyes flashed to the sleeping Sparky. "Those puppies deserve better. It's not their fault they were born with bad genes."

"Should I meet you at the acupuncturist's office, then? Just provide me with her location."

"I have a better idea, Mimi. We can caravan. And since you'll be at my place bright and early anyway, you can make my morning shake."

Fair enough. I agreed to her condition. One smoothie for a pack of pain-free dogs? I'd take that deal any day.

CHAPTER

thirty-four

REMEMBERING THE GREEN smoothie routine after my previous time spent assisting Nicola, I re-created Lauren's early morning wake-up shake. I made sure to put in extra green apples to suit
Lauren's palate.

She seemed satisfied with the drink and was complimenting my
use of stem-free kale leaves when the doorbell rang.

Magnus with the dogs, I bet. I'd confirmed his availability with
Zel right after the yoga class.

When Lauren opened up, Magnus stood framed in her massive
doorway. With his large build, the huge double doors seemed ap-
propriately proportioned for his girth. I introduced them to each
other.

After making small talk, Lauren checked the time. She filled up a
travel container with her smoothie and said, "Time to go."

We headed out to the acupuncturist's office using two cars. Lauren led the way in her sleek white Benz, and I sat with Magnus in his

enormous van. The dogs were in the back, secured in crates. I could smell the sachets of lavender Magnus had strewn all around the vehicle.

I envied Marshmallow, who'd opted to stay home. Transporting a bunch of dogs in the very early morning hadn't appealed to him. Riding in the car now, I realized the front seat wouldn't have had enough space for Marshmallow anyway, and he'd have hated getting jostled around in the back with the pups.

The trip proved short, and our destination turned out to be a bland strip mall. Most of the shops remained closed at this hour, but a light shone in the storefront at the end. The banner above its door read, "Dr. Silvia Li, Veterinary Acupuncturist."

Between the two of us, Magnus and I brought the dogs into the acupuncture center. Walking inside the store felt like entering a serene spa. Dim recessed lighting set in the ceiling shone down in gentle beams. Soft pan flute music piped in from hidden speakers.

A carved teakwood table near the front held a slim computer next to a small potted bamboo. The plant's flexible stalks twisted up in an elaborate weaving of green.

The rest of the business space appeared sectioned off into smaller private areas divided by the placement of shoji screens. I couldn't see anything through the tall, opaque rice sheets.

A woman wearing a crisp white smock walked toward us with gliding steps. Her glossy black hair was piled on top of her head in a sleek bun. She'd secured the hairstyle with bejeweled chopsticks.

"Hello." Her voice rang out in the air like a tinkling bell. "I'm Dr. Li."

Magnus and I shook hands with the acupuncturist, while Lauren gave her a tight hug.

Dr. Li counted the dogs in the room. "You brought in six."

Magnus nodded. "These are the ones showing signs of the most pain right now, but I have more dogs at my place."

Dr. Li pursed her lips. "I can do a session for each of them today. However, be forewarned. They'll need ongoing treatment in the future, but at least I can start realigning their energy flow right now."

She led the way to one of the screened-off areas I'd noticed before. Instead of a massage bed behind the folding panels, I discovered a padded table. Blue Chux plastic liners covered its soft surface. In the corner, a pedestal table held a tiny fountain, which bubbled with soothing water sounds.

"I'll need you to place a hand on the dog to keep it still," Dr. Li said to Magnus.

He nodded, and placed his large palm over Sparky, the first pup getting worked on. From a nearby drawer, Dr. Li retrieved a case of needles.

I looked closely at the metal points. Thankfully, they appeared smaller than I'd feared, more of a filament width than the size of a sewing needle.

Dr. Li placed the needles into Sparky using a gentle but firm hand. The puppy didn't make a single sound. In fact, he acted as though he hadn't felt the pinpricks.

She repeated acupuncture on each of the other puppies, using the different sectioned-off spaces. We then waited the requisite amount of time before she could remove the needles from the dogs.

Afterward, I couldn't believe the frolicking behavior of the puppies as they scampered around the front room. "That's absolutely amazing."

"Acupuncture works with the central nervous system," Dr. Li said. "It takes away their pain. But if I see patients after things have gotten

really bad, I need to go beyond the plain needles and use electroacu-
puncture."

"They're really energetic," Magnus piped up, watching one of the
dogs jump in the air.

Lauren beamed from near the teakwood table. "What did I
tell you?"

"You're like their fairy godmother," I said. "You've granted their
deepest wish."

"If only I could give them homes, too . . ."

Magnus sighed, a heavy groan coming from the depths of his dia-
phragm. "I would help, but I've got no contacts. The folks who come to
me want perfect specimens, purebreds."

"How about organizing a pet adoption fair?" Lauren said.

"I don't know." Magnus shook his head. "Wouldn't it take time to
put together an event? How long will the acupuncture last?"

Dr. Li said, "Depends on the dog, but I usually recommend weekly
treatments."

Seven days or less before the next acupuncture session? Lauren
would only pay for their first session, so the word would have to spread
fast to help get the puppies rescued while they still felt well. We'd need
assistance that moved at the speed of technology.

"I might know a way," I said.

· · ·

It took a short call to Pixie for me to arrange the meeting at PetTwin
headquarters. I decided to bring Marshmallow along on my field trip.

At the sprawling campus, we looked around in awe. PetTwin's
sleek mirrored building lay next to a field of luxurious grass. Even I
wanted to roll over in the fresh-cut turf.

Mock fire hydrants stood at various points so dogs could do their business in designated areas. Near the front entrance, we discovered a pet drinking fountain. Bowls could be positioned under the low spout for refreshing, clean water.

As we approached the mirrored building, the automatic doors opened with a smooth whish. Right away, a woman with braided purple hair marched toward us wielding a clipboard. "Mimi Lee?" she said.

I nodded, and she continued, "This way, please, for your appointment with Stacy."

She led Marshmallow and me into an all-glass elevator. As it rose to the second floor, I felt like I was levitating.

The doors opened, and she walked us over to an intimidating conference room. "Our founder is already waiting for you."

The meeting area housed a large reclaimed wood table with swivel chairs. All the furniture nestled against the back wall, and the rest of the space held a tall object that looked like nothing short of a glowing telephone booth.

"Have a seat," Stacy said, her trademark red mermaid hair curling down to her waist.

I sat in the office chair with its ergonomic molding, while Marshmallow took a spot on the polished floor below the table.

"Thanks for meeting with me," I said. "Here are pics of a few of the puppies." I showed Stacy the photos I'd taken of the dogs after their treatment at the acupuncturist's office.

"What a bunch of cutie-pies."

"I hope a lot of people think the same way. They need good homes. And I hope your app will match them with great owners."

"PetTwin is excited to help out. Do you have information on their background?"

"Not really. The puppies were left all alone when their breeder, uh, suddenly died." My description sounded a lot better than murder, and I'd managed to omit the fact that I still had a cloud of suspicion hanging over me.

"Sounds tragic," she murmured.

I wanted to put the puppies in the best possible light, but . . . I took a deep breath and said, "The puppies do suffer from a genetic problem."

"Rescue dogs all have issues. I believe people will trip over themselves wanting to adopt these poor dogs."

"Thanks again for partnering with me."

A glint entered Stacy's eyes. "Of course, I'm meeting with you as a favor to Pixie. She's a generous donor to PetTwin. I must tell you, though, that we usually deal with organizations and shelters, not individuals. We also charge those companies a fee to use our app."

I swallowed hard. Of course there would be a catch.

"However, I'm willing to waive the cost—if your puppies will showcase our new technology."

"Which is?"

She pointed to the telephone booth–looking object. "Our 4-D simulator. This is one of our prototypes. It comes preloaded with a sensory experience. Go ahead and try it."

Maybe Marshmallow would go inside the booth with me? I peeked down at him and implored him with wide eyes.

"No way," he said. "You're on your own with that Area Fifty-One souvenir."

I stood up and walked with glacial steps over to the booth. Gripping the metal door, I slid it open—to reveal a cushioned bench opposite a mounted screen. The interior looked a lot like a fancy photo booth.

This didn't seem so bad. I sat down, and the door closed on me.

Due to either a weight or a motion sensor, the screen flickered on. Words scrolled past my eyes: "Please adopt me."

A video of a cute tan bunny with floppy ears filled the monitor. Statistics about the male bunny appeared in the lower-right-hand corner.

More words appeared. "This is how it will feel to play with Posy."

The sharp smell of clover filled my senses. Warm rays of friendly sunshine caressed my face.

The screen started enlarging and wrapping around the walls. A brilliant blue sky with ethereal clouds displayed above me. I caught a bouncing motion near the bottom of the booth. Looking down, I realized that the ground had transformed into a field of clover.

Posy hopped closer. He paused before me, as though waiting for me to reach out. The bunny twitched his nose at me. My heart melted. I bent down, and my fingers reached toward Posy's velvet fur.

Again, the same words appeared on-screen: "Adopt me today." Contact details followed.

Darkness covered the screen. It retracted to a normal size, and the door slid open. I stepped out and blinked at the bright office lights.

Turning to Stacy, I said, "That video really drew me in. I forgot I was even in a booth."

"The 4-D experience practically teleports you, right?"

I nodded, unable to encapsulate my thoughts into words.

"We could make some 4-D videos of your little rescue dogs right in this building," Stacy said. "Then, using the material, we'll be able to set up the other prototype pods for the public to enjoy."

"Definitely. The more that word gets out about those puppies, the quicker they'll be adopted."

"There's only one hiccup." Stacy bit the tip of her pinky nail. "It's such new technology that we're still searching for a stellar legal consultant to double-check and make sure our patent paperwork is in order."

A happy smile spread across my face. "Well, you're in luck," I said. "I think I have the perfect contact for you."

CHAPTER

thirty-five

THE APP MUST have worked its magic, because Magnus soon called me up to say three dogs had been adopted. In fact, he invited me to watch them meet their new owners on Saturday.

I had several errands scheduled for that same day, but I went first to Magnus Cooper's house. He stood on his porch with the PetTwin founder by his side. Marshmallow and I joined them, greeting the new owners with unbridled enthusiasm as they came to pick up their new pets.

Sparky, Tigre, and one of their littermates were all swooped up. I didn't need Marshmallow to translate the puppies' happy vibes. Their tails wagged as they each went off with their respective owners: a smiling family, two kind-looking spinster ladies, and a burly fireman.

After the new owners and their animals had left, Stacy turned to me. "What a success, Mimi. Can you imagine how many more potential owners the 4-D experience will draw in?"

"I take it that the legal consultant worked out for you."

She nodded. "Josh Akana and the whole team at Murphy, Sulli-van, and Goodwin have ensured an airtight patent application on our technology."

"I know they're top-notch." I'd referred Josh without telling him. He didn't know I had intervened, and I hoped the new collaboration had been a pleasant surprise.

Stacy continued, "We'll be creating more 4-D units soon. A few organizations have requested models from us, and there's growing buzz. I think we'll be establishing a long-term relationship with the Goodwin law firm."

Did that mean Josh had now secured a steady client? I couldn't wait to find out.

After Stacy had left, I excused myself and stepped to the far edge of the porch to dial up Josh. He answered at once. "How's work going nowadays?" I said.

"Super, and you would know."

"You found out I was involved?"

He chuckled. "The founder mentioned a Miss Lee had referred us to collaborate with PetTwin. I'm really enjoying the new work."

"Since things are stable at the law firm," I said, "will that mean a less extreme schedule for you?"

"I know what you're trying to get at, Mimi." His voice took on a gentle tone. "Yes, we'll have more time to see each other."

I flushed but felt pleased he'd gotten my hint.

He continued, "Actually, my schedule's freer already. I even had the chance to dig into Tammy's lawsuit again. Looks like her case against Russ Nolan got dismissed."

I glanced down the street. Russ Nolan's neighborhood wasn't too far from here. My voice quieted. "Yeah, it didn't go through be-cause he died."

"No, actually." Josh cleared his throat. "The fine print on the original contract between him and Tammy banned any suing. Her attorney should never have filed the lawsuit in the first place."

"Guess she should've hired you. You would never have made that kind of mistake."

A grin crept into his voice. "I don't represent just anybody. And you, Mimi, are always my number one client."

I hung up with Josh and felt so elated that I did a jig on the porch. The PetTwin collaboration turned out to be a win-win for everyone involved. Dogs got adopted. PetTwin advanced its amazing technology. Josh fared better at his workplace. And I earned extra face-to-face time with my intelligent lawyer boyfriend.

Brimming over with gratitude, I decided to channel some of that positivity to someone who lived nearby. Besides, I had time before my appointment with Indira, the next scheduled visit of the day.

I wanted to drop by Shirl's house because I hadn't gotten around to thanking her when I'd visited the neighborhood last time. I'd been too focused on figuring out more details about the cash-filled cereal box by chatting up Henry. And I'd been distracted by watching the two neighbors meet each other for the first time.

"You can do a trick to show my gratitude to Shirl," I said to Marshmallow.

He bristled. "I'm not a circus animal."

"Fine, I'll say thank you by myself."

When we arrived at Shirl's house and she opened the door, my prepared mini speech flew out of my head. Because Shirl wasn't standing alone on the threshold of her home. She had company—Henry.

"Oh, I didn't mean to disturb you two," I said.

She held up a tub of buttered popcorn. "You caught us as we're about to watch a YouTube marathon. I'm teaching Henry about new tech."

Henry fiddled with his suspenders. "Look what I got from Shirl," he said, his thumbs pointing to the YouTube logo shirt he had on. It looked at odds with the rest of his traditional newsboy outfit, but he seemed pleased with her gift.

"We're matching," Shirl said. Indeed, she wore an identical shirt. And instead of her usual drawstring pants, she wore a tight elastic-banded version. She'd dressed up for this watching extravaganza with her neighbor.

Henry leaned close to me and whispered, "By the way, I took your advice and got Shirl an item she needed."

She must have overheard with her sensitive hearing, because a flush crept up her neck. Shirl lifted up her wrist and showed off her new jewelry.

"Wow," Marshmallow said, giving a mental whistle. "That's a medical bracelet?"

"Pretty," I told Shirl, admiring the sleek silver design with its medical cross symbol. It even had a unique twist—an extra hanging paw charm. "Cute, a dog print."

"Cat print," Marshmallow and Shirl said at the same time.

"There are no extra pointy marks coming out from the pad," Marshmallow added. "Which makes sense. Only cats have retractable claws."

Shirl peered back into the interior of her potpourried home. "Did you need something from me, Mimi?"

"Actually, I came to thank you because you retracted your statement about the receipt. And, basically, for telling Detective Brown that I was innocent."

"I wouldn't go that far, Mimi. The detective pressed me for details about the night of the murder. I ended up telling him the truth about Russ Nolan's female visitor—or, maybe, visitors." She took a handful of popcorn and munched. "He kept asking me about the height of the last visitor who showed up."

"Sounds like he wanted a detailed description."

"He did. And he asked whether the woman had been really petite. I didn't think so but couldn't say for sure from my vantage point. It was pretty dark that night."

Marshmallow and I looked at one another. Out of all the recent female visitors to Russ Nolan's house, I knew I was the shortest of them, at my five-foot height. Seemed like Detective Brown hadn't let me off the hook yet. Instead, he lay biding his time, waiting for something concrete so he could haul me to the slammer.

CHAPTER
thirty-six

T O ARRANGE A visit to Indira's house, I used the excuse that I wanted to focus on our discussion without customers around. I figured she'd open up more in the privacy of her own home. Maybe she'd even let slip whether she'd known about Russ Nolan's secret money stash.

Without any extra pet owners in it, the house seemed more spacious and relaxed the second time around. Through the open French doors, I spied her sparkling pool.

Indira invited me to sit on her microsuede sofa and then bustled into the kitchen. I made myself comfortable and watched Marshmallow curl up next to Ash on the Persian carpet.

Tracing the rug's elaborate pattern with his paw, he said, "Indira may be a murderer, but at least she's got excellent taste in textiles."

When Indira returned, she was balancing two teacups on porcelain saucers. She handed me one, and I breathed in the fragrant milk tea spiced with cardamom pods.

"This smells heavenly," I said. "And thanks for letting us meet on a weekend."

"You're very welcome. And you won't find anything in the cafés better than my fresh-brewed chai." She settled on the couch with her cup and crossed her long legs. "Now, tell me what's going on with the pooch pouches in your store."

"Honestly, I'm not really moving much inventory." I blew on the steaming tea. "But you seem to be getting lots of interest."

She gave a half shrug. "My excellent work naturally draws in buyers. But I admit I do have years of sales experience."

"If only I could market your bags better . . . What if I told the customers which fancy materials you use in crafting the pouches?" I figured that the fabric Indira used for her carriers might indicate to me the cost of manufacturing them. That, in turn, could inform me as to whether she'd actually needed an extra infusion of cash to make them.

She sipped her hot chai, and I wondered how Indira didn't scald her tongue. "I use all different sorts of material in my work. Polyester, silk, cotton, et cetera. It's hard for me to be specific. Every design is unique."

The heat emanating from my porcelain cup seemed to singe my fingers. I perched it on a side table to let the tea cool down. "Maybe you could say where you purchased the materials. I could market your pouches as, say, locally sourced."

She looked into her cup as if its contents fascinated her. "I don't think that will be possible, Mimi. I'm sure you understand that I can't give away my creative secrets."

I edged closer to her. "Come on, you can tell me something. One businesswoman to another. How do you manage to do it? Afford to make these luxurious carriers, turn a profit, and still manage to look amazing?"

A Mona Lisa smile played at the edge of her lips.

Indira didn't seem to want to spill. I nudged Marshmallow's tail with the tip of my foot. Maybe a little feline snooping could help me understand her creative processes better.

Marshmallow purred at Ash. They set off together, with the hobbling Chihuahua in the lead.

In the meantime, I decided to try the chai again. Picking up the teacup, I sipped. The drink burned my lip, and I had to set the cup back on the table.

Well, two could play with fire in this conversation. "Can't you give me a tiny hint, Indira? After all," I said, "I don't have to carry your line of pouches in my store . . ."

My threat lingered in the air.

Indira pressed her lips together tight.

We stared at each other in silence until our pets returned. Ash carried a half-finished doggie pouch in her mouth. A thread trailed from the side of the bag.

"What? Bad dog," Indira said as she tried to stand. However, she still had to balance her teacup, so I had the advantage. I sprang up and removed the pouch from Ash's mouth.

As I took it, I noticed a small neon sticker on the bottom of the pouch. "'Ye Olde Thrift Shoppe,'" I read.

Indira's cheeks flushed. "So, you've caught me."

Examining the bag, I noticed a shoulder seam. "Did you make this out of an old shirt?"

She touched the pouch and leaned in toward me. Her mouth quivered. "That's my big secret, Mimi. This pouch and all my other designs? The material comes from fashion rewear stores."

I tilted my head. Why was she ashamed? "How very green of you."

Her eyes sparkled with fire. "A side consequence. My real intent? That I build my empire on the trash of the upper crust. Think about it: They're buying their old junk again and paying me extravagant prices for it."

Marshmallow bobbed his head. "She's got a wicked sense of revenge."

"Mm-hmm." I nodded at Indira's ingenuity, even though I couldn't support her intense dislike of others.

She seemed relieved to find that I hadn't judged her. In her mind, maybe she even thought I stood in solidarity with her since we both owned local businesses.

I pondered over the new piece of information. If Indira used thrift store finds for her carriers, then she hadn't needed much capital investment to launch her new line of pooch pouches. I said goodbye to Indira and readied myself for my next stop, a surprise visit that might shed light on another possible culprit.

● ● ●

I expected Nicola to be at home on the weekend. After all, she didn't have a boyfriend, a job, or an easy means of transportation.

Climbing the rickety staircase to her cramped one-bedroom unit, I reflected on Lauren's comments about her character: Nicola had seemed morose after Russ Nolan died. Was that from grief, or guilt?

I recalled that Nicola hadn't wanted to meet at her apartment the last time. Instead, she'd asked to connect at a nearby café. During our lunch, she'd also steered the conversation away from Russ Nolan. What could the diversion have meant?

Before I knocked on her door, I knew she was home. I could already hear loud singing from inside the apartment. Nicola's soprano voice drowned out the soundtrack playing in the background. The tune came from a popular musical, but I couldn't remember the exact lyrics.

I knocked, and the music shut off. Nicola opened the door a crack and craned her neck around the edge.

I smiled at her, while Marshmallow purred from near my feet.

She blinked at me and didn't open the door any wider.

"May I come in?" I asked.

"Now isn't a good time, Mimi. I wasn't expecting visitors."

I gave her a wider smile and said, "But I'm here to pick up your résumé. You said you wanted me to have it." I'd known I would need a good excuse to show up unannounced.

"I still have to update it," Nicola said. "I can bring it to Hollywoof on Monday."

I cleared my throat and said, "Gee, I drove all the way here to pick it up. Maybe I can get a sip of water before I go?"

Nicola gave a short cough and covered her mouth. "Sorry, I'm feeling under the weather today. I wouldn't want to pass my germs to you."

Marshmallow and I exchanged a glance. If Nicola's pretend coughing was any indication of her acting skills, it was no wonder she hadn't landed any major roles yet.

I tried to peer over her shoulder into the apartment. "I thought I heard you singing a moment ago. Loud and clear."

"Oh, that must have been the radio." She started a coughing jag. "See you Monday," she said, closing the door.

I turned to Marshmallow and lowered my voice. "What do you think that was all about?"

"Something must be inside the apartment that she doesn't want you to see."

"Could it be the money?" I pictured piles of cash teetering on her armchair. If she and Russ Nolan had been an item, she'd know all about his secret stash. Had she been singing with glee, having counted all the cash she'd taken from his house?

CHAPTER
thirty-seven

TAMMY SHOWED UP at Hollywoof on Monday. She carried Kale in her arms and asked if I could provide teeth cleaning.

Lowering her voice, she said, "Between you and me, her breath stinks. And I'd like her to smell nice for her upcoming leg surgery."

"I'm honored to be your dentist." I rubbed the top of Kale's head. "Tammy, do you want to drop her off or wait around?"

"I doubt it'll take very long, so I'll stay." She handed Kale over to me. On her way to the waiting area, Tammy halted. A look of horror crossed her face.

She sidled toward me. "Mimi, I think my cousin Scarlet is visiting. Do you think you can help?"

I wrinkled my brow. "I'm not sure—"

"My *Aunt Flo* has come to town," she said. "Maybe you have extra supplies in your purse?"

Oh, right. Now I understood about those pesky regular visitors ... that only women receive. Guess the same euphemism crosses cultural lines, because Ma also referred to her time of the month as when relatives came to visit. "My bag is underneath the counter with the cash register." I pointed to its location.

Marshmallow must have been following our conversation, because I saw him shudder. He crawled over to me and said, "I'll tag along. Because sticking your hands into a dog's mouth—not the brightest idea. Plus, Tammy needs privacy."

I nodded. Who knew male cats would feel uncomfortable around feminine hygiene talk?

Before we walked toward the back of the store, I said, "Bathroom's down the hall, Tammy. First door on your left."

"Okay, thanks," she said, moving toward the space beneath the cash register.

I marched Kale into the back room, with Marshmallow following me. After easing the puppy onto the table, I said, "This won't hurt a bit, Kale. Just a regular cleaning. I'll make your mouth feel fresh."

Marshmallow translated and then gave a soft, continuous purring that soothed even me as I gathered the tools I would need. I brought out a dog toothbrush and some poultry-flavored toothpaste. Then I proceeded to place a dollop of paste on the soft bristles of the toothbrush.

I knew I only needed to brush the exterior teeth. Kale's tongue would naturally work the paste around to clean the inside of her mouth. She didn't even need to spit out the toothpaste like a human would.

I finished brushing and checked her teeth. They seemed clean. "You've been such a good sport," I said to Kale.

When I returned to the front with Kale, her teeth sparkling, I found Tammy sitting on the pleather bench watching a movie play on the flat-screen TV. She looked much more comfortable than when she'd first come in.

"Kale smells so much better," Tammy said as she paid the grooming bill.

"I'm glad you're getting out," I said. "You seem in a healthier place. I mean, emotionally."

She looked at me with a steady gaze. Her eyes didn't appear teary or red-rimmed. "Yes, things are improving," she said. She cradled Kale in her arms and rocked her like a baby. "Everything will be fixed soon."

• • •

No walk-in clients or phone calls came for me the rest of the day. Instead, I handled some lookie-loos who'd walked in because of the local beach volleyball tournament. The curious observers came into my store to check out the fees and riffle through my merchandise. As a result, I did ring up a few collar and doggie pouch purchases.

Around four o'clock, Nicola showed up. True to her word, she actually brought in her résumé. She even wore a proper pantsuit, as though she'd prepared for a formal interview. Seemed like Nicola had really fallen for my excuse when I'd dropped by her apartment. Maybe *I* deserved an Oscar.

"You look like you rested up," I said, as she handed me the thick ivory paper listing her recent jobs.

A delicate pink hue colored her cheeks. "Must have been one of those twenty-four-hour bugs. I feel much better."

I looked at her résumé. My finger tracked her list of recent positions, mostly duties at fast-food restaurants. She'd also listed her crew work on a few local productions. She'd placed them at the end of the page under the "Other Experience" heading.

"Have you worked with animals before?" I asked her.

"Only Sterling," Nicola said. "But you remember how much he adored me."

"Actually, I'm not sure I can hire new staff at the moment."

She grasped my hands with hers. "I know you're biased against me, what with my sour attitude toward Mrs. Dalton and borrowing her jewelry—"

"It's not that." I just didn't want to hire a possible killer. Plus, I really couldn't afford it. I decided to tell her my second explanation. "I took a closer look at my finances and can't justify the expense."

"I don't believe that's your real reason. Please give me a chance." She squeezed my hands tightly.

I wondered why she even needed an income now. Couldn't Russ Nolan's money tide her over? But maybe he hadn't kept a lot of loose cash in the house. Or perhaps he'd depleted it by bribing too many people. I disentangled her hands from mine and peeked over at Marshmallow.

"Why are you looking at me?" he said. "You're the one with the psych degree. I can't tell if she's a good candidate or not. I wouldn't know where to begin figuring out that mess you call the human mind."

"People can become improved versions of themselves." Nicola's gaze flitted around the room. "That's one of the reasons I fell for Russ. I knew I could change him for the better."

The classic rescuer mind-set. How many people acted in a like manner? Thank goodness I didn't fall victim to the *My Fair Lady* sort of thinking that got people into trouble. Besides, my wonderful Josh didn't need improvement.

Nicola continued, "My personal philosophy is that you can always start over and begin again."

"Tell you what, I'll hold on to your résumé," I said. "Maybe I can use my connections to find an open pets-related position."

"Thanks, but I guarantee you won't regret it if you take me on. I can work real hard." She pumped my hand. Ouch. She had some muscle behind her gazelle frame.

I waved to Nicola as she left. Her words about wanting to "start over" rang in my head. Had she meant with this new job? Perhaps getting fired had propelled her to start looking for different employment.

Likewise, her recent loss of Russ Nolan could lead to a new relationship in the future. The question remained, though: Had the loss been predetermined—one which Nicola herself had caused?

CHAPTER
thirty-eight

Around closing time, I started cleaning up the back room. Marshmallow stayed nearby, watching while I worked.

"If only you could hold things with your paws," I said.

"What can I say? Cats are meant to be served, not the other way around."

I grunted at him as I wiped down the table with antiseptic. Suddenly, the lights turned off.

"A power outage?" I said. "That's never happened before."

"How bad is business if you can't pay the electric bill?" he asked.

"Not funny."

I'd never had issues with the electrical system in the past. Hollywoof had its own subpanel, so I wondered if it had gotten shorted somehow.

A faint chime sounded from the distance. Could it be the front door? But no customer would walk in so late for my grooming help.

I sighed. I'd better call the power company to figure out what had happened and how to have the electricity restored. Too bad I couldn't see well in the dark. I groped my way back to the main room by placing my hands against the walls to guide me.

As I passed by the waiting area, I thought I heard a soft plopping noise. I shook my head to clear it. The darkness must be heightening my imagination.

Near the front of the store, dusk let in some dim light through the glass window. I could make out the bulky shape of the cash register. Staggering over to the counter, I fumbled for the phone. When I finally lifted the receiver to my ear, I couldn't hear a dial tone. Strange. Had I tripped on the cord and unplugged it?

Oh well. I could use my cell. Bending below to reach under the counter, I found my purse and started digging through its contents by touch. I felt odds and ends in there, but nothing shaped like my phone. Where could I have put it?

That's when I heard the muffled footsteps. Straightening up from the counter, I found the silhouette of a female figure looming over me. She held up some sort of slender tube. A weapon?

Grabbing the item closest to me, I ended up lobbing the doggie biscuit jar at her. The woman shrieked, dropped whatever she'd been holding, and fell back into the shadows. Disaster averted.

From the sitting area across the way, a familiar tune started playing. "Chapel of Love." Ma's special ring tone.

I could see the top of my phone glowing in the dark, poking up out of a handbag. What was going on? I moved toward it, but something—or, rather, someone—tripped me.

Ouch. I landed on my side. A sharp pain seared my right ankle. I must've twisted it during the fall.

Sprawled close to the waiting area, I glanced at the nearby bench, already knowing what I'd see. My phone had been pickpocketed, and

I recognized the metal-studded bag it lay in. Aunt Flo had been a decoy.

Tammy marched over to me. "I put my bag down on the bench so I would have my hands free to deal with you." So the soft plopping noise I'd heard earlier hadn't been my imagination.

She continued, "But you still startled me by throwing that jar. I even dropped the syringe. Good thing I don't need it anymore. That fall knocked you down flat."

Wait, she'd said something about a *syringe*? Injections. The cap I'd found had come from a needle. "Ketamine," I said. The medication Dr. Exi had prescribed to numb Kale's leg pain. "You used it on Russ Nolan."

Tammy chuckled. "Sure I did. I knew it would make him drowsy."

"You mean, make it easier for you to kill him?"

She shook her head. "No, I only wanted to knock him unconscious. He's a big guy. I figured I'd need to drug him first to conk him out. I must have swung too hard."

I tried to wriggle my foot. My ankle pulsed with pain. "Why didn't you just wait for the lawsuit to go through? Do it all aboveboard?"

"Mimi, it was a frivolous claim."

Josh had told me the lawsuit had been dismissed. Why again? The original contract terms had forbidden suing. What if it hadn't been Tammy's inept lawyer who'd made a mistake? "You knew all along the lawsuit would never work."

"Of course I did. It was a brill move on my part, don't you think? Filing it cast suspicion away from me."

My phone rang. "Chapel of Love" again. Tammy reached into her bag and silenced the song.

"You must have hated Russ Nolan for tricking you with an inferior puppy," I said. "And the canceled dog show fundraiser didn't help, either."

She huffed. "I bet nobody could stand that doofus. It was only fair he paid for the problem he introduced."

"That's not a good enough reason to kill him."

She shrugged. "My only real regret is that you got curious and followed my trail. Pretended to be Soo Yi at school, talked to my vet, and even impersonated me over the phone."

I gritted my teeth so I could endure the pain in my foot while I inched toward the bench. Maybe I could snatch my phone and make an emergency call. Three simple numbers.

Tammy wagged her finger at me. "You were trouble from day one, Mimi. You even blocked my way at the house."

A sudden realization hit me. "So that's why I ran into you the day after the murder. You came back to look for the cap from the syringe."

"I didn't realize I'd lost it until way after and figured I'd have better success searching for it during daylight."

"But a man dying for your sense of fairness, to cover Kale's surgery?" I shuddered. "It's not like you even need the cash. You married into money."

Her voice turned bitter. "And that fairy tale has ended. I've no regrets Russ Nolan died. An eye for an eye. After all, he killed my marriage."

"He did?"

Coldness seeped into her every word. "Yes, by selling me a horrible pup. Kale was supposed to be a substitute for the child I couldn't conceive. A new pet that would help our ailing marriage."

"Your fur baby."

"A wonderful addition to the family," she said. "Instead, Kale broke things and chewed on wallets. And then the leg problems showed up and added too much stress to my marriage."

"That's why you tried to take Kale back to get a refund from Russ Nolan, but he refused."

"So I did the next best thing by taking Russ Nolan's money to pay for the surgery. I thought if Kale got better, somehow everything would go back to normal."

"Why did you want your money back from the surgical center, then?" I asked.

"I need everything I can get to survive, now that he's filed the divorce papers." She pointed at me. "By the way, you're not looking too hot."

I had, however, managed to drag myself to the edge of the bench during the past few minutes. If only I could sit up, then I might reach my phone. I had to keep Tammy talking to distract her.

"I don't understand," I said. "If your husband doesn't like Kale, why is he paying for the procedure now?"

"His brat of a daughter whined about it. Ironic. He'll keep the dog but kick *me* out."

She rummaged in her bag and retrieved something. A water bottle. "Mimi, it was so easy to sneak up on you. People are very clumsy in the dark."

I narrowed my eyes at her. "You were the one who shut the lights off?"

"Easy squeezy. I asked an electrician who's part of the PTA. He walked me through how to access the subpanel over the phone."

She lifted her bottle up.

I flinched and tried reaching for her bag. It was still too far away. I'd have to sit up to get it. "What's in your bottle?" I asked as I pulled myself up.

"Some seashore."

Panting, I rested my back against the bench. Then I processed her previous words.

A memory flashed before me. The first doga class I'd attended, when Lauren had borrowed Tammy's water bottle and wiped off—"Sand," I said.

"You figured it out. I weighted this bottle down. But don't worry, I know exactly how to make the strike quick. Second time's the charm."

"The police will catch you," I said.

"Not that clueless detective," Tammy said. "Excuse the pun, but he's always barking up the wrong tree. How confused will he be when his prime suspect goes kaput."

I tried to shrink back but found myself stuck against the bench with nowhere to go.

She lifted the bottle high above her head. "I'm not going to prison because of some meddlesome pet groomer."

Before she could come any closer, blue eyes glinted in the dark. A giant fluffball launched at the woman from out of nowhere. Marshmallow started clawing Tammy. But like a woman possessed, Tammy kept pressing her attack.

It was too late for me to grab the phone now and call for help. I had to defend myself.

CHAPTER

thirty-nine

WITH THE BOOST of adrenaline, I snatched the bag off the bench and swung it hard at Tammy's knees. The combo of Marshmallow's clawing and my smacking pushed her off balance. As Tammy stumbled, I threw all my muscle into whacking her in the middle of her stomach.

She doubled over in pain, dropping the water bottle. It rolled away, out of her reach. Thank goodness for her own bag's hard metal studs. They must have made strong contact with her body, because Tammy lay on the floor, groaning.

I heard the wail of a siren approaching. Tammy continued to moan and curled herself into a fetal position.

A few moments later, the door burst open. The shop bell jangled with fury.

A man's figure filled the doorway. "Miss Lee, are you all right?"

I knew that voice. "Twisted my ankle, Detective Brown. But still alive."

He tried turning on the lights but couldn't. After cursing under his breath, he used a mini penlight to shine a faint beam around. Maybe he kept the small tool handy in his magical jacket pocket.

"What happened here?" he asked.

I pointed to Tammy and said, "She tried to attack me, to kill me the same way she did Russ Nolan."

Detective Brown strode over to Tammy and handcuffed her. "Sounds like you and I need to have an in-depth conversation."

First, though, he called for extra police. Once he'd finished talking to headquarters, an insistent meowing filled the air.

Detective Brown swung his light in the direction of the sound. Marshmallow sat near a tube-like item: a medical syringe. The cap at the end of the needle looked exactly like the one I'd discovered in Russ Nolan's backyard.

"What do we have here?" Detective Brown bent over it and read the label. "Ketamine. The autopsy report finally came through and showed the very same chemical in the victim's body."

"Uh-huh," I said, not disguising the I-told-you-so tone of my voice.

He cleared his throat. "I was in the process of following up on ketamine prescriptions, I'll have you know. That doctor-patient confidentiality is a tough nut to crack."

All of a sudden, the lights came back on with full force. Backup must have arrived, and somebody had restored power to the store.

Detective Brown turned toward Tammy, who still remained in a huddle. "Time to take your statement."

Her eyes grew wide. "If I confess everything, the judge will be lenient, right? After all, I didn't mean to hit Russ Nolan so hard. And I didn't actually kill Mimi or anything."

"The police department will value your full cooperation," Detective Brown said. Which really didn't promise her anything, but

Tammy nodded at him. She let Detective Brown haul her up from the floor.

He pivoted to me. "Miss Lee, I'd advise you to get some rest. You've had a rough night."

"I have a question for you, Detective," I said, searching his face. "How'd you realize I was in danger so fast?"

"I didn't. But your mother kept calling the station, wanting us to check on you. She said you weren't answering your phone and hadn't told her you'd gotten home safely tonight." He gave me a wry grin. "When I heard your name being tossed around, I volunteered to check Hollywoof myself to see what trouble you were causing."

Huh. Ma's constant worrying had come in handy for once.

Before we could leave, a few paramedics checked out my foot. Diagnosing it as a mild sprain, they provided me with an ice pack.

Then they proceeded to fuss over Marshmallow, who hissed at them.

I patted his head. "After your *paw-some* attack, they're just making sure you're *fe-line* okay."

He groaned. "That fall made your sense of humor get even worse."

Although the paramedics had cleared us to leave, I didn't want to drive home. Besides, I had zero desire to be alone. I asked an officer take me to my parents' place.

When the patrol car approached the house, the lights inside my childhood home glowed bright, like a friendly beacon guiding me to safe haven. The door flung open even as we eased onto the driveway.

Three faces peered into the car's headlights from the doorway. When I got out and placed Marshmallow onto the paved ground, Ma rushed to check on me.

She inspected me at arm's length to make sure everything was okay and then hugged me. Alice soon ran over and added to the huddle. Finally, Dad lumbered over and crushed us all in his signature bear hug.

They spoke at the same time:

"Make me worry to dead. *Sei-ah*," Ma said.

"Glad to see you safe and sound, Princess One."

"Mimi, what happened?" Alice asked.

Dad ushered me inside and insisted I sit at the dining table. Ma brewed me a mug of strong oolong tea.

I sipped it as I figured out how to answer Alice's question. With my family crowded around me, I tried to summarize my experience at Hollywoof. Of course, I downplayed the danger.

I rushed over the details of Tammy's attack and sped straight to the police arriving on the scene. Everyone stared at me, aghast. Why had a customer tried to threaten me?

I didn't tell them about the murder case or how I'd gone snooping to clear my name. Why had Tammy come after me, then? I spun a story about how she'd entered my shop to chat. Overwhelmed with taking care of her sick dog and angry about her looming divorce, she just snapped. They shook their heads at me.

Finally, Ma tutted and said she'd fix me some herbal chicken soup to restore my scattered energy. Dad slung a comforting arm around my shoulder. Alice held my hand.

At my sister's gentle touch, I said, "Alice, why are you here, anyway? Was Ma so worried that she called you when I didn't answer?"

A sweet smile appeared on my sister's face. "Oh no, I was already here. I came over to tell Ma and Dad some good news from Roosevelt Elementary."

"Tell me, too." It'd be nice to hear something positive for a change.

"Principal Hallis resigned."

I squeezed my sister's hand. "It will be a less toxic environment for you to work in now. I don't understand, though. I figured she'd want to rule the school a long time with her iron fist."

Alice wrinkled her button nose. "Somehow the school receptionist convinced her to leave. Said Principal Hallis and her pet hedgehog might enjoy life better in a different state."

I thought back to when I'd threatened Principal Hallis in her office. I'd deposited the exotic pets brochure in the recycling bin in full view of the receptionist. She must have picked it up and read it. Then she had continued the good fight. Well done, her.

Ma deposited a bowl of soup before me. "Drink." Then she wagged her finger at me. "If no help, you no go back store."

CHAPTER

forty

THOUGHT ABOUT MA'S semiserious condition for my returning to work. Like she said, it would be nice and probably feel safer to have another pair of hands around. Especially if trouble sprang up again at my store.

I even had a willing applicant. But I also needed someone whom I could trust. What had Nicola been hiding in her apartment that she hadn't wanted me to see?

In the early morning, I called her up to find out. "Why were you so cagey during my last visit? What are you hiding in your apartment?"

She sighed. "I thought you might notice I was acting suspicious. Don't worry, I returned it."

I recalled the banging noises I'd heard from the backyard when I'd discovered the plastic cap. "Did you happen to go into Russ Nolan's the day I talked with Shirl to retrieve the bracelet?"

"Yes." She hesitated. "I stole a memento from his old house. But I gave it back to Henry."

Nicola seemed to be on the up-and-up. After all, how else would she know the new renter's name unless she'd met him?

I should check out her story, though. I'd already taken the day off to recover, so I could fit in a visit to Henry.

With my car still stuck at Hollywoof, I asked Alice to drop me off at Henry's house. It would be on her way to school, so my sister agreed.

When I knocked on Henry's door, he answered right away.

I shuffled my feet. "Hello again. I'd like to check on something, Henry. I have a job applicant who took something from your house ..."

Henry nodded. "Young Nicola? She came and apologized to my face. Turns out this was her old boyfriend's home. Can you wait here a minute? I want to show you the item."

He rummaged inside the house and returned with a fancy domed night-light. "This is what she brought back. I didn't even notice it when I moved in. She found it in the bedroom closet. It's a light that projects constellations onto the ceiling."

In a soft tone, I said, "Nicola must have wanted to keep it as a reminder of her boyfriend."

"A natural sentiment. I told her she shouldn't have bothered to bring it back. I wouldn't have minded if she kept it, but she said it was better for her to start fresh. She mentioned wanting to do the right thing from now on."

The theme of beginning again, Nicola's philosophy, echoed back at me. She was trying to be a better version of herself.

I heard a zooming from behind me. Looking over my shoulder, I saw a news van hurtling down the street. "Is something happening around here?"

Henry scratched his chin. "That's right. I talked to that dog walker the other day. She told me her uncle had some interviews today. Something about rescued dogs."

"Exciting." There must be another puppy getting adopted. "Thanks for letting me know about Nicola," I said.

He touched my shoulder. "Give the girl a break. She seems to want to turn over a new leaf. Goodness knows I did a lot of stupid things in my youth."

"Ha. You seem like you were born a gentleman."

He scoffed. "You're seeing me in my current state. Trust me, I'm making up for lost time."

I waved goodbye to him before jogging over to Magnus Cooper's house to catch the breaking news. Journalists lined the street, but I managed to use my small stature to slip past people.

Magnus had just finished passing over a puppy to its grinning new owner. Reporters took turns asking Magnus questions. Some covered the adoption on live air. A few focused on the feel-good features story, while others emphasized the introduction of the ground-breaking technology used in PetTwin's 4-D experience booths.

As Magnus answered, his eyes roamed the crowd before him. Spotting me nearby, he stopped in midsentence and waved me over.

"This is Mimi Lee," he bellowed. "Owner of Hollywoof, the finest pet grooming studio in the Southland. Actually, she orchestrated the adoption of these puppies and handled the technology side of things." Cameras clicked at me. Shocked at the sudden attention, I tried to grin and not look like the dazed zombie I felt.

After the hoopla had subsided, Magnus clapped me on the back. "Wonderful publicity event. Zel contacted the local TV stations. Said media coverage would help get the word out about my breeding business. And now maybe your business, too."

My cell phone rang right then. I picked it up to hear the irritated voice of Detective Brown speaking. "Did I just see you on live news?"

"I have a free day, and I wanted to see the rescue dogs getting adopted."

"You never rest, do you, Miss Lee?" But his voice held a note of admiration. "Well, if you're done hamming it up for the cameras, I'd like to give you a ride back to Hollywoof so you can collect your car."

• • •

Detective Brown picked me up from Magnus Cooper's house in his unmarked car. On our way to Hollywoof, he summarized what had transpired in the police station the night before. Tammy had given the police her full cooperation, like she'd said she would, and had confessed to everything.

Relief flooded my body. Justice would be dealt, and my life could return to normal.

When we arrived at Hollywoof, Detective Brown placed a hand on my arm to stop me from getting out right away. "One moment of your time, Miss Lee."

I froze. Was I in trouble again? But the detective handed me a small wrapped gift.

An enormous amount of tape kept the shiny paper on the box. "Let bygones be bygones. I'm sorry I pursued you relentlessly in the Nolan case."

I nodded and ripped the sloppy wrapping. Opening the box revealed . . . my favorite mug, the one that said "Stay PAWsitive." The detective had nestled it in soft tissue paper.

"Thanks for returning this, Detective." I pulled the mug out, already dreaming of brewing a hot cup of tea. "Wait, what happened to the crack? There's beautiful gold paint covering it."

"Kintsugi," he said. "I wrote down that term you mentioned when I searched your place."

I'd first admired kintsugi at a local Asian museum. The art of ceramic repair revived broken pottery through lacquer and gold pigment. Detective Brown must have used his precious time, and possibly police contacts, to locate an artist skilled enough to create this ceramic transformation.

"Detective, I'm floored." I fingered the gold line. "Thank you."

He scratched behind his ear and nodded in the direction of my car. "Okay. You're all set."

I turned to go, and he spoke up again. "And, Miss Lee, try to stay out of trouble in the future."

CHAPTER

꞊ forty-one ꞊

MARSHMALLOW DRAGGED HIS paws when it came time to go into Hollywoof the next day. He'd been acting strange ever since I'd broken the good news to him about the murder case being wrapped up. Did he miss the excitement of investigating?

When we arrived at the store, I expected to see Nicola, whom I had hired to satisfy Ma's condition. Instead, I found a line of people and their pets waiting outside the door. Were these new customers?

"What's up with all the *pup*-arazzi?" I whispered to Marshmallow.

Instead of his usual snarky comeback, he stayed quiet. He didn't even let out an irritated grumble.

The customers gave a collective cheer and greeted me by name. Every single one said invariably the same thing: They'd seen me on TV.

Swamped with customers, I soon filled up the seating area—and more. A lot of them squeezed together on the benches, but others stood to wait.

A few milled around, checking out the merchandise. When they swept up all of Indira's pooch pouches without a second glance at their price tags, I knew I'd be partnering with her for a while. Maybe I needed to negotiate a fifty-fifty split.

I also finally got the chance to use the side room, taking several dogs and placing them in crates to wait their turns. While grooming, I heard the business line ring multiple times. Thank goodness Nicola had arrived by then. She managed the front while I handled the direct pet duties.

Hollywoof was an overnight success. In fact, Pixie even had a fancy potted orchid delivered to me. The note in her elegant cursive read, *Heard the media hype. Congrats! Let's meet up soon. XOXO.*

Grooming tasks kept coming without end. I couldn't close up like usual for my lunch break, but I did manage to nibble on the "sweet wishes" chocolate-dipped fortune cookie Josh had given me for returning to work.

Around three in the afternoon, I felt exhausted and told Nicola I needed a quick breather. I leaned against the grooming table in the back room and stretched out the crick in my neck.

Marshmallow sidled up to me and said, "Heard you insist on a break. Guess it's finally time. Well, I'm ready to go."

"And where exactly are you going?"

"Don't be a smart aleck, Mimi. I know you're taking me back to the shelter."

"What are you talking about?"

He looked at me with doleful blue eyes. "Our deal, remember? You said you'd keep me around only until you found the killer. And now the case is closed."

"You can't be serious." I cupped his furry face in my hands. "Marshmallow, you saved my life. I wouldn't give you up for the world."

"Not ever?"

"Nope. You're family now, Marshmallow Lee."

He groaned. "Marshmallow-y? Again with the silly name."

I let go of his face and tsked at him. "That kind of *cat*-itude is why you don't get to come along on tonight's date. That, plus I don't think they allow pets."

• • •

Josh and I went to an elegant restaurant called Montagne, located inside a skyscraper, for our first official fancy date. The upscale dining establishment offered French-Asian fusion dishes with names I couldn't even begin to pronounce.

Plus, the restaurant provided a superb vantage point for admiring the city lights. Sitting together at a cozy table on the building's highest floor, we took in the gorgeous view. I felt like we were perched at the top of the world.

Josh adjusted his dark blue tie and ordered champagne from the waiter.

"Lavish," I murmured when the waiter came back to pour the bubbly into handmade crystal flutes.

The waiter retreated, and Josh turned to me with sparkling eyes. "You're worth any extravagance. Besides, thanks to you, I can afford it with my new promotion at work. The partners loved how I handled the deal with PetTwin."

"Let's toast to your success at the firm."

"No." He gripped my hands with both of his. "We'll celebrate you being alive—I know I could have lost you the other night..."

"How about to Life, then, with a capital 'L'?"

He lifted his glass but cocked an eyebrow at me.

I raised my flute and said, "Because Life capitalized is full of wonders. Things we work hard for, like amazing dream jobs. And also unexpected joys, like my two handsome fellows."

His hand wobbled. "Two?"

"Charming you . . . and feisty Marshmallow."

He laughed and clinked my glass. "Cheers, Mimi."

We sipped our champagne and held hands across the table. Turning my gaze to peer out the large glass window, I took in the view. The lights of Los Angeles dazzled me with their shimmering brilliance, reminding me that Hollywoof-size dreams really do come true.

ACKNOWLEDGMENTS

First off, thank you to sassy cat supporters everywhere! I love to stay in touch with readers through my newsletter or on social media. Find ways to connect with me at jenniferjchow.com.

If you enjoyed M&M's adventures, please leave a *paws*itive review on Amazon and Goodreads. (Marshmallow says a steady diet of praise keeps his ego well fed.)

I'm blessed that Mimi got a chance to live out her Hollywoof dream and shine in mine. Special thanks to Lily Choi for the initial inspiration.

A huge thank-you to agent extraordinaire Jessica Faust for supporting me and other diverse writers. Props also to James McGowan for his hard work and to the rest of the BookEnds team, including Buford, the literary hound.

Revising under the professional eyes of Grace House and Martha Cipolla was an absolute pleasure—thank you for making insightful additions and smoothing out the story. Heartfelt gratitude to Angela

Kim for her enthusiasm about this series. Much appreciation for the marketing and publicity efforts of Brittanie Black, Jessica Mangicaro, and Natalie Sellars. I continue to be amazed by Lindsey Tulloch and the whole publishing team at Berkley for their bookmaking magic.

Love to my extended family, particularly the Ngs, the Chows, and the Lims. Hugs to my critique group (Lisbeth Coiman, Robin Arehart, Sherry Berkin, and Tracey Dale), who keep my creative juices flowing. Sweet wishes to my sixth-grade teacher, Mrs. Okada, who delighted in my first mystery story.

Finally, I'm indebted to my husband, Steve, for believing in my dreams and helping me persevere. And to my kids, who tagged along on my research outings, including doggie readings and cat cafés.

JENNIFER J. CHOW grew up reading Garfield comics and adores creating sassy kit lit. She also writes the Winston Wong mysteries, which feature a regular meowing cat. Her other Asian American novels include *Dragonfly Dreams* (a *Teen Vogue* pick) and *The 228 Legacy*. She's involved in Crime Writers of Color, Mystery Writers of America, and Sisters in Crime.

CONNECT ONLINE

JenniferJChow.com

Ready to find
your next great read?

Let us help.

Visit prh.com/nextread

Penguin
Random
House